Psychedelia Gothique

Selected Short Fiction by
Dale L. Sproule

Arctic Mage, Toronto
2013

Reviews for "Fourth Person Singular"
(1994 Aurora Award Nominee for best short form work in English)
Edward Bryant, Locus Magazine:
"The imagery is bizarre here, the pain tangible, the occasional smiles uneasy."
A.J. Fox, Ottawa Citizen:
"An eerie glimpse at the ugly legacy of violence."
Derryl Murphy, Edmonton Journal:
"A contender for best speculative fiction story of 1994."

Review of "Memory Games"
(1997 Aurora Award Nominee for best short form work in English)
(Dragonlance Author) Nancy Varian Berberick, Tangent Magazine:
"The story asks a simple and haunting question. Are you sure the person with whom you're about to sleep is who he says he is?"

Reviews for "At Fort Assumption" (now "Exposure")
John Degen, Quill and Quire:
"...a hallucinogenic ride that mixes film and dream sequences quite expertly."
John B. Rosenman, Tangent Magazine:
"A harrowing psychodrama."
Edward Bryant, Locus Magazine:
"The sense of distance and isolation reflects terrifically from physical location to internal alienation."

Praise for "The Onion Test"
Kristine Kathryn Rusch from the Introduction in Pulphouse #1:
"...one of the few stories I've ever read which forced me to go back to the beginning and start all over again. I couldn't believe what I had just read."
George Hatch from Noctulpa Journal of Horror:
"...sent me through the roof of the subway car and I'm still trying to figure out the damage done to my brain was from the roof of the tunnel or "The Onion Test"."

Published by Arctic Mage Press, 222 Parkview Hill Crescent, Toronto, ON M4B 1R8

Psychedelia Gothique, Copyright 2013 by Dale L. Sproule

Cover copyright 2013 by DLSproule

Interior design and layout by DLSproule.

Prologue copyright 2013 by David Nickle

Published in Canada

Library and Archives Canada Cataloguing in Publication

Sproule, Dale L., 1953 -

Issued in print and electronic formats.

ISBN: 978-0-9919406-0-8

A whole host of huge thank yous to:

My wonderful life-partner, Laura Belford – for all your support, for giving me some low/no-pressure time to put this collection together and for your inestimable contribution as copy editor.

All the members of the Cecil Street Writer's Group since I first joined in the mid-90s. And to the members of the Victoria Writing Group, especially Gerry Truscott. You've all seen and helped me with at least one or two of these stories.

All the editors and publishers who have considered, accepted and printed my work over the years, especially Don Hutchison, Dean Wesley Smith and Kristine Kathryn Rusch.

Mark Lefebvre at Kobo Writing Life for valuable advice putting this package together and getting it onto the market.

The folks on Wattpad who have shared opinions and advice.

My kids Lauren and Sheena, my step-kids Carly and Connor and my former step-kids, Jen and Jason (and his whole family) for making it imperative that I be a good role model and finally finish a big project or two.

Sally McBride, for remaining my friend and colleague.

And thank you at last to the Toronto Arts Council for their 1998 grant which enabled me to complete a number of these stories.

Contents

Foreword by David Nickle

Dale Sproule and I met face to face for the first time in Winnipeg in 1994, for the Worldcon there. I admit that I was predisposed to like him. Earlier that year, he'd sent me a note, telling me he'd read and dug one of my stories, and asking me to send him a new story for a magazine he and his [then] wife Sally McBride were starting up. And I sent him one, and sure enough, there it was in Issue #1 of *TransVersions*.

Dale was living in Victoria at the time, and I was in Toronto, so the science-fiction bacchanal that is a World Science Fiction Convention was our only face-to-face contact for awhile. Really, we didn't catch up much at all until he upped stakes and moved to Toronto a few years later, and we started hanging out more regularly.

But I started regularly paying attention to Dale's artistic output – both fictional and otherwise – immediately. How could I not? Dale Sproule's stories and paintings travel to dark and surprising places.

I remember first reading "Fourth Person Singular" in 1994, when it appeared in Don Hutchison's *Northern Frights 2* (the same anthology that contained the story of mine that Dale had liked so well) and shivering with equal parts horror and writerly envy, as he laid out the terrible childhoods of Barry and his brother Wren in a house haunted by their monstrous father.

That story's in this collection, right near the start. If you start with it, it might lead you to believe you're in for a run of Faulkner-esque journeys into the pain and madness of shattered families. But follow that line too long, and you might just pull a ligament, trying to parse it with the metafictional flights of "Labour Relations", the splatterpunk excess of "The Onion Test", the pure gonzo comedy on display in "Showdown in Kitschtown" and "Flushed".

Some of these stories haven't seen the light of day for some time, but when they appeared, they did so in a spotlight. "Labour Relations" first appeared in *Ellery Queen's Mystery Magazine*; "The Onion Test" in the long-lamented and highly respected *Pulphouse: The Hardback Magazine*. "Flushed", as well as "Exposure" and of course "Fourth Person Singular" were showcased in the *Northern Frights* series.

There's also innovation on display. As long as I've known him, Dale has aimed to innovate in a way that allows him to take more control of his work and how it appears than is considered seemly, at least among the more timid of our brethren. In a climate that was not friendly to speculative fiction pulps, Dale and Sally started up *TransVersions* and kept it alive for years before passing the reins along.

The novelet "Razorwings" appears later in this collection, and originally it saw life as the beating heart of a website that Dale put together in the late 1990s. The site was meant to document the adventures of Jaynie Razorwings, a twisted denizen of Faerie, both blessed and cursed with a glamour that hides then reveals her true nature as she's grown. The website didn't take off, being as it appeared more than a decade before the time of Wattpad and Amazon and all the ways that a creator can reach an audience today.

But "Razorwings" is here, in all its dark and terrible glory. Like the other stories in this collection, it invites you to join in on a dark and surprising ride – to sip a potion that will show you worlds that skew deep and strange and wonderful.

So what are you waiting for? Climb aboard, drink deep and keep your eyes open. Dale Sproule has some things to show you, and trust me when I say you won't want to miss even a blink's worth.

"Your Brain Must be THIS Big to Go on This Ride"

When I first started putting pen to paper, I wrote science fiction because it was pretty much all I read from the time I was able to parse sentences on my own. But I am no rocket scientist, and while I was capable of using the genre to express my sense of wonder, I pretty much sucked at the science.

Despite that hard reality, I continued to dream of being a science fiction writer like Robert Silverberg or Phillip K. Dick. When my sf stories collapsed like dust bunnies, I should have hung a sign above my keyboard saying, "Your Brain Must be This Big to Go on This Ride," and gone directly on to something else. Not smart enough to do that, I kept trying to scale Mount Everest in my bellbottoms and sandals.

In response to the lack of respect my genre writing received when I took Creative Writing at University, I decided to look for a more redoubtable literary style. Nobody from my generation questioned the post-modern masters like Borges, Cortázar, Tom Robbins, James Joyce and Donald Barthelme. Along with a few gonzo writers like Ken Kesey and Tom Wolfe, they were mainstream of "psychedelia" in literature. So I declared myself a fabulist, which allowed me to cling to my quirky vision. The ruse was successful. Fellow students and professors alike were unable to understand my stories and felt ill equipped to judge them at all. So I got As and Bs on everything and the anti-fantasy criticism pretty much stopped.

On the downside, there weren't many post-modern publishers – and the major ones immediately saw through my smokescreen and realized that I was actually just writing genre stories with a post-modern approach. So in the mid 70s, I cast aside the pretensions and started looking for a genre where my work would fit more comfortably.

Horror wasn't really considered a category unto itself in the early 70s. HP Lovecraft had never really enjoyed popularity with the masses, the Twilight Zone was fading to black and 50s/60s paranoia was wearing thin. Stephen King hadn't quite happened yet. There was lots of room to do something new that didn't require a PhD in Physics!

So I started taking my psychedelic prose poems to the dark side. Purple Lovecraftian prose swirled with hallucinogenic nightmares. Some of the stories impressed people and raised a few eyebrows. When my stories worked, they worked well, but I was still so focused on "style" from my post-modern experiments that I hadn't really recognized the value of telling an exciting story with well developed characters.

It wasn't until I was able to add that to my repetoire, that my fiction was able to evolve from psychedelic to gothic to full blown Psychedelia Gothique.

"What is that exactly?" you ask.

My PR person, Dee Leonard explains it like this – "Psychedelia Gothique adds a mind-altering dimension to the gothic tradition, opening the gates of perception, to demonstrate that fear is closer to the surface of our everyday reality than most of us ever suspect. All you need to do is shift your perceptions, just a little bit."

What's that? A misspelling? Okay fine, then, my PR "persona." But one day I will be able to afford a professional spin doctor. Until then, all I can do is put my humble little tales in front of you and hope you like them.

Dale Sproule

Toronto, 2013

Nice Day for a Trip

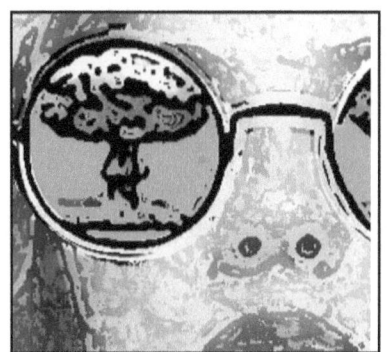

Preamble – Nice Day for a Trip

This postmodern quickie prompted the editors at Seattle's *Sign of the Times Magazine* to say in their acceptance letter, "Watch out Tom Wolfe!" I framed the letter.

Drugs, apocalypse, pop culture and a post-modern sensibility…this little story has it all. And it has just the right sentiment to start the collection. It is a nice day for a trip, dammit. And for those of you who come along, I sure hope you enjoy the ride.

Nice Day for a Trip

Ball slapping asphalt followed by an outburst of soprano shouts. Dull thud. Voices swell and then the rhythm starts again. On the street, staccato-clicking rumble races past and in its wake a monstrous roar changes pitch and merges with the hum-drum hum at the periphery of awareness. Faintly at first, but mounting like panic, a siren wail splits the soundscape. The fissure spreads. And from the deep recess, the meaning of life whistles past in a single, never-ending scream. The sky disappears.

Either they've finally dropped the bomb or Pink Floyd has attained world domination. There's always a choice. Life is a series of choices. And there is evidence to support the latter option.

Time has reversed. Sometime in the summer of '85, it turned around. There were signs. The new taste of Coke® yielded to Coca-Cola Classic®. Live-Aid re-united the Who, Led Zeppelin, Crosby, Stills, Nash and Young. The public affection for Trivial Pursuit® became a fervour. They should have called the game Wish Fulfillment.

Look around. It's all coming back. *I Dream of Jeannie*, *I Love Lucy*, *Mayberry R.F.D.*. Even *Mr. Ed* is on his way. Or is that just someone playing coconut shells?

Turn on the radio. Who do you hear? Moody Blues. Yes. The Monkees? Keep listening. You never know when they'll play something from the new Jimi Hendrix album. New? Now you're catching on. Davy Jones is crawling out of his locker. The Days of Future Have Not Passed.

Walk to the newsstand. Watch as the vendor snaps the twine on a bundle of *Esquire*, *Life*, *Look*. And over there, *High Times*.

Now you understand.

Maybe it started when Speilberg decided to take us *Back to the Future.* Back. He knew where to find it. You could see it even in his earlier films. The nostalgia. The wish.

Now it's your turn. Make a wish. Make a choice while there's still time.

It's a straight line, from the days of acid rain to the days when acid reigned. For over ten years after high school, you worried about flashbacks that never came.

Well, here they come now.

Ummagumma.

With a hiss and a snort, the guardian of the underworld closes in. A horizontal monolith with laughing windows and blast-furnace breath. Number nine…revisited. The destination changes as you watch. From "Crosstown" to "1967". *Magical Mystery Tour.* All aboard! Passengers in long hair and woolen ponchos turn to stare out the back window at the mushroom cloud, secure in the knowledge that it's just a hallucination. Far out! The road ahead is paved with black light posters. The oblong sun is glowing purple.

The future is a funny shade of bright.

Fourth Person Singular

Preamble – Fourth Person Singular

I loved cyberpunk in the early 1980s, but didn't have the chops to write it. I felt like I had missed the boat, but cyberpunk very quickly went the way of dinosaurs and slide rules. Only the best of those writers went on to enjoy long, lucrative careers. And I was no William Gibson. So missing the wave wasn't such a bad thing.

When I finally decided to take a run at horror fiction, I observed that it really wasn't very scary. So I dedicated myself to being as scary as possible. And being a young man, I loved the idea of shocking and offending people. For a few years in the mid 80s I dedicated myself to the pushing the envelope until it was no longer recognizable as an envelope.

By the time splatterpunk (extreme horror) came along, I still wasn't a consistent enough writer to make a real splash. Again, fortuitous, because despite introducing the world to Clive Barker, the movement vanished in the blink of an eye.

Really, this should be the introduction to my breakout "extreme horror" story, "The Onion Test." But in fact, that story did the job of shocking and offending a little too well and when I started putting this collection together I realized that "The Onion Test" deserved to be in the volume, but would not set the tone properly for the fairly eclectic collection of stories to come. So I've bumped that one back to the middle of the book.

"Fourth Person Singular" is my best known story. It appeared in *Northern Frights 2* alongside such brilliant Canadian horror stories as David Nickle's "The Sloan Men", Gemma Files' "A Mouthful of Pins" and Garfield Reeves Stevens' "The Eddies". It not only held its own in such heady company, it garnered an Aurora Award Nomination and was selected for *The Year's Best Horror Stories 23* - which never appeared because Mr. Wagner died that year. It also appeared in *Wild Things Live There - The Best of Northern Frights*. You can even listen to an audio version at Pseudopod.

The compliment that sticks with me the most was delivered by my good friend, Gerry Truscott (the creator and original editor of the *Tesseracts* SF anthology series) who made an offhand comment during our fiction workshop that he wouldn't be surprised if it went on to become a horror "classic" - words you always want to hear from your peers, but pretty much never do!

If curiosity overwhelms you and you want to see why I shy away from using "The Onion Test" at this juncture, please feel free to fast forward and read it out of order.

Fourth Person Singular

"And he is the mad eye of the fourth person singular
of which nobody speaks
and he is the voice of the fourth person singular
in which nobody speaks
and which yet exists
with a long head and a foolscap face
and the long mad hair of death
of which nobody speaks
And he speaks of himself and he speaks of the dead..."

Lawrence Ferlinghetti "HE"

Every night since I was seven years old he's swooped down at me out of the darkness of sleep: a pale, skeletal boy with thin arms thrust out like wings, eyes like white domes in black craters, mouth open as he screams acceleration.

His name is Wren.

■

It's been over thirty years and the images haven't even begun to fade. Maybe writing it down will help exorcise my ghosts.

In 1961, when I was six and my brother, Wren, was nine, we would huddle together on his bed pulling his thick blue bedspread over our heads on those nights when the screams came from the basement. Several times each year, tortured voices wavered up the heat ducts, sometimes sounding like men, sometimes women. Sometimes they would wail for hours although one night, a single excruciating plea of "stop!" was followed by silence. Wren and I put our ears to the metal vent in the hardwood floor, listening for more, but instead heard the door downstairs slamming and Dad stomping up the stairs. I barely had time to scramble back to my room and pull up my covers before my door swung open and Dad came in and kissed me goodnight.

He smelled like the stuff they use to clean hospitals, the scent of pine heightened until it makes your nose smart and your eyes water.

Smashing, cursing sounds told me he was going into Wren's room. Dad hardly ever came upstairs, so he didn't remember Wren's forty or fifty model airplanes hanging on fishing line from the bedroom ceiling; a network of filaments like a massive spiderweb.

The next morning at breakfast, Dad spoke. "Renfield," he said, being the only person who ever used my brother's full name, "I want you to take down those airplanes."

"You broke four of them," Wren replied sullenly.

A spoonful of cornflakes stopped en route to my lips as I watched Wren mirror Dad's stare, a shrunken reflection of our father's stubbornness and passionate intensity.

"Move them or suffer more losses than you already have. Understand?"

"Yes sir," he muttered, playing it safe for once. My relief slipped out in a sigh. Then, with no more trepidation than saying "pass the milk", Wren asked, "What is that screaming we always hear coming from the basement?"

I wanted to grab my brother by the shoulders and shake him and shout "Shuttup you idiot! This man made Mom disappear. He'll make you disappear too and then I'll be alone with him. Don't leave me alone with him!" But I didn't move, didn't breathe.

Looking up from his magazine, Dad sounded genuinely puzzled. "Screaming?" He turned to me. "Have you heard screaming, Barrymore?"

Avoiding Wren's glare, I said, "No Dad."

"He hears it just like me. Tell him, Bear."

I couldn't.

An interminable silence later, Dad suggested, "I have a proposition for you, Renfield. Come into the basement with me when I get home from work tonight and I will show you everything there is to see."

I hoped Wren would somehow read the silent plea in my eyes, but without according me even a scornful glance, he flipped his long black hair out of his eyes and said, "Naw. Guess I don't want to know all that badly."

"We will see." Dad nodded, then looked at us one by one. "Neither of you have mentioned this imaginary screaming to anyone outside of this house, have you?"

"No," I answered, hoping Wren would chime in and we would speak in a single voice like we once did.

Instead, my brother wondered aloud, "How could we tell anybody, if you won't let us out of the house, Dad?"

"You sneak out sometimes while I am at work during the day. I found that yellow plastic bowl you left beside the garage the other day."

We had used the bowl to feed our neighbour's Irish setter. Their house was around the bend in the road and we never wandered that far, so we'd never been close enough to overhear the dog's name. Going over to inquire might start them asking why we weren't in school. So I blessed the dog with a second name; Robin, like in that song Mom used to sing. "When the red, red robin comes bob, bob, bobbing along..."

The lecture droned on, "...going out any more. I have to trust you to be good boys," Dad gave Wren a fatherly smile and tousled his hair. "If you told anyone about this screaming, they would quite likely send you to a psychiatrist. Do you know what the psychiatrist would do? Perform a lobotomy operation. Just like they did to my father. They drilled a hole in his forehead, inserted a knife, and sliced off the front of his brain. We don't want anyone doing that to you, now do we? I want my family safe and sound. Keeping your mouth and eyes and ears shut is the best way to stay safe and sound, Renfield."

"I thought keeping the door shut was the best way."

"Are you being smart?"

"No sir. You told us..."

"Do not ever get smart with me."

"Yes, s..."

"Mouth *shut*, correct?"

Wren nodded.

Dad got up and walked straight out the kitchen door. My brother and I listened to the rattling of locks and latches, the departing footsteps, the uneven rumble of the Rambler's engine and the crunching of gravel as Dad backed out the driveway. Then Wren said, "I'm going down to the basement. You wanna come?"

I shook my head and pouted. "You'll scream," I warned.

"Huh?"

"Going down there will make you scream like all the others."

"Dad goes down there," said Wren. "He doesn't scream."

I trailed my brother upstairs, unable to muster a better argument than his. We struggled to lift the window in his bedroom.

"Get something to prop it open!"

I brought the wastebasket from the bathroom and watched as he climbed onto the porch roof. His legs, his head, and finally his hands seemed to sink into the greenery as he climbed down the trellis.

After a few scary minutes by myself, I decided to follow, but on my way out, I hit the wastebasket with my shoulder and the window came shuddering down at me. Certain I was about to be decapitated, I threw myself back into the room, escaping with no worse injury than bruised elbows and a sore bum.

I'd seen the wastebasket bounce off the gutter into the yard, where Dad was sure to find it. My struggles to open the window couldn't budge it.

Had I locked my brother out forever? I had no idea what to do next. Break the window? I scanned the room for a tool, in case it came to that. On the floor were clothes and empty boxes from his model planes, but no balls, bats or other outside toys. Being too young to assemble the many models Dad had given me as gifts, I'd passed mine along to Wren who had thrown out the cars and boats, but added the airplanes to his collection.

I looked up. Even if I could reach them, Wren would kill me for throwing one of his planes through the window. I'd once broken a wing on a model he was working on. He didn't talk to me for a week.

I looked down. I was standing on the furnace grate. Kneeling beside it, I tried unsuccessfully to pry it out of the floor. Then, lying flat on my stomach, I put my lips to the open vent. "Wren?? Are you down there?" I shouted timidly. Receiving no answer, I yelled again and again. When I stopped, I could hear my own small, hollow voice still echoing through the ductwork.

The door behind me opened and I whirled, surprised that Wren had found another way in.

But it wasn't Wren.

Dad stared down at me, his face blank and grey as usual. He was still in his blue suit as if going off to work but he obviously hadn't gone.

"We were...uhhm...playing hide 'n' seek," I stammered, unable to lie quickly or convincingly enough. "I'm IT. Wren is hiding."

Wordlessly, Dad turned and headed back down the stairs.

How had I failed to hear him return? Dad must have read our minds again. He must have parked the Rambler on the road and snuck into the house on tiptoes.

I laid there on the cold floor until Dad called me for supper hours later. Wren wasn't there. Hopefully, he'd seen Dad coming and run away. I never asked, never spoke at all, never even looked up from the canned spaghetti cooling and congealing on my plate. Dad sent me to my room.

I curled on my bed, clutching my knees to my chest as I listened for my brother's screams. There were screams; although not those of a child. A man's voice gibbered and wept for a long time before his screaming started. It was loud at first, his voice gradually weakening, becoming hoarse and merging with the rustling of leaves in the nearby trees, the rushing of water in the creek, the pumping of my own heart.

Wren was in bed when I peeked in on him next morning.

Needing to know if he was alive, I slipped through the doorway, crept up beside the bed, reached out and tentatively touched him on the shoulder. He didn't move. I shook harder, then tried to roll him onto his back, but he resisted.

"Go away," he said in a voice I barely recognised.

"Are you hurt?" I whispered.

"He made me watch."

"But he didn't hurt you?" I asked.

"He made me watch." Wren said again. "Now go away."

"What did you see?"

"The screams. I saw the screams."

"Who was screaming?" I asked.

He didn't answer so I grabbed his shoulder again, shook harder, asked more loudly, "Who was it? Why were they screaming?"

"Breakfast," said a man's voice from behind me. Dad had stuck his head in. I turned and saw him smiling warmly. As suddenly as he'd appeared, he went away and I heard a number of distinct thumps as he descended the stairs two at a time.

Dad must have heard me asking Wren about the screams, which, even from the sanctuary of my bedroom, sounded full of pain and fear. I didn't really want to know what the screams looked like. I didn't want to talk to Wren anymore. I didn't want to go downstairs for breakfast. I didn't know what to do.

Wren got up and I followed him down to the breakfast table. My brother stared vacantly at me as we sat down, although I'm sure he didn't see me. Dad whistled and made "a hearty breakfast" of bacon and eggs. I concluded he hadn't heard me asking about the screams. Dad chattered throughout the meal about nothing in particular.

The next few weeks were lonely. The only time I saw Wren was at supper. After we ate, Dad would present him with a new model plane. Wren added it to the stack against the wall at the bottom of the stairs before retreating to his privacy. After a while, my brother began to act like himself again. The tower of boxes shrank, then disappeared.

I went to his room, but Wren was so caught up in the process of building his new models that he hardly talked to me. So I stopped visiting. The next day the banging and hammering sounds began. Wanting him to know how hurt and offended I was, I refused to give into my curiosity. He didn't seem to notice. One afternoon as I was just about to give in and visit him, Wren appeared at my door.

"Come see my invention."

I did.

His model airplanes had been taken down and were heaped in and around his closet. A single plane hung from the knob at the bottom of the light fixture in the centre of the ceiling. Leading from there into the corner where Wren stood on top of his bed, was what looked like a railway track which Wren had constructed out of coathangers. At the end of the track, hung another plane. Wren reached up and grasped it firmly.

"Watch this," he said, hurling the projectile as hard as he could. I could actually hear it whistle through the air as it flew across the room and collided with the stationary plane. Bits of plastic sliced through the air in every direction and I turned away, covering my eyes.

"What'dya think?" he asked.

"Uhmm, neat, I guess."

"It's the neatest thing ever," he corrected. "I'll show you again."

I watched Wren untwist the lines, dropping the wreckages carelessly to the floor, before replacing them with new airplanes.

"You know what this is called?" he asked just as he was about to throw the second plane. I shook my head.

"A dogfight." Smash.

"What is?" I puzzled, as Wren replaced the casualties with new sacrifices.

"Airplane battles. No kidding. I dunno why. A birdfight would make more sense. Or flying tiger fight. But it's called a dogfight. Wanna try?"

I could barely touch the fuselage with my fingertips let alone grab hold of the plane.

"Can you make the string longer?"

Wren shook his head. "Took forever to get everything just right. Don't wanna start over."

I couldn't throw very hard. On my first attempt the plane ended up flying in circles around the target after missing completely. Wren let me try again. I managed to break one strut off the propellor on the target plane. Wren laughed. I stomped out, leaving my brother to the bewildering and solitary pleasure of destroying the only thing he'd ever cared about.

A month later, Dad took him downstairs for a second time.

The screams went on for longer than usual that night and I imagined I heard more than one voice wailing. I didn't recognise either of them though.

Wren was withdrawn the next day, but not at all as bad as he'd been that first time. He even came to breakfast. Dad had made pancakes.

"What do you want for your birthday on Sunday, Barry?"

"It's my birthday?"

"Seven years old. Both my boys are growing up."

I didn't respond.

"If you don't ask for something I can hardly get it for you can I? What would you like?"

"A puppy?"

"You know we don't have pets in this house. Don't be so stupid. Now what would you really like?"

I shrugged.

"Would you like to come to the basement and see what daddy does downstairs?"

"A colouring book."

"We could have a party down there. All three of us."

"He says he wants a coloring book instead, Dad," Wren cut in, the boldest I'd seen him since his first trip to the basement. "I don't think Barry's old enough. He wouldn't understand."

Dad pushed his plate of uneaten pancakes into the center of the table and wiped his lips with a napkin. Then he stood, not moving from his place at the table, and stared at me.

I'm sure Dad saw that I was crying, no matter how hard I tried to hide it. With a nod, he grunted, "Perhaps," then strode to the door and out.

"Why can't I have a puppy?" I sobbed once he was gone.

"He'd kill it. He killed Robin, you know?"

I didn't know. I hadn't been outside in weeks.

"He keeps the body in the basement," Wren continued.

"Maybe it was another dog that looked like Robin."

"I'm sorry, Barry," Wren said, coming around the table to give me a hug. "I'd get you a puppy if I could."

Wren's hammering resumed late the next morning, but he wouldn't let me see what he was up to. "Secret," he explained.

That Saturday, Dad brought home a yellow cake with red writing on white icing. It spent the night in the fridge.

Sunday at noon, Dad brought out the cake, singing "Happy Birthday" as he carried it to the table. He watched for my reaction and I pretended that it was a big surprise. He smiled and kissed the top of my head.

"I guess I should get some candles to put on there," Dad said.

"Aren't you supposed to light the candles before you sing?" asked Wren.

"I think there's some in the hutch. Be right back," Dad continued, as if my brother hadn't said a word. He went into the dining room to look for them.

Wren saw me staring at the top of the cake and said, "What are you looking at?"

"The words."

"What for? He'll never let us learn to read."

Wren had been to grade one but I'd never gone to school. Dad said that insolence and apathy were all we would learn in school. Teachers know nothing about respect, he would say. How to give it or how to earn it. I'd like to teach the teachers, he would say. And he would laugh.

When Dad returned with the candles, he also brought my presents; a stack of coloring books and what seemed like a hundred packages of crayons. I picked one of the coloring books off the pile and studied the cover wondering if I could learn to read by studying those letters. If I looked at them long enough, would it suddenly come to me and start making sense? I looked at the second coloring book down. It was blue with a cartoon dog on the cover.

"You like Huckleberry Hound, Barry? Did I pick you some good ones?"

"What's Hucklederry Hound?"

Dad put his hands on his knees and bent down to look me in the face. He smiled broadly. "Like on TV?"

"Barry's never seen TV, Dad."

"Yes, I have," I protested.

"Well, you can't remember it, can you, twerp?"

I had no answer to that one.

Dad just kept smiling. "Maybe that's what I should buy for Christmas. A television set, a family present."

Wren and I nodded eager assent.

"Now let's get back to that party," Dad grinned as he held a little box of candles beside his ear and shook it.

After I blew them out, Dad asked, "What'd you wish for?"

"That Mom would come back."

"Oh." Dad's smile disappeared. He busied himself cutting big pieces of cake, then said, "I have to go to work."

"It's Sunday," I protested as he was leaving, but Wren held a finger to his lips.

"Shhh. Let's just eat."

Wren gave me the biggest piece and I crammed a big forkful into my mouth. After a minute I looked up at Wren, who simply sat with his empty hands face down on the table on each side of his plate. He stared at the cake without eating any. After a few more bites my appetite disappeared.

"What's the matter?"

"I got you a present," Wren said.

"Why didn't you bring it to the party?"

"Party? This isn't a real...aw, hell Barry. Dad wouldn't have liked it, that's all. I got you something he wouldn't have liked, so you have to keep it a secret. Okay?"

"What is it?"

"Guess."

"I dunno. What color is it?"

"Mostly black. But his tail and one foot are white."

Was Wren talking about some sort of stuffed toy? Where would he have found such a thing?

"C'mon. I'll show you."

I followed my brother to his bedroom which looked empty except for the pile of plastic which had once been model airplanes. The carpet was squishy underfoot.

Wren saw me looking down and said, "He messed the floor."

"Who did?" I said, starting to get genuinely excited. Had Wren somehow smuggled in a real puppy? He started hauling something out of the closet. A box? A cage? No...a big piece of plywood; with a puppy nailed to the wood by its paws.

"His eye is gunky," Wren was explaining. "I thought you could fix it with that big green marble you were showing me the other day."

Not wanting to believe what I saw, I asked, "is it dead?"

Wren was offended. "He WAS dead. Now he's your puppy."

I covered my mouth with my hand, not knowing what to do.

Wren kept talking, earnestly, desperately, "it feels a bit funny when you scratch him behind the ears. And he has these little white bugs crawling around in his fur."

My brother was making a sincere effort to give me what I wanted. I knew that. I could see love and concern in his eyes, hear it in his voice. Wren cared about me. But then, so did Dad.

"...maybe we should give him a bath."

"Did you kill it?"

"What?"

"The puppy. Did you kill it?"

"I *found* him. Beside the road. Alone. He needs someone to love him. Somebody like you."

I wanted to thank him, but I felt like throwing up.

"I thought we could name him Razzmatazz. Why don't you..."

I turned and ran to my room, slamming the door behind me. I leaned against the door and burst into tears.

Wren pounded and pushed on the door. "Barry? Are you okay? What's the matter, Bear? Don't you like him? What's wrong?"

Realizing that Wren genuinely didn't know what was wrong, I braced my feet against the side of my dresser. My socks left red footprints on white paint. I remembered how I felt when Wren said, "He messed the floor." Now I knew what he meant. "Go away!" I screamed.

But he didn't go away. Nor did he try to break in. He kept knocking and asking what was the matter until I stood up and yelled. "Because the stupid puppy is dead and that's the dumbest present anybody ever got and you're the dumbest brother anybody ever had! Now leave me alone!"

Without another word, Wren went away.

I couldn't sleep. Sometime in the middle of the night, I snuck into his room to apologise.

"Wren?" I whispered, stepping into absolute darkness.

I stood there and listened for the sounds of his breathing. Nothing. I brought my hands up defensively with each cautious step, half expecting to run into something in the middle of the room.

As I approached the bed, feeble moonlight sliding through the crack at the edge of the curtain allowed me to see that the bedspread was still pulled all the way up, neat as could be. I backed up to the door and flicked on the light. The room was empty.

I walked through the rest of the house in darkness, everywhere except the basement. Then I went back upstairs.

Maybe Wren had run away. Maybe I had driven him away.

Wren wasn't just my brother, he was my protector, the only thing between me and Dad. Between me and the basement.

He didn't show up for breakfast.

"Where's Renfield?" asked Dad.

I shrugged.

That day, the pounding and hammering started again. This time it reverberated through the whole house. I couldn't tell where it was coming from and I was afraid to call out for Wren, in case it was actually Dad again.

When Wren didn't show up at dinner, Dad asked me, "Where's your brother?"

"Said he wasn't hungry."

"Is he sick?" Dad pushed his chair back and walked to the stairs.

"Said he was tired. He's sleeping."

"You're sure he's not sick?"

I nodded. Dad came back to the table.

"You bring him up some dinner later."

I nodded again and ate the rest of my meal in silence.

Dad wouldn't accept the same explanation a second time. I had to decide what to do.

As far as I knew, Wren had only one exit; the window in his room. He'd been outside to get me the puppy so it followed that he must have managed to pry the window back open.

After Dad went out that night, I got up and went to Wren's room. I entered in darkness, in case Dad was lying in wait again. Ready to catch us again.

There was a gust of cold air. The window was open. A new airplane was hanging from the light fixture. The wind slammed the door behind me as I walked to the centre of the room.

"Wren?" I yelled, turning circles as I stumbled back toward the light switch. Flick. A second plane slid along the track. Crash. But no one was there to throw it. The room was empty, except for me. Except for me and the airplanes, now swaying silently on their strings; two wreckages dangling from their strings.

"Wren!" I screamed, lurching from the room.

I searched the whole house calling his name; checking every door and window; looking in closets and cupboards, behind curtains, even in places I knew were too small for him to fit.

I flopped face down on the sofa and was still sleeping there when Dad found me, hours later, and carried me up to bed.

At breakfast the next morning, Dad put my bowl of cereal down in front of me. "Where's Renfield, son?"

My throat tightened up like it was stuck with airplane model glue. Able to neither swallow nor talk, I shook my head.

"We're a tight-knit family. You two are always together. Your brother wouldn't have left without telling you where he was going. Where was he going, Barrymore?"

"I...don't..." my words seeped out.

"What are you afraid of, son? Do you think he's gone to the police? Is that it? Are you afraid they'll send him to a psychiatrist and slice up his brain?"

It hadn't occurred to me. Suddenly I was truly afraid for my brother.

Dad's moist brown eyes oozed fatherly love as he reached out, cupping my whole jaw in his big hand. "I can't protect him if I don't know where he is. You tell me, so I can bring him home safely."

The air felt so warm and thick I could hardly breathe. "I don't know," I said. "I've been looking for him."

"You don't know?" Dad asked. "If you don't know, who does, Barrymore?"

"I don't..."

"Tell me where he is, son."

"I don't..."

"Tell me!"

As I shook my head, tears ran down my cheek into his cupped hand. He let me go. Then he got up and stared out the window, into the morning sunshine. "What are we going to do? We can't call the police."

Recalling his story of where the police would send him, I nodded.

"But if the police find him and Renfield mentions that he has a brother, they might come looking for you, I'm...I'm going to have to hide you. I'll put you in the basement. Won't let them look in the basement. This wrecks my plans. I was going to have guests tonight. Damn that boy."

Dad's stare made me feel transparent, like he could see the fear gushing around inside me. "Let's go. Before the police get here."

I bolted from my chair, planning to lock myself in the bathroom, but Dad caught me before I reached the stairs. "What the hell is the matter with you? I'm doing this for your own protection. To keep you safe and sound."

I squinted in the bright sunshine as he carried me out to the porch, then down the steps to the basement door. He inserted a key in the lock and the door swung open, letting some darkness out. But somehow no light came back in when we entered.

Dad didn't even turn on the light when he pushed the door shut behind us. The air was cold. My legs swung with the rhythm of his stride as I pried at the hairy arm clamped around my chest and listened to my father's footfalls clop across bare concrete. Abruptly, he stopped and reached up. As a light directly above us blazed on, I struggled to get free.

"Am I going to have to strap you down like I did to Renfield? Like I did to your mother?"

Peering through the incandescence of my fear, I saw a table; a giant version of the puppy board, its wood was riddled with nail holes and covered with dark splotches.

Dad spun me around to face a wooden wall. No, it was an upright board; like the table, except with belts instead of nails to hold someone by their arms and legs.

The board wasn't propped up from behind, it was nailed to a beam above us. As I stared up at the ceiling, I could make out something else; some sort of metal track, like the one in Wren's room. My gaze slid along it into an impenetrable darkness. This had to be where Wren got the idea to build his track. I wondered what sorts of things my father sent rumbling toward whomever was strapped to the board. Things that made people scream.

My gaze searched the perimeter of our pool of light. I saw shapes along the wall. Just jars and bottles I finally realized; milk bottles, pop bottles. Maybe there were horrible things in them. I couldn't tell.

On the other end of the table was a workbench. It was painted green, just like the one at our old house. All of Dad's tools were hung up neatly along the wall above it; I'd never seen pliers and drills before, so I didn't know what they were. But I had seen knives, and there were lots of knives; some funny ones with big square blades and some hook shaped ones and some really skinny ones along with all the regular knives. There were a few empty spaces at the bottom. I wondered if Dad had brought some down for me.

Dad put his arm around my shoulders and walked me up to the edge of the table. I backed away, but he held onto my upper arms and turned to face me. Crouching down, he looked me in the eyes and smiled. He shook me very gently for emphasis as he spoke. "It's a father's responsibility to protect his family. I'll teach you how to make people respect you, Barrymore. Because people who respect you will never hurt you. There's only one person you should fear. You know who that is?"

Wide eyed, I answered, "You, sir?"

He laughed and kissed me. "No, Barrymore. It's you. That's right. People hurt themselves sometimes, son. Even kill themselves. Like your mother. She could have lived as long as she wanted. But she knew I couldn't let her go to the police. So, you see? For all intents and purposes, her own hand held the knife that slit her throat. She killed herself. I guess she didn't have enough respect for herself. I loved her, just like I love you and Renfield. I would never hurt either of my boys. But I have to teach you not to hurt yourselves."

As he stood up again, I heard a whistling sound like the ones during the dogfights in my brother's bedroom. Dad noticed the sound at the same time I did, only he had to turn around in order to see what I saw; Wren soaring toward us, his arms straight out to the sides like wings. In one hand, he held a fireplace poker and in the other, a knife. My father and I stood transfixed.

Any sound the metal shaft of the poker might have made as it plunged into Dad's throat was drowned out by a terrible thump and clatter of the ropes breaking free of their guides. My brother flew overhead, his body slamming into the plywood board. The knife clattered at my feet.

I bent down and tried to turn Wren onto his back. His head lolled loosely, just as the dead puppy's head had done two nights earlier. But how could Wren be dead. He wasn't bleeding or anything.

Dad was bleeding. He was lying on his side and I could see the tip of the poker coming out the back of his neck.

"Wren?" I said, but he didn't answer.

I remembered somebody saying that when a person is dead, they stop breathing. And I couldn't see Wren's chest going up and down like it usually did when he pretended to be dead. I put my ear to his mouth and listened as hard as I could. I could hear a breathing sound, I was sure of it!

As it got louder I realised that the sound wasn't coming from Wren.

I looked at my father, half expecting him to pull the implement from his neck and stand up, but he didn't move.

The sound was coming from deep in the gloom of the basement. A voice? I sat up, holding my own breath as I peered into the darkness.

It was a voice of a sort; the growl of a dog floated toward me, turning into a whimper.

"Robin?" I said. And the big red dog stuck his head around the edge of the board and sniffed at Wren's hair. It licked my dead brother's face. Then it staggered toward Dad and started lapping blood off the floor.

"Robin! Don't!"

Wren had told me Robin was dead. He'd seen the body. But Wren was wrong.

The dog's tail pounded against the wooden table leg as I stood up. He began walking slowly towards me. I reached out to push him away. His fur felt stiff, the same way the puppy had felt a day or two earlier.

Backing away from the dog, I looked at the bodies of my father and brother. "How long will you stay dead?" I whispered. Then I turned and scrambled toward the line of sunlight streaming in through the door which was standing slightly ajar.

Sensing Robin close behind me, I looked back. In the light, he looked worse than he had when I'd first seen him – horribly skinny and his fur was all matted and crusty.

Robin followed me when I ran. His limp prevented him from catching up, but he was still there every time I glanced back. The dog on my heels kept me running. I don't remember stopping. I don't think I ever stopped.

Although my brother has been dead a long, long time now, he comes back night after night; as cold and familiar as the moon.

Labor Relations

Preamble - Labour Relations

Mostly what I remember with this story is what it was like selling my first story.

Since I had started sending out manuscripts, I had become an obsessive mailbox checker. I even came home from work at lunchtime (it was only a 15 minute walk) to check the mail for responses on my submissions.

My rejected stories would come back in their big manila envelopes and I would repackage and resend them before I'd finished lunch.

One day, I found a business sized envelope with the *Ellery Queen's* logo! My hands started shaking as I took it out of the mailbox. Editor Eleanor Sullivan was asking if I'd be willing to reword a couple paragraphs. They wanted to publish it in their "Department of First Stories". She specified that it paid less than their standard rates.

Nothing could have mattered less. I remember whooping and throwing my hands in the air for the better part of an hour. I think I hyperventilated. The neighbours must have thought that a team of rodeo clowns moved in next door.

"Labour Relations" appeared in the May 1984 edition of *Ellery Queen's Mystery Magazine*, which hit the shelves in April, one month after my daughter Sheena was born. It was available on newsstands across North America, so all my friends and relatives were able to find it at the local drugstore.

Labor Relations

"Trapped in a short story. Now that's a dead-end job. No wages, lousy conditions, and the author thinks he's Raymond Chandler the Second." Grimknuckle mumbles to himself as he stops and peers into the darkness. Dilapidated tenements rise on either side, casting menacing shadows across the narrow street. As he stands there, hands thrust deeply into the pockets of his rumpled trenchcoat, he nods knowingly. "Rumpled trenchcoat. Great start. Surprised he doesn't have me drinking my breakfast right out of the milk carton. But he's got something better in mind. After all, we're still in the first paragraph and he's already got me risking my neck walking through the slums.

"You're on a case, Grimknuckle. So just get on with the story," I reply coolly.

"What kinda case? Doncha think you shoulda filled me in a bit before you started typing?"

"You're...ah, looking for the killers of...Jimmy Hoffa," I offer.

"Hoffa? I've worked on cases where the trail was cold but this one's been around so long it's like trying to peek under a glacier. Why Hoffa, for crying out loud?"

"I had to justify the title somehow. And besides, you're a terrific detective. You'll find evidence everyone else has missed."

"If I'm so good, how come I can't afford a new trenchcoat."

"You can but you're in disguise."

"Jeez, is this guy confused. First it's Columbo, now it's Mr. Dress Up. I'm afraid to check my driver's licence in case it turns out I'm really Angela Lansbury."

"Don't be ridiculous. Let's just get back to the action, okay?"

"Action? You mean this sad excuse for a story? Hey, what's gonna happen next?"

"Sorry, that would give you unfair advantage."

Grimknuckle glares out from his barrio backdrop. "Now don't give me none of your bull. So far, I'm the only pigeon you've got. Y'know, I'd be the last guy in the world to say anything about a lack of plot, but it seems to me you need all the help you can get. There's gotta be a little give and take here, if you know what I mean."

"Well, all right. I'll give you a hint. You're about to come face to face with four Mafia hitmen."

"Four! *Four*! You ever hear of overkill? You put one unarmed man up against four wise guys and you call that a *story*?"

"Don't worry, you have a black belt in karate."

"Oh, really?"

"That's right, you studied under Bruce Lee way back when he was working his way through acting school doing a part time gig with the Green Hornet."

"Yeah?"

"If I say you did, then you did."

"I never had any trouble believing you. I'm merely overwhelmed by the improvement in my odds. But lemme ask you, have YOU ever tried to karate chop a bullet?"

"This is my story and everything will work out fine. Just let me handle it, okay?"

"It ain't safe. I'm reporting you to the Worker's Compensation Board!"

"Forget it, Grimknuckle. If they find out you're fictitious, they'll know you invented your own Social Insurance Number and you'll end up in jail for fraud. Face it. You're nothing more than a few scribbles on a page."

"I'd be more three-dimensional if you were a better writer."

"I'm not and you're not, so let's just..."

"I'll go to the Fictional Character's Union! You'll look like a real creep when Anne of Green Gables, Mary Poppins, Shirley Temple – the whole lot of them start following you around with pickets."

"Shirley Temple's real."

"You're kidding?"

"No. Honest to goodne...wait a minute. We're getting off the subject. You're a product of my imagination and you'll do whatever I decide. Now that I've made myself clear, we're going back to the story."

Most of the streetlights have been broken by vandals, or shot out by gangs during drive-by shootings. In the dim light, Grimknuckle can't see the front door of a nearby apartment building swing silently open. Or the long, black Cadillac drifting slowly up behind him. Glancing nervously back, Grimknuckle increases his pace.

"Grimknuckle increases his pace!" I repeat, patiently. "That means walk faster, you moron!"

"This is dumb. I'm not gonna be a participator in this nonsense."

"Okay, have it your way."

The Caddy guns its motor and pulls within a few metres of the sullen detective.

"Roll down da window," Eddy 'The Jackal' DiGiaccomo orders his driver. Two more figures in black pin-stripe suits emerge from a nearby tenement doorway, brass knuckles and switchblades gleaming in the headlights.

Eddy signals his man in the front seat to 'turn on da heat.' In response, the thug reaches under the dashboard and pulls out a sub-machinegun which he sticks out the open window and levels at the now preposterously motionless Grimknuckle.

Sweat leaps off the end of the pouting detective's ski-jump nose. "Look," Grimknuckle's treble voice trembles, "maybe we can make a deal after all."

"What kind of deal?" I ask, disinterestedly.

"Suppose I go along with you. Think you can get me outta this with a few fleshwounds?"

"Well – I don't know."

"I'll even go along with a shot in the leg. Us private dicks gotta *live* with that sorta thing, if you catch my drift here."

The Cadillac pulls up directly beside him.

"Well c'mon," Grimknuckle squeaks, "whattdya think?"

The chauffeur slouches down in his seat, out of the line of fire.

"Please?" Grimknuckle hits a note that would have been the envy of anyone in the Vienna Boy's Choir.

"Oh, all right."

"Whattdya mean, all right? How do I get outta this?"

"First you pull the Magnum out of your shoulder holster. Then you dive down to the pavement and blow them all away."

"If'n I was you," growls a voice from deep in the bowels of my CPU. "I'd replot dis here bit before my frens on da outside take youse on a tour of da riverbottom inna new pair of heavy-duty overshoes."

Eddy the Jackal stares out from the monitor, aiming his heater at my right eye. His cohorts pull weapons of every description from beneath their jackets. "Jus' becuz we ain't real, don' mean we're stoopid."

Four very mean looking guns are pointed directly at me. I stare in astonishment at the screen. I mean, I don't exactly have some sort of fancy graphics program. Pure word processing, y'know. But right there on the monitor are what looks like the mouths of four very large cannons.

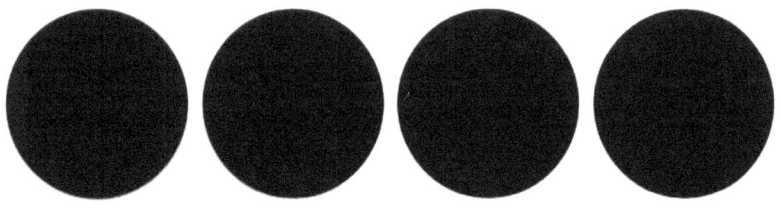

"Git in here," Eddy commands.

"Who, me?" I reply.

"Naw, Wendy da good witch a da Nort. Now move dat pansyass in here 'fore we got no choice but splatter yer ugly mug all over yer keyboard."

"Is this irrational, or what?" I ask myself as I write myself physically into the plot.

The courageous author is grabbed and held by two of the hoods as the other two pace back in forth in front of him – uh, I mean me (this situation could lead to serious point-of-view problems). Grimknuckle sits down on the tenement steps, forgotten and grinning in obvious satisfaction at the turn of events. He lights up a Player's Light® and begins hacking violently.

"Why'd you put these things in my pocket if I don't smoke?" he asks me as he flicks the butt onto the pavement.

"Isn't that the package you got from your secret agent friend in the last story? Gee, I hope you haven't forgotten about the ones with the cyanide filters."

"The what??"

"One puff and..." I shrug. Grimknuckle is on hands and knees beside the tenement stairs. "But don't worry, Grimknuckle, your odds are almost one in five that you're perfectly safe..."

"Shaddup." My arm is twisted violently behind my back. I wheeze with pain. "You can't do this to me unless I write it..."

"Oh, no???"

"No. I'm. In. Control. Here." I say, unconvincingly.

"Dat a fact?" Eddy manages to spit out before he and the chauffeur collapse in hopeless hysterics.

"Well, if I'm not, who is?"

The laughter stops and we all stare out from the page directly at – *you*.

"Who're dey?" Eddy whispers.

"Readers."

"Dey mus' be makin' dis up as dey go along, den, eh?"

The author winces. "Well, I didn't think so."

"Hey – youse, out dere. Ya youse." He points at you, then jerks his thumb in my direction. "My five year ol' kid can write better dan dis birdbrain. So, if he ain't doin' it, whattdya say ya give it a go, huh? Leastwise, till my kid gets here."

Lifestreams

Preamble – Lifestreams

In my early years as a writer, "Lifestreams" was my calling card story. Both psychedelic and postmodern, it was the story that gobsmacked my fellow creative writing students into silence, and it never failed to get me a detailed critique from markets where I submitted it.

Problem was, no one would buy the damned thing.

It was too genre for the literary markets, too post-modern for the genre markets and too psychedelic for the mainstream and family oriented magazines. After they had published a William Burroughs story in one issue of *High Times*, I sent them "Lifestreams" and got an encouraging reply from the editor saying that publishing fiction was a one off that only happened because it was William Burroughs, but he thought "Lifestreams" was wonderful and wished he could have accepted it.

Between 1985 and 1987, I had sold three stories to a bizarre, alternative-lifestyle literary magazine called *Sign of the Times, A Chronicle of Decadence in the Atomic Age (SOTT)*. Since they paid only in copies, I never submitted "Lifestreams" to them until the end of 1987. I had exhausted all the paying markets and I figured the least I could do was sell it to a publication that had been very supportive of me and my work.

To this day it is available at www.sott.com. Where – just above the content warning – the website creator says, "Published for twelve years, *SOTT* truly was a "sign of the times. I don't believe that a magazine could exist today dealing with all the weirdness in society without the FBI raiding its offices." Mike Gunderloy at the small press review zine *Factsheet Five* described it as, "A literary 'zine that bills itself as 'A Chronicle of Decadence in the Atomic Age.' I'd say they fill the bill, with a mix of twisted sexuality and twisted reality filling the pages."

Twisted reality? Well, perhaps a little…

Lifestreams

Too much coffee. How could I do this to myself? I feel sick enough, without turning my guts into a churning caldron of caffeine.

Well, this is IT. (I'm starting to sound like Samuels.) The cathodes are all in place. The eye on the machine is glowing green.

"Ready David?" Shawna's question is superfluous. She's already dabbing the alcohol on my arm, sliding the needle in.

"I'm terrified." That sounds dumb, considering my attitude up until now. Not that I haven't the highest respect for Edwin Samuels, but – Jesus, I'm tempted to reach over and pull out that IV. No. I've gone this far. Shawna's already got the sensory shields in place. Here IT goes!

IT. That's Dr. Samuels' clever little acronym for Intracerebral Therapy. He's a delightful guy, but he has a terrible weakness for puns. "IT's no laughing matter." That was his favorite. He didn't think I took the dangers of IT seriously enough. Still has his doubts.

"IT's like a river," he told me. (He's fond of analogies too.) "A river with an infinite number of tributaries. Each stream is an individual psyche. Some wind through jungles, some cross deserts or tumble down mountains, some simply dissipate into swampy deltas. But they're all dangerous. At the best of times, it's easy to get swept away by a strong current, or find yourself trapped by steep canyon walls. Once lost in an alien terrain, you could well be stuck there permanently. And with our comatose patients, it's even worse. If you accept that coma is a form of mental suicide, then maybe you won't be caught by surprise when the stream takes a sharp turn and heads straight into the desert. It's the state of the psyche. These patients would love to evaporate in the hot desert sun. Poof! No more problems." Then, Samuels would waddle over to the liquor cabinet or create some other diversion before making his point. "If you expect a joyride, forget it. You'd be as suicidal as the patient you're trying to help."

I'm looking now. But I don't see any rivers. So much for analogies. Nothing seems to be happening. Nothing. That's a bit strange in itself. David. I'm the only reality in this universe. What am I supposed to be exploring? How do I get my bearings. There's no north, south, east or east. Or west. There. I've got to get a grip on myself. Can't lose track of the only...only what? Oh, yeah. Name. It's coming back now. I am Eric, bound tightly into my horizontal womb. A womb of ether. It penetrates; it is almost a part of me. My nostrils are like wind tunnels, where the ether has coated the walls for slip-ease. The sandman chants as he dances into the distance, but I can't hear what he's saying.

I see lines moving like heartbeats. They have promised to become images and I am a subjugated voyeur.

Physical movement is a treason or a sacrilege. I could be a fixture; a statue or lamp stand. I am motionless. Turn me on.

Click.

A billion bodies on a spherical stage writhe like paste white snakes. Desecration in Jello. The ritual quivers with mockery and fades. False start.

A room, choked full of people. They are dancing; holding hands and turning in a huge, slow circle. It is a cabaret or discotheque. I see faces running in and out of focus. Paint dribbles along the ruts in their masks. Faces splinter and greasepaint oozes from their lips.

I am Eric. And I see Eric, sitting. Gyrating bodies crash into his table and glasses smash and shatter on the cold tile floor. He tries to move, but his feet are stuck – must be the beer. It's like glue.

A fat man with a large, pink Band-Aid® on his cheek walks up to the bar. "I'd like two glasses of Elmer's Glue-All®, please."

The bartender replies, "Will that be white or amber, sir?"

The smell of alcohol makes me salivate. I like to pour it on my wounds.

"There is beer, beer, strong as a wino's tears in the store ..."

I hear a voice asking if there is brain damage. I don't know, lady, but if I see some, I'll call. Ha-ha, I wish I could laugh.

A girl I once knew is sitting beside myself. Eric smiles and mumbles something, as she runs her hand down his leg and asks if he wants to take her home. My alter-ego declines. Stupid bastard.

Wait. She's hiding something. Eric grabs her arm and pulls it from under the table. In her hand is a syphilis brochure. Eric smiles knowingly and I finally understand my logic. I want to applaud, but I have no hands.

Is this what they mean by "Theater of the Mind"? I wonder if I have to pay the actors.

The cabaret again. My best friend, Lorne, is sitting at a table with half a dozen of the brothers he doesn't have – and who all look miraculously like him. They call my name and Eric walks over and sits down at their table. He listens. Lorne's obnoxiousness is multiplied by his images. They are having a loud argument which is turning into a brawl. Eric can't stand to watch Lorne destroy himself.

I'm glad I only have to experience my own perceptions. As Eric gets up and walks away from their table, I follow closely.

"Eric, meet Eric. Eric – Eric."

"Don't I know you from somewhere?"

Eric goes up on the stage and stands in the heat of the light; the people seethe like mealworms in a tomb. Fights are starting and ending at every table and all of the participants are being forced to leave. Eric sees his mother being hauled out on the arm of a muscular bouncer. He runs up and asks the man what she's done and the bouncer replies that she ripped the bandage off a fat man's face and jammed a beer-soaked facial tissue into his cut. He takes her away.

"Do they beat them up outside?" I wonder. For a moment I am angry at myself for not having the courage to defend her, then I remember what Mom always told me. "Never cry over spilt milk, Eric."

"Okay, Mom."

Eric is searching for his lover. He surveys the crowd. The people are swaying in some black psalmody. Eric is drawn in, submerged. The mass squeezes tighter and Eric sees his lover's face. She is hiding in the ambiguity of faces. Old lover, new lover – a blur where only the sensuality remains. She sees him, and realizing the inevitability of their meeting, she presses forward to greet him. They embrace and she takes his hand and leads him outside.

As they pass the washroom, the door swings open and Eric catches a glimpse of the interior. A fat man is standing in front of a mirror, holding the leg of a corpse against his cheek. It must be a better pain killer than alcohol, Eric decides.

There are comets and meteors and novas in the cluttered vastness of the space. A cougar is waiting by the door. There is also a man pissing against the wall and someone lying on the ground, bleeding.

Eric and the girl caress one another. I am jealous, she is my lover. I want to touch her soft skin, feel the warm friction of her tongue against my lips. I can only watch.

The smell of flowers enshrouds me. Roses? Gladiolas? I search for the source. Eric-with-the-girl is looking too.

While he was distracted, the girl escaped from his grasp. He swivels his head around slowly – and spots her in the parking lot – between cars. Laughing, she yells to him, "Meet me." She is driving off in her McLaren Mark IV when Eric decides to follow.

"Meet her where?" I ask myself.

I must know. I see Eric smiling as his Fiat bounces from the lot and onto the gravel road to town. He is going 110 mph – 112 – a high speed chase! Her tail-lights are out of sight. That mother is *fast*! Eric's car hits a bump, skids into the ditch and back out again. Something is burning. He slams on the brake and the car slides to a precarious halt at the edge of a chasm. The Fiat backs up. Eric gets out and builds a ramp by kicking dirt into a pile and laying boards across it. He climbs back in and slams his heel into the accelerator. The ramp disintegrates beneath the clawing treads – the machine churns helplessly into the void. It flips slowly as it plummets, swinging sideways just before it careens into the rocks at the bottom. Glass, gasoline and twisted metal are spewed in every direction.

Naked corpses stand in a circle around me.

"What do you want?" I scream.

They answer in a collective voice, "We are Death and we have been waiting for you." The voice quivers with mockery.

"I am only a child," I wail.

"You are a fetus," the voice replies.

"Let me live," I plead.

"Make us," the faces sneer.

I think for a moment, then say, "Husha, husha."

They all fall down.

Eric's unharmed body lies beside the wreckage. He gets up and walks away. He has no time for miracles; he is too preoccupied with the pursuit of happiness. I admire my fortitude.

Eric runs. With Herculean speed, he passes automobiles and villages. He upsets cyclists with the sheer force of his jet stream. He knows the police must be chasing him. He can see the red light flashing – hear the siren. The dull crescent of city lights glows. There are dead-end signs ahead, checkered; yellow, black, yellow, black yellowblackyellowblackyellbl.... .

He stops. There is a building in the road. A white tower. The police must have given up. The commotion of their emergency has quieted.

People rush at Eric from the doorways. Hundreds of hands lift him and voices cheer. A hero's welcome. Eric beams proudly and talks about the Olympics.

Triumph is a vicarious experience. I am a second-hand hero.

The crowd thunders down the ramp and into the building. Inside – the city. Narrow streets criss-cross symmetrically. A blur of patterns and voices. The light is dim and amber. A multitude of old derelicts lie prostrate on the sidewalks and within the traffic. There are whores in white silk dresses. There are pox-ridden faces and ugly cops. Silent guns are firing into the street and people are falling like dominoes – white eyes staring into space. Blood is running in the gutters and there is blood on Eric's hands and feet – his eyes are clouded with it. He sees his lover in a doorway, in a lace dress. There is a man clutching her, tearing at her clothes. She is screaming like the sirens were and Eric runs to help.

I am upset. I try to lash out, then realize I must let my other self do the fighting for me. I cannot lend him my energy, but I can give him moral support.

A Supporting Moral: If rapists were grown from rapeseeds, they could be pulled out by the roots.

I cheer on the sidelines as Eric carries the play.

I will do the same for myself some day.

Then the girl says, "Not now," and pushes Eric away. I feel disorientated, lost and tired.

A wino offers Eric a bottle of Canadian Club® and Eric lies down beside him on the street and says, "Thank you, brother."

The man replies, "Here comes another...."

"The whole scene is running over again. Cabaret...girl...syphilis...Lorne... mealworms and mother. Something has changed. This time – I follow in a Volkswagen. What happened to the Fiat?

"Eric, what happened to the Fiat?"

After the accident, Eric pedals with Herculean speed. The flashing red light is attached to his skull, my mouth is the siren. When Eric lies down in the traffic, the bum says, "Here it comes again."

Again? It's happening again. I am Eric. Eric sits. Eric moves. Eric loves. High speed chase and accident. Another accident ... it must be a different one ... different lover ... different tower ... different street. It must. Eric steals an ambulance and lands like a kamikaze pilot in the street. The wino cracks Eric's head open with the bottle. And the contents jack in the box into Eric's lap. My lap.

Inside are:

1. Confetti.
2. Several computer cards (spindled and mutilated).
3. Streamers (reading "Happy New Year 1952").
4. A shredded blueprint.

We sift them through our fingers. Maybe we should call out for a doctor. Maybe we are a doctor. Is anybody here a doctor?

A fat man with a corpse on his shoulders trundles up. He is clutching a black bag.

The corpse looks down and says, "We're a doctor. Where does it hurt?"

I wave my arms in a semi-circle.

The fat man pulls a bottle of Elmer's Glue-All® from his bag.

The cadaver leans down and stares into my eyes. "Don't I know you from somewhere?" he asks.

I stumble back, shaking my head. Then look him in the sockets where his eyes used to be.

"Not me," I say, pointing. "Him." Eric stares back – cocks his head like a dog. Cocks his head like he doesn't know me from David.

There is a chorus of whisperers, chanting, "Husha, husha."

I look around me for the source and then look back at David. No. There is no David here but me.

Eric stands among the corpses.

"Husha, husha."

"Eric!" I scream. "It's okay! I am a doctor!"

"Husha, husha." The sound is a river.

I hold my hands out to him.

Eric smiles and moves deeper into the crowd.

I reach out as far as I can and feel cold flesh press against my arms. A hand slithers over my wrist. A hundred hands, gripping. Pulling me in.

"I don't belong here! I'm just looking for Eric."

Bodies writhe like paste-white snakes and I am one with them. Now, against the blurring necroscape, a solitary warmth comes forth. Radiating. We touch.

"I need a guide!" I hear myself shouting over the roar of the river.

"*Husha, husha.*"

Eric thrusts an oar into my hand.

"Show me the way," I plead.

As he turns and walks away, I feel the river churning.

"*Husha, husha.*"

"I can't make it alone. I need your help."

Eric hesitates. Looks back.

The request still hangs in the air between us. He inspects it and finds it sincere. He cries and when I touch him, I'm relieved to feel the warmth, still radiating. When we walk together, I'm surprised to see how quickly we reach our destination. The exit is a hazy mist of light, stretching from horizon to horizon. Eric refuses to go any further. He shrinks away from the light, becoming less and less substantial.

"Wait! There's something I have to ask you. I'm coming back. Will you be here, to make sure I don't get lost again?"

His answer is like an echo of itself. Too distant...too faint, to make it out. The light is getting stronger. It's featureless but welcoming. Shapes define themselves. Shawna, Dr. Samuels.

The crook of my left arm is throbbing. The wad of cotton covering it feels as insubstantial as everything in Eric's world. The needle is gone.

"Your arm will probably be bruised." Shawna's hand slides behind my head. I don't even have the strength to help her lift me into a sitting position. "You were thrashing around so much, we were worried that you'd rip out the IV."

My head hurts almost as much as my arm.

Dr. Samuels leans forward, beaming. "IT went well." A statement rather than a question.

"How do you know?" My voice sounds like it's coming from somewhere else.

Samuels steps aside. Motions at the patient in the other bed. I can't see Eric's face from here.

"He spoke."

"Spoke? Out loud?"

"There's some other way?" Samuels is grinning broadly. Shawna is tucking Eric's sheet under his chin. "Just two words. But it's a start. Do you know what he meant?"

"What the hell did he say?"

"I'll wait."

Metropenance

Preamble – Metropenance

"Metropenance" represented a huge breakthrough for me. By the time I sold it the first time, I already had three other stories published and at least one of those was in a much better-known and more prestigious market. But this was an honest-to-God literary magazine – the kind of magazine I had long been striving to get into. A respected little Canadian publication called *Waves* bought it and printed it beside a story by *Field of Dreams* author, W.P. Kinsella.

I later sold it to *Pulphouse* after it became a quarterly newsprint magazine.

But it took me a long time to wrap my head around the reason that this particular story was so salable.

It was a prose poem, without a discernable plot or story arc or a single named character. I was surprised to have sold it the first time. After a while, I realized there were several reasons it sold.

It was well written. Always a plus.

It was extremely short. That often works in the favour of the author. *Waves* was a little publication that published a lot of poetry and liked to showcase new writers. "Metropenance" was the perfect length. In the second instance, *Pulphouse* had been holding a much, much longer story of mine for a very long time and I think this was a peace offering. He wasn't able to publish the big one – yet. But I was grateful for the show of faith, and the chance to show "Metropenance" to a bigger audience.

"Metropenance" gave a genuine and somewhat chilling glimpse into madness – a typical cycle of illogical "logic" that people get trapped in. I'm fascinated by insanity and once managed a boarding house where one of the tenants was a sweet, earnest and badly-in-need-of-medication, young man named Vincent. The night when I gave him his eviction notice was the night that he told me the story that inspired "Metropenance." Heaven was perpetually at his fingertips. Ultimately, I'm sure it stopped eluding him. He solved the riddle and found the answer.

I'm actually pleased that this got published before the internet came along and allowed people to fact check. Because I'm sure I got virtually all of the biblical details wrong but the fact – maybe even the point – is that it doesn't matter. All the facts and all the knowledge in the universe can't hold a candle to the truth.

Metropenance

The house next door has curving stained glass windows. The light behind them flickers as I watch and I don't know what to make of it.

The designs I draw on the paper look like the patterns of light on the windows. Only, I'm not drawing the windows. I draw the sunshine reflecting off the clouds in Heaven; where the angel Gabriel stands, sounding long plaintive notes on his graceful horn of gold. Deep-resonating notes which echo within the myriad of crisscross planes within me.

The word "GOD" is etched in blood on all the panes. I am a window into Heaven. I have watched the passion plays and nativity scenes until I know all the movements by heart. All the movements – from the most minuscule twitch of a goat's whisker in the stables....

I have seen Lucifer losing paradise and Moses eschewing it. Most people don't know that; about Moses' disillusionment at the critical moment. They don't usually believe me when I tell them.

John the Baptist may have touched me once, his hand brushing past my window. And I think I heard his fingers tap lightly on my surface. My hand trembles uncontrollably as I light a cigarette. My palms are sweating and the pencil stub slips from my fingers, creating an ugly black smear across the paper. Disgusted, I sweep it onto the floor. My fingers caress the wound upon the page and when it's healed, I bend to recover the pencil from the carpet, but the lead is broken.

Now...now I have no way to write it down when the message finally comes (this time it is a question): would you trade your best friend for a thief?

Which thief? Which friend? Does it matter? I repeat the question again and again. Not too loudly, because my neighbours all think I'm crazy and I don't want to wake them up. They don't know that God sends me these questions – fashioned to elude me. He is the Sphinx and the Boatman. He is the Monolith and the Answer. The answer. When I finally get the answer right it will pay my fare to Heaven. I envision hard, filthy coins clattering into the glass fare box of a bus and I do not smile.

"Would you trade your best friend for a thief?"

The answer fills the air around me. "No." "No." "No, no, no!"

"No." I repeat.

There is no answer. Maybe there is no answer.

The light behind the windows has gone out and now my room is dark. I slump down into my chair, reach over to the bed and pull my rumpled grey blanket across my lap.

Maybe God has his own bureaucracy; a staff of incompetent saints still putting my request through channels. Or maybe they just didn't hear me.

I stand up and shout, "*No!*"

But what am I denying? I stare around my room. Papers are scattered across the small arborite table. My eviction notice is among them. I can't stay here and I won't go back to the hospital. My place is someplace else.

I pick up an ashtray. It smacks loudly against the wall, breaking the smooth surface and showering the room with chalky flesh.

I stare at the scar. My ears ache from listening for the clarion call and hearing nothing. Finally, I stoop and pick up the cigarette butts and broken glass. I hope no one heard. I will fix the wall tomorrow.

Showdown in Kitschtown

Preamble – Showdown in Kitschtown

The biggest horror involved with this story was figuring out how to spell kitsch. Not for the faint of heart!

Honestly, this story brought me back to visiting my grandparent's house when I was "knee-high to a grasshopper". I remember my grandfather calling me Buffalo Bill in his thick Quebecois accent. I remember sleeping in my uncle's room, which was full of girly magazines and "selected" issues of *National Geographic*. But mostly, I remember the hordes of garden gnomes and plethora of strange (mostly mechanized) knick-knacks that populated the living room and dining room. It was a fun place to visit thirty years after the fact.

When I had the opportunity to teach speculative fiction at the Victoria School of Writing in the late 90s, I had the opportunity to read this aloud in front of over fifty students and instructors including Leon Rooke and Susan Musgrave. I am delighted to say it brought the house down.

Showdown in Kitschtown

1) Hans and his Delusions of Grandeur.

Hans stared out through the glass door of the liquor cabinet where he lived. A white-haired, jolly faced, mustachioed Aryan in lederhosen. He was the largest and most talented knick-knack in the house. Touch his switch and Hans would mechanically raise his arm, lift a shot glass to his lips and tilt it back. Then his nose would light up and smoke would issue comically from his red ears. Hans liked to think of himself as the God of Alcohol. On the cupboard beside him stood Santa and Rudolph. Elf and reindeer. Maybe they had the power of myth but Hans towered over them nonetheless. If they got uppity, he'd start smoking.

"Yes, Hans. You are the God of Alcohol," Santa would quickly agree.

Rudolph didn't say much. But then, he was about as smart as your average dairy cow. His nose wouldn't even light up.

It occurred to Hans that the reindeer's batteries might be dead.

"Hans is the God of Alcohol," Santa would repeat, wishing he too could blow smoke out of his ears.

2) Sparky and the Gun.

Sparky was a mule who lived on the big burl coffee table. He was made of plastic and when his tail was lifted, a cigarette would slide, filter-first, out of his butt. All cigarette filters in the sixties were splotchy brown, the darker the funnier.

He grew dependent on the laughter which inevitably accompanied a session of tail-lifting and ciggy sliding. He even grew to enjoy the feel of each stiff length being pulled out of him. Before he reached his first birthday, Sparky experienced orgasm.

Then came the gun.

It wasn't really a gun but a cigarette lighter shaped like a silver derringer. Just like the derringer on *Maverick*. It found a permanent home on the coffee table beside Sparky. It pointed right at him, in fact. At first it was just plain scary, but after awhile, the sensuous mule began to enjoy riding the razor-edge of erotica. It doubled his pleasure. Tripled his fun.

3)   High at Noon , Home by Nighty-night-night.

When Hans, the erstwhile God of Alcohol was moved from the liquor cabinet to a dominant position in the centre of the coffee table, beer bottles congregated around him. But Sparky would have nothing to do with the barbarian (although he secretly admired the Aryan's curvy legs from afar).

A showdown was inevitable.

In retrospect, it was plain to see – as black and white as *Our Show of Shows*, as simple as *Leave it to Beaver*.

It began with taunts. One night after everyone had gone to bed Sparky said to the lush, "Sooner or later your batteries will give up the ghost and no-one will bother replacing them. You'll end up in a trunk in the attic beside the remote control cars, crammed in underneath the electric blanket with the short-circuit."

"Oh, ja?" said Hans arrogantly. "Vell, you know vut vill to happen to you? None of zeez cotton picking people vill lift your tail any more and ven they do, they von't laugh. Your cigarettes vill dry out. Small children vill crush them in your rectum, filling your hollow feet mit dry tobacco. Oh, vell. At least you vill still haf your gun, zo you can blow out your brains. Ho ho ha!" Abruptly, he lifted a tankard to his lips and tossed back another beer.

The derringer's proximity was meaningless unless Sparky figured out a way to take advantage of it. He reached out telepathically to the stalwart knick-knack.

"Hey Derringer! Are you interested in being a hired gun? *Like Have Gun Will Travel.*"

No answer.

Sparky wondered for a moment if his psychic powers were on the blink. But on his second attempt he made contact, and found out why the gun was so stalwart. That saying "thick as a sack of hammers" didn't apply, because the derringer had an intellect of less than one of those hammers. The derringer didn't know its own trigger from a hole in the ground.

But wait!

Sparky had another idea!

Telepathy was useless. It was telekinesis he wanted!

Concentrating his full attention on the derringer, Sparky willed it to rise and point itself at Hans. It twitched and spun a little on the glossy surface of the coffee table.

This was going to be harder than he thought. Sparky put every tiny bit of his strength into pulling that trigger. As the hammer drew back, sparks rained down onto the fluffy, bone dry wick. There was no smell of lighter fluid. Nothing. The gun was empty!

"Gaaaakk!" screamed Sparky in frustration as the hammer of the gun seemed to snap down on his consciousness like a wire trap. The mule's poor mind went permanently blank.

Hans had a celebratory drink. His nose was a victory beacon. Ultimately all his challengers defeated themselves. It was because they over-reached their capacity.

Transformation has its limits, and through his willingness to settle for altering nothing more than his mental state, Hans became the God of Alcohol every night (until the day his batteries died and they put him in the trunk under the electric blanket).

The Onion Test

Preamble – The Onion Test

When *Pulphouse* was announced, editors Kristine Kathryn Rusch and Dean Wesley Smith said they were looking for material that would push boundaries in the manner of *Dangerous Visions.* This is the only time I successfully wrote a story for a particular anthology. It was also the fastest trip in my writing history between submitting the manuscript and seeing the story in print. I got the acceptance letter less than two weeks after I mailed the story internationally. The signature sheets arrived within my days of my returning the signed contract and I felt like a celebrity autographing two hundred and fifty pages. The finished book arrived in my mailbox within a few weeks.

I bought several copies and convinced a number of friends and family members to do the same. Their reactions were varied. My mom just blushed and congratulated me repeatedly but wouldn't say anything about the story. My best "writing" friend said it was the best story I had ever written and declared, "I can't imagine you'll write a better one in your whole career." My co-worker's fiance instructed her to quit immediately because he couldn't handle the idea of her working with such a pervert. The rest of the reaction was somewhere between those points.

For me, it broke the long drought with paying markets and I got to see my own story in a hardcover book alongside many of my literary heroes including Harlan Ellison, Kate Wilhelm, Michael Bishop, Ed Bryant and Charles de Lint. My euphoria at making the sale wasn't as hysterical as it had been with my first story sale, but upon seeing the printed version I experienced true rapture.

The Onion Test

Dr. Helen Sheperd found an island of grey-green mold floating in a pool of coffee at the bottom of Del Winter's cup and a meticulously hand-written poem on the table beside it. She read:

The Onion Test
They peeled back scalp and then skin,
To find out what lurked within,
To see what made Del tick.
He doesn't *tick. He's sick.*
Del's sick!
Instead of a brain, they found a prick.
No blood, just sperm, off-white and thick
No logic but lust.
Del knew he must
find
the girl
with the vaginal mind
and thrust and thrust and thrust and thrust
and plant his seed inside.

It was dated August 22nd, months before anyone but Dr. Strasse himself knew about the experiment, let alone that it would be nicknamed The Onion Test. Helen took a deep breath and noticed for the first time how the room stank. The cadence of footsteps from the corridor stole her attention from the page. Suddenly terrified that it might be Del, even though she knew it was impossible, she swung the beam around, frantically probing the tiny cell for a hiding place and finally just turning off the flashlight and standing rigid and silent in the darkness. The heavy door swung open.

A prison guard's familiar face defined itself in the thin light from the corridor. "Is that you, Dr. Sheperd?" he whispered as if even he had considered the possibility that the occupant had somehow returned. "It's almost shift change."

"Jimmy." She sighed. "Yeah, I got what I came for." Helen made a show of folding the paper and sliding it into her sweater pocket.

Undoubtedly bewildered why someone with complete access would want to sneak in after hours, Jimmy had readily agreed to an exchange of favours. It was vital that he not to tell anyone about her visit under any circumstances. If Strasse had found out about her rifling Winter's cell, it would confirm his suspicion of her growing paranoia. Helen hurried back to the infirmary. She couldn't resist peering in through the porthole window into cell three to confirm that Winter was where he was supposed to be; lying on the bed with all the wires and sensors attached. She flinched as the monitors burst into a flurry of activity, before calming herself that he was merely entering REM sleep and Layer One of the dream therapy.

They surrounded him, grey as the concrete walls and as strong. This. Couldn't. Be. Happening! But it was. All his victims were here. Even the one from the seawall in Stanley Park that he'd never told anyone about. Del had been so sure she was the one he was looking for – he felt her need, bad as his own, but suppressed. Then, they'd heard voices from the sidewalk and Del knew with absolute certainty she was going to scream. He had to stop her. So he had done the only thing he could. He hadn't meant to kill her, only cut out her voice box so she couldn't scream or share their secrets with anyone else. And now she was one of these…ghosts or zombies or vampires or whatever they the hell they were, who were dragging him to the floor with arms like steel bars. They held a weapon in front of his face and he thought at first it was a knife, before recognizing it as something from a disturbing news story he'd once heard about a native woman from the Queen Charlotte Islands who got revenge on her old man by cutting off his hardware with a tin can lid. And Del told himself it was just some sort of nightmare dredged up from his subconscious, but couldn't grasp the significance of that realization as they fondled him and his erection grew despite the fear, and the ragged edge bit in….

Helen not only knew the content of Del's dream, she had watched it being created; actresses in grey paint, POV camera whirling in simulated panic within the encroaching circle of bodies. Helen had seen the video images translated into the idiom of the computer and all the necessary details programmed in so that the inmates would perceive the faces as those of their own victims. Even the emotional reactions had been built in so that the "dream" would have approximately the same impact on each of the subjects.

Thinking about the terror that Del was experiencing as she watched the gauges fluctuate, Helen felt a certain satisfaction. As she turned, she saw Jimmy waving at her as he made his way out of the building after work, and she realized how long she must have been staring in at Del Winter. She acknowledged that she enjoyed his suffering. He deserved it, not only for what he had done to those women, but for what Helen was going through now.

However afraid she might be, Dr. Helen Sheperd could not allow herself to give up this job. When she was hired, she left the rest of her graduating class in the dust. While they took low paying research jobs and donated their time to social service organizations just to get credentials for a real job, Helen had already made it. She was the interface between the scientific team conducting the experiment and the twelve inmate/volunteers who were their subjects. It bothered Helen at first that her centerfold looks and her willingness to use them were at least as important to her getting the job as her doctorate in psychology had been. But it was only a means to an end. Everyone had assumed that she had slept her way to a degree, despite her virtual celibacy the whole time. Why should she feel guilt or shame for finally making use of her natural attributes? Her colleagues, like her fellow students and professors, were hypocrites. They would condemn her even as they used her. The inmates, on the other hand, had surprised her. They all seemed polite and friendly and every bit as normal as most of the men she had ever known. Despite her understanding of rape as a hate crime, she couldn't help but wonder if they were merely men who lacked the innate power and finesse to approach women in a more socially acceptable way. They seemed truly sincere about their desire to reform. Then came Winter.

"I've seen A Clockwork Orange twenty-seven times." He had beamed as he sat on the far side of her desk in the oversized office. "But I never thought I would have a chance to be in it!" Then, he carefully scripted his signature on the release form. As Helen leaned forward to take the form from him and start her speech about how his quarters would be temporarily moved to the infirmary area and how he would be briefed before each session, she looked up into his eyes and saw death and something worse and the words refused to come. He made no move toward her and didn't say a word, but Helen was petrified. After a long, unbearable moment, Del finally smiled and said, "You're the one, aren't you?" And at the time Helen hadn't understood but was chilled nonetheless, as Del got up, opened the door, and turned around to look at her before the guard took his arm and led him back to his cell.

When he was gone, Helen went in to confront the team leader, who had been watching all the interviews from his office next door. Dr. Strasse had barely raised an eyebrow when she burst in.

"Winter's dangerous," she said, bluntly.

"How so?" the old man asked.

She hadn't thought about how to explain it and finding herself without an answer, Helen stammered, "I ...dunno. It was like he could see inside me. Like he knew exactly what the experiment was all about."

"So, he's psychic, our Mr. Winter?" Strasse cocked his head with a bemused pursing of the lips. "Even true, it wouldn't matter. Or perhaps, it would be just the thing. Really put us to the test. He might be our most valuable subject." Then Strasse emptied his pipe into the wastepaper basket. "Thank you for sharing your...intuition...Doctor Sheperd.

Her panic turned to humiliation which turned to anger.

After leaving Dr. Strasse, Helen finished her remaining interviews and then headed to the prison psychiatrist's office to dig out the file on Del Winter.

His history was as predictable as a story made up from the headline's of True Homicide Magazine: "Watching Mom have Sex with a Thousand Men turned Streetwalker's Son into a Maniac!" But Helen had grown up in the same city which had supposedly spawned Del Winter and she knew the neighbourhood where he said he'd been raised. A prostitute in those streets would be about as welcome as some hairy biker loose in the girls' shower at old Ross White High School.

■

Two weeks later, Helen still had no way to prove her suspicions. Del's poem was perverse and disgusting, but anything he said in it could be excused as poetic licence.

Helen hurried out to the parking lot that evening and slid into her new cherry-red Supra. Compelled to read the poem one more time, she switched on the interior light. Half an hour later, she was still staring at the page. She tried to tell herself that hers was no more than the fascination of a bored suburbanite at the scene of some gruesome accident. That thought was less reassuring than she had hoped. So she reminded herself that the experiment was all but over. Tonight was the final night. She shuddered and turned the key. Del's words kept going through her mind.

"...they peeled back scalp and then skin..."

She tried to set a new land-speed record on the way back to her rented condo. Home at last, she hurriedly locked the front door behind her, but felt even less safe than she had in the car.

"...to find out what lurked within..."

She spoke to herself. "Do you know what's bothering you? That fucking dream you starred in. You can't handle it. You never should have done it."

Her real role in the Onion Test was that of seductress. Tonight during Layer Twelve, all the subjects would share the same dream, in which the experiment is over and, supposedly rehabilitated, they are released back into society where they track down the woman who has dominated their sexual fantasies since the beginning of the experiment. Helen. For weeks, she has deliberately tantalized and taunted them. In the dream they would come for her...and their fantasy would turn into the worst nightmare they ever had.

The thought of Del in the role of rapist while she played the victim made her more nervous than she had been when she and the actor had taped the scene.

Helen poured some rye into a tumbler just as a sound came from the bedroom, a cross between a hiss and a rumble...like the sound of a french door sliding open...like Layer Twelve coming to life.

He'd forced the French doors out of the tracks and couldn't get them back in, so he left a gap and as he crouched beside the bed, a cold breeze whipped intermittently at the curtains. Del prayed that the draft wouldn't alert her to his presence before she came into the room. Rolling the knife from hand to hand, he was soothed by the weight of it, the surety of the grip. He listened to footsteps padding in the hall, the clinking of glasses and the thunk of the refrigerator door. Doors opened and closed. Then, after a long silence, Del could hear her approaching. She was tiptoeing, betrayed only by the soft creak of the floorboards and the barely audible popping of her joints as they strained through this unfamiliar exercise. Then there was a whoosh of the pressure equalizing as she opened the bedroom door, followed by the click of the light.

He lunged, slamming the door behind her, throwing her violently to the bed, jumping her and pressing his blade to the soft flesh of her neck. Her right arm hung off the side of the bed and he saw it ascending, hammer clutched between white knuckled fingers and he slashed the soft flesh of her upper arm and watched the deep red meat of her muscle slide apart and heard the clunk of the weapon hitting the floor, louder even than the squeal of pain which bled between his fingers clamped roughly over her mouth.

"Where's you smile now Miss High and Mighty?" he hissed as he dug the fingers of his free hand into the mound of a breast and ripped away the fabric, pleased at the red welts which now marred the whiteness of that perfect tit. Then, looking back to savor the horror on her face, he found the horror all too real. Flesh slid gelatinously from the bones of her face and Del felt her body giving way beneath him...collapsing with an obscene slurp. He saw the tentacles emerging from the sockets where her eyes had been and felt the liquid mass curling up around him, slithering under his clothing, burrowing into him, and he screamed...

The real Helen had no such defense. No script written for the conditioning of criminals. This was no dream, she told herself as she stood motionlessly in the kitchen. And still the poem played in her head, drowning out any sounds from the bedroom.

"...he doesn't tick. He's sick..."

Then she heard the bedroom door brushing the fibres of the carpet. There's no way it can be Winter, she told herself, yet knew, somehow it was.

He was now a shadow walking boldly down the hall toward her. She saw her largest, sharpest knife amongst the dirty dishes in the sink and wrapped her fingers around the black plastic handle just as he reached the doorway. She swung and plunged the blade deep into his throat...and thrust and thrust and thrust and thrust, what seemed like a hundred times before he hit the floor and she saw that it was Jimmy, the guard who had snuck her into Del Winter's cell and now she remembered the deal they'd made.

She stared down at the body and the white substance that was pooling beneath his head, too thick to sink into the fabric of the carpet and this time, she heard Del's voice out loud.

"...instead of a brain, they found a prick...."

Helen peered down the dimly lit hallway, leaned out to look around the corner, but couldn't see him anywhere and the voice was coming from the walls themselves.

"...no blood, just sperm...."

She looked down, amazed, to where the semen had dribbled from carpet to tile, becoming a sluggish stream, clinging to her skin where it touched her foot and now, crawling up her leg, in its purposeful voyage toward fertilization

Memory Games

Preamble – Memory Games

I was raised in Edmonton Alberta, home of one of the world's best and longest running science fiction magazines, *On Spec*. The only stories of mine that haven't been rejected by *On Spec* are the ones that sold before they got there. I'm sure *On Spec* would have rejected those too.

Having started in the early 80s on Vancouver Island, where I lived, the *Tesseracts* anthology series is now up to #17. One of the original editors was best man at my second wedding and was the founder of my writer's group. The publication was taken over by Candas Jane Dorsey and moved to Edmonton after issue two. I was truly desperate to sell them something, but it looked for the longest time like it was going to be another *On Spec*-like experience.

The fifth *Tesseracts* volume was edited by Robert Runte and Yves Meynard. I had my hopes up when they were still holding my story very late in the process. I recall that Robert sent me one of the nicest rejection letters ever, saying that he wanted the story but that they were limited to a defined word count and there was no room to fit it in. I think he said he was still trying to talk Candas into making the book longer. I was pleased as punch when he called to let me know that he got his wish and they were accepting the story after all. I was even more pleased when "Memory Games" was nominated for an Aurora Award for best short work in English. I didn't win the award – but I felt like a winner. I had finally broken the jinx. I even had an inquiry about film rights from a young woman with the last name of Coppola (calm down – not the one you're thinking!)

So now there's just one more bit of business to take care of. If anyone at *On Spec* is amenable to bribes, I'd appreciate your calling me.

Memory Games

She grabbed Daniel's fingers as he unfastened her jeans. His hands were cool, almost cold. Even though he was little more than a shadow, she could see his eyes glinting in the starlight. Moonlight. More. A glare of headlights swept into the bedroom from the street, catching Daniel in their photographic flash. Something about his visage looked wrong.

Celine said, "We should talk first."

His arm turned to stone, refusing to be moved. "Why're you starting that again?"

Celine shrugged and began rebuttoning her blouse. "Did you know that Alan Winston was one of them?"

"Don't start again," he said.

"You remember Alan Winston, don't you?"

"No. I don't remember Alan-fucking-Winston!" When she didn't respond, he continued. "This is a crock. Sometimes I wonder what you'd really do if I failed one of these tests."

"Kill you."

"I mean what you'd *really* do! Know what I think? You wouldn't kill me, Celine, because you wouldn't trust your own judgement. You'd tell yourself you were being paranoid. You wouldn't kill me."

He undid the buttons she had just fastened.

She didn't stop him. Even if the stories were true about the Morphs absorbing the short term memories of the bodies they'd sucked the life from, the sorts of things Daniel knew about her were more than superficial. Weren't they?

How could he fake something like that?

He'd known about her paranoia. But then, who wasn't paranoid these days? Daniel's bluster and bravado didn't conceal his fear, they magnified it. If he was a morph, why would he be afraid?

He unfastened her brassiere, cradling her heavy breasts in his hands, rolling her nipples between his fingers. Closing her eyes, Celine tried to not to wince at the sensation of Daniel's hot breath and tongue gliding like a wet eraser down her neck and between her breasts. His fingers didn't feel so cold anymore, as they slid up her back, gripping the base of her skull and holding her like that as he kissed her. His other hand moved down, over her buttocks, his big hand squeezing the flesh of her ass, pulling her firmly to him.

She felt his erection through his jeans and squirmed away with a surge of terror.

"I may not kill you," she babbled. "But I won't be with you any more. Not until you tell me about Alan Winston."

"We worked with him," Daniel replied sullenly.

"Which department did he work in?"

Celine could see his anger quite clearly because the headlights had lit up the room again.

Only morphs drove cars anymore. She squinted at the window. "What are they up to?"

"I called them, when you started freaking out. We're never gonna catch this woman by surprise, I told them. Might as well take her now. "

A joke. Celine cringed at her uncertainty. Truth was impossible to recognize anymore. Celine wasn't sure it had ever existed.

He spoke again. "We should make the most of the short lives we have left." A familiar Daniel sort of sentiment. "If you send me away, you'll never make love to another man. You'd never be sure. You'll be afraid of living."

The air in the room felt thick and hot.

He was right.

Celine walked to the window, peering out into the empty street. After ensuring that the car didn't stop in the neighbourhood, she looked back into the darkness where Daniel stood. "You think I can't live without you? I've lived alone for half my adult life, Daniel. I'll survive."

He didn't speak for a long time. Celine began to wonder if he'd left the room.

"Yeah?" was all he finally said.

Celine immediately said, "We were talking about Alan Winston."

"I'm not playing tonight, Celine," Daniel said, walking up to her.

"Suits me fine. Neither am I."

She turned and walked down the stairs to the living room, where she sat down in the candlelight and stared blankly at the smouldering ashes in the fireplace.

The room was filled with things which were becoming more and more important as each day passed. Things made by human hands, which would soon be little more than artifacts. The raku vase her mother had bought her as a housewarming present, the once-valuable blue depression glass water pitcher she'd found at a garage sale, the painting on the wall – a vibrant cityscape, filled with people and cars and buses. She could read the names of the streets, the headlines on the newspapers and the signs. The buses had destinations.

Celine began to cry again. She derived little solace from the thought that if Daniel really had been replaced by a morph, this crying fit would probably drive him away. Negative emotions at the time of 'conception' spoiled the pre-natal environment – or so the stories said. But what did anybody really know? Who had actually been on a breeder ship and returned to tell about it? Who had ever seen a morph hatch, flesh of human parents bursting like balloons of blood and bone?

But there were many, many stories. A whole morph lore.

The shapeshifting invaders could take on all sorts of interesting disguises, like the angels they'd first appeared as, announcing that Judgement Day had come.

Millions of people, from radical sects of dozens of different religions followed them to hundreds of different heavens. The converts filled the alien birthing pods... .

Then Daniel was there, sitting on the couch beside her. In this light, he no longer looked as strange as he had upstairs. Not strange at all in fact. He was wearing that boyish look of contrition she'd always found irresistible.

On the one hand, it made her even more determined not to give in.

But then again, it made him seem more like Daniel.

"I need you," he said earnestly. "You're all I have."

When she didn't respond, he continued. "I thought you felt the same..."

"We don't love each other," Celine said. She stared at the tall dark-haired man beside her and really wondered for the first time whether this was actually the man she'd been sleeping with for eight months. Surely they didn't make duplicate people *this* perfectly? "We only stay together because we're afraid to find someone else. It's too dangerous. But it might be worth the gamble."

"I do love you," he said, as he put an arm over her shoulder and tried pulling her toward him.

But she pulled away, standing up and staring him in the eye and practically hissing, "Then stay and answer my questions."

"Okay. Alan Whateverhisnameis. Tell me more about him. Maybe, I'll remember."

"You really don't remember, do you?"

"I know the name, I just can't put a face to it. Gimme a kickstart. It'll come to me."

Celine shook her head but complied just the same. "Medium height. Sort of stocky. I think he was into weightlifting or something."

"Wait, wait, wait. He was...an analyst from Systems Support."

"No, that was Ernie Williams."

"Ernie, Alan, what's the difference?"

"Alan was the expenditure coordinator from Investment Administration. He and Gary from Payroll were known as the two musketeers cause they couldn't keep their swords in their scabbards. What was it Gary always used to tease you about?"

"It was so long ago, Celine."

"Come on! You know the answer to this one."

He grinned again. "It was about you."

"That's better. Why did you ever open your mouth to him in the first place?"

He shrugged.

"He might have said something to your wife. What would you have done then?"

He shrugged again.

"Daniel??"

"Never thought about it."

She backed away from him. "I want you to leave right now."

Daniel grinned. "Come on. I'm only teasing. I wasn't married. I figured that if you could make up a cast of characters to test my memory, I could play the same game. To show you how stupid this whole thing is, how willing you are to believe everything you hear from everywhere."

Celine rolled her eyes. If this was a morph, it argued exactly the same way Daniel did.

He'd once seemed so gallant and romantic, but now Celine wondered what she had ever seen in him, how she had come to believe that she loved him.

During the years she'd worked with him at the Department of Finance office, Celine's imagination had claimed and redefined him. And for most of the next eight months she'd visited his apartment once or even twice a week. Her husband had left her after finding out but Daniel had declined her invitation to move in with her.

Only in bed did their chemistry still seem perfect. Only there did she still need him. Even now, despite her fear and revulsion, Celine still found herself having to fight the urge to give herself to him. He was talking, but she had been tuning him out. "...for so long, it's getting hard tell the difference between fantasy and reality anymore. You know that?"

She shook her head. "I don't buy your explanation, Daniel. You should know those people I was just talking about. You worked with them for almost as long as I did."

Daniel nodded, then went to the closet and got out his jacket.

"What are you doing?" Celine asked.

"Going home."

She stared at him as he fastened the snaps. Christ. She never thought it would really happen, or what she'd do about it. It was only the long term memories which were rumoured to be notoriously incomplete.

"Look, we don't have to leave just because we're not going to make love. If you really need me and love me why can't we just sit and talk?"

"Because you'll just be playing memory games the whole time. Trying to trick me into slipping up. You know what I just thought of?" Daniel mumbled.

"What if they've found some way to erase chunks of our memories? All of us? If we've both forgotten all sorts of things, then if even one of us has been affected, we'd be all screwed up. We'd be sure to have the kind of disagreement we've just been having."

Suddenly realising she'd been nodding, Celine looked up, as disgusted with herself as she was with him. "Why would they do that? Look. I may be gullible, but you're pushing the bullshit meter a little high even for me. Maybe you should leave. We can talk about this tomorrow."

"They'd do it to make us afraid of each other. Maybe they even started the story about morphs having incomplete memories," Daniel said. "If we're afraid of each other, we'll be less likely to mount an effective resistance."

"What resistance?"

"Precisely."

"You can't bafflegab me anymore. If you won't humour me by answering a few questions, then you don't love me enough. Period. This isn't going to work, Daniel."

He turned and left without further protest.

Maybe it really was Daniel she thought, as she watched the door close behind him.

He expected her to believe this stupid memory-wipe theory he'd hatched out of the blue?

She would have laughed if it wasn't so tragic. For six months, Daniel had been the only male on the planet whom she had dared to trust. And now, he was being taken away from her.

By her own paranoia? Daniel's well-aimed wisecrack had shaken her. As he knew it would. He was armed with a quiet brutality and even if he was really human, Celine knew she was better rid of him.

She had trouble sleeping that night and while she lay there staring into the darkness, she started to see the logic of Daniel's assertion. Maybe the stories about the aliens really were propagated by the aliens themselves. That would certainly answer her questions about how any humans had lived to tell the tales. She wondered if there was any way to test the large-scale memory loss idea.

Encyclopedias! That was it. After Google took over the knowledge brokering industry, Celine's Mom had found an entire set of the old tomes for ten dollars. Not wanting to tell her mom she'd been ripped off, Celine had accepted them. Historical artifacts themselves, they had anchored her bookcase in the living room for the past ten years. She'd check it to see if she could find historical facts she had forgotten.

Pulling on a housecoat to hide her nakedness, despite the fact that she was alone in the house, Celine descended the staircase slowly in the dim candle light. Once in the living room, she walked straight to the bookcase, grabbed an encyclopedia at random and opened it.

A bit more than an hour later, there was a knock on the front door. "It's me," was all he said.

He grinned when she opened the door for him. "So you couldn't sleep either, eh? Look, Celine. I think we've got to work this out."

She nodded. "I think so too. In fact, that's what I was doing now." She displayed the volume in her hand. "The letter 'S'.

"In case they really ARE tampering with all our memories." Walking back into the living room, she left Daniel standing at the door as she sat down on the couch, peering at the book in the dim, flickering light. "I want to see if there's anything I've forgotten. Anything important. Anything I should remember."

She opened the big book to the middle. "South Dakota."

Daniel grinned. "I think you should look for something a little more obscure."

Running his hand through his hair like a cowboy, he sauntered into the room and sat down beside her. "An event or something. How about that?"

"Slipperwort?"

He sat down beside her and pointed. "How about this? Stone Mountain."

"Oh, come on."

"No, really. Tell me about Stone Mountain. I don't..."

"C'mon, Daniel, quit shitting me. Nobody's ever heard of Stone Mountain."

Daniel's eyes opened wide. "You're serious?"

"Cut it out," Celine squeaked.

"Look here," he said, pointing to the encyclopedia entry. "One of the largest granite masses in the world. The Confederate Memorial is carved into the eastern slope, for crying out loud. The figures of Robert E. Lee, Jefferson Davis and Stonewall Jackson carved into the mountain. You at least remember Mount Rushmore, don't you?"

Celine nodded mutely. She could not for the life of her remember ever hearing of Stone Mountain. Being a Canadian, maybe it was simply a point of ignorance on her part. Or maybe she really had lost chunks of memory.

She continued through the pages. "I know about almost everything else in here."

"Oh, yeah, Mrs. Einstein. Then who's Snorri Sturluson?"

"A famous medieval Norwegian writer. Ha!"

Daniel nodded, obviously amazed that Celine had known the answer to such an obscure bit of history.

"You weren't expecting that were you? I think that's the first time I've ever had a chance to use anything I learned in that Mythology course I took in university."

He shook his head and kissed her on the nose. "You're a marvel. Now let's continue with the exercise. What's the capital of Paraguay?"

She punched him in the arm.

"Give me the book. Now it's my turn."

Reluctantly, he handed it to her. After a moment, she said, "Tell me about the Suez Canal. Where is it?"

"It's in...Arabia or somewhere in the middle east. It connects the Mediterranean with...some other big body of water. The Indian Ocean, the Red Sea, something like that."

Nodding Celine turned some more pages. "How 'bout the Spanish Inquisition."

"And how about those Blue Jays."

"Come on. I'm serious. Who was Torquemada?"

He shook his head. "The designated hitter? I dunno. That's a bit too obscure."

"Then tell me something else about the Inquisition."

"It was in Spain..."

"Good start. What else?"

"Something to do with religion, Christians being persecuted or something?"

"Come on, Daniel. It was the Christians who were doing the persecuting."

"Maybe that's why they never talked about it much in school."

"Hmmmm..." she conceded. Somehow his ignorance was more convincing than his knowledge would have been.

"Besides, history was never my forte. I preferred sex education."

This time, Celine laughed as he kissed her neck. "I'll bet you did."

"That's the thing about memory," said Daniel. "You can never be sure about something you've forgotten." He kissed her lips. She kissed back, wondering in the back of her mind whether she'd just been conned.

She remembered how lonely she'd felt when Daniel had gone away – the shock and discomfort of the realization that she'd never find anyone else she could be sure about again in her whole life.

When she kissed him back, the book slid off of her lap, landing with a soft thud on the carpet.

She let him untie the belt on her housecoat and run his hands over her breasts. He was right, the only way she'd ever know for sure would be to take the chance.

"I love you," he said as his hand slid down between her legs. She clung to Daniel, to the idea that he really was who he said he was and he really did love her.

She nuzzled her face into Daniel's neck.

"I'm sorry," she said. "I love you too."

They undressed right there on the couch.

As he entered her, his eyes gleamed in the candlelight and despite her determination to believe him, she couldn't prevent herself staring into those eyes, mining for secrets.

Flushed

Preamble – Flushed

My enduring affection for the work of H.P. Lovecraft and appreciation for parodies of the Lovecraftian aesthetic by folks like William Browning Spencer in his wonderful novel *Resume with Monsters* inspired me to put this story together.

It would be a more amusing preamble if I could tell you that I wrote the entire story while sitting on the toilet, but I didn't (although I may have thought much of it up in there). I actually wrote this for Don Hutchison because I wasn't satisfied with just doing the cover art for *Northern Frights 5*. I really, really wanted a story in it – after all, the Northern Frights books were the best horror anthologies ever published in Canada (and they are in my opinion among the best in the world) – and Don had revealed a weakness for silliness in previous volumes.

Flushed

The toilet bowl was less than six inches in circumference above the trap and it funneled even narrower into a four inch sewer pipe, and yet Lawrence had seen his wife getting sucked down. Had touched her.

How could he go to the police or even call a plumber about this? Hearing such a story second hand, he himself would not have believed it. But he had heard the shriek from the bathroom; and the flushing, screaming and gurgling as he tried to break down the heavy oak door with his shoulder before running for the crowbar.

The wood cracked like gunshots, door popping open just in time for Lawrence to see Christine's arm reach up out of the toilet, grabbing the rim with whitened fingers. He stood gaping in disbelief, spurred to action only when he spotted the wedding ring on her finger. The implications of what was happening sank in. At the very instant she lost her grip, he reached out, catching her by fingertips which wriggled and clawed at the palm of his hand, then finally, slippery with the residue of cheap toilet cleanser, oozed from his desperate grasp.

The blue water in the bowl burbled, then chugged repeatedly. An unbearable stench rose from its depths and the water turned purple before congealing to a thick, rusty brown. Something pink broke the surface. Lawrence fished it out with the pole end of the plunger, washing the slime off in the sink to find Christine's sock, the one with the hula-bears around the rim.

Spending the next ten minutes dragging and plunging the toilet to no avail, he pulled the lid from the toilet tank and heaved it into the bathtub, but could see nothing inside to help him figure out what had happened or what he could do to get his wife back.

Running to the roll top desk in the kitchen, Lawrence sat down at his computer and hammered on the keys, making several attempts before successfully logging onto The Psychic Explorers Hotline.

"Emergency! Anyone ever heard of disappearances involving toilets or waterclosets? Esp. supernatural. Need help in Pacific northwest, BC lower mainland area. E-mail or phone response. (604) 380-7150. Reward offered for any information. ASAP. Ask for Lawrence."

Then, he went down to the basement to see what he could see. Half way between the floor and ceiling, the sewer pipe bulged out around the object it was digesting.

"Christine!"

Had the metal somehow softened? Lawrence tried to sink his fingers in, then tapped, and ultimately whacked at the swollen surface of the pipe with a crescent wrench, but it was as thick and strong as ever. He ran to his workbench, found an axe and contemplated it for a moment before spotting the hacksaw, which had no blade. His eyes lit on the blowtorch before he realized that any attempt to cut the pipe would heat it up, thus poaching his wife.

The phone rang and Lawrence ran to answer it. Glancing back at the pipe from the top of the stairs, he saw the bulge sinking into the floor. The concrete seemed to have become elastic around the base of the pipe, because it didn't break or buckle.

On the line was a man with a uncannily deep, yet squeaky voice. Like Mickey Mouse on steroids. "Mon nom est Monsieur Clarrisse. I am responding to your electronic admonishment."

"You know something about disappearances of this nature?"

"Mais, oui. I have encountered them before."

"No, I don't think you quite grasp ...I'm saying that...I mean..." He decided to just come out with it. "The toilet ate my wife."

"Hers was not the first such disappearance, Monsieur Lawrence. Was she, par chance, a cheerleader?"

Lawrence gasped so hard he choked. "How could you...possibly...?"

"I share not only your area code, but your prefix. It seems I am nearby. And eager to investigate this phenomenon. But my knowledge is not the sort which can be dispensed over the telephone."

Hesitantly, Lawrence divulged his address, wondering the whole time whether this was some sort of elaborate scam to get appointments for vacuum cleaner demonstrations.

The gaunt, goateed man with the hypnotic gaze who showed up at Lawrence's door was dressed like a plumber, but looked as absurd in his crisp, clean blue coverall as God in a tutu.

"I am M. Clarrisse," he said, holding up a box. "Et voila, this is my snake, Maximillian."

He named his plumbing snake? Lawrence wondered again if it had been a good idea, inviting this man into his home. But then, what choice did he have?

As Lawrence ushered the man to the washroom, Clarrisse explained how he knew so much. "You see Monsieur Lawrence, my own wife, Trixie was an earlier victim. She was employed by the franchise de la Dallas Cowboys, eh? The police were determined to charge me with murder but no evidence could be found. After one year, they allowed me to depart. For four more years, I studied with mystics in Nepal and the Phillipines and learned to project my consciousness into the body of Maximillian.

"But during my absence, Trixie's brother, Ace had built an apartment block where my house had been, changing the whole sewer system in the process. The trail was lost. But perhaps now, we have discovered another route, n'est ce pas?"

As he lowered the snake into the thick, brown water of the toilet bowl, M. Clarrisse instructed Lawrence sibilantly, "I warn you, do not disturb me when I am one with Maximillian. Such interferance would be disastrous and tragic. Just listen and I will describe whatever I see or touch or smell."

The python's head creased the water's slimy surface, long, silver body arcing up as it dove and its disappearance left a dimple.

"Merde," muttered Clarrisse.

As Lawrence stood beside Clarrisse, watching Maximillian slide like a strand of spaghetti into porcelain lips, he reflected upon how lucky he had been to find M. Clarrisse so quickly.

Clarrisse, meanwhile, appeared to be in some sort of trance. His voice provided a droning commentary, "Maximillian has reached the sewer main without encountering any major obstacles. Wait. He's being channelled off, sucked down and down and now...he is emerging into a pool...a fountain, surrounded by cherubs and angels with gargoyle faces. A fountain of excrement. The walls are ornate, pebbled with tiny bones, trimmed with skulls, human and otherwise. Heavy trellises of big bones form gothic archways. Most of the bones on the floor of the chamber are human and recent, some still with strips of flesh and sinew attached.

"There's something dark and...massive. A monster so large that the air in the chamber gets thin when it inhales. And whistles out in a fetid hurricane.

"And, Tabernacle! There they are. Women. Dozens of beautiful young women, half naked, their hands blossoming with human entrails. One of them is Trixie. Ma belle, I have found you at last!"

"Does one of them have red hair?" Lawrence asked anxiously. "A gorgeous mane of bright red hair?"

But instead of answering his question, the snakeman said, "The monster looks at the women hungrily with each of its thousand eyes."

Lawrence grabbed Clarrisse's arm and shook it excitedly. "Is Christine there? Can you do anything to save her? You must save her!"

Clarrisse turned and stared at him with beady snake eyes. "You idiot! You have broken the connection! Because of you, Maximillian is now trapped in the same netherworld as my beloved Trixie!" The man turned purple with rage. Grabbing the soap-on-a-rope from the bathtub caddy, he whipped it at Lawrence's head, catching him across the temple.

Lawrence fell heavily, smacking his forehead against the rim of the toilet bowl. Groggily, he clung to consciousness, his ear pressed against the cold porcelain which conducted the sounds from the unspeakable depths. In the instant before Lawrence was beaten insensible with an economy sized shampoo bottle, he heard sounds that would be imprinted in his memory forever: the ululating chant of the cheerleaders, ripe with terror and despair – drowned out by the roar of the monstrous crowd that filled the subterranean chambers like aural sewage.

Corrosive Agents

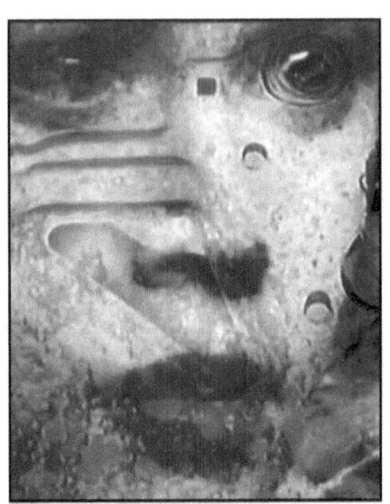

Preamble – Corrosive Agents

This is another story that took me a long time to write, probably because it has so many parallels to my real life in eighth grade.

It went through a number of false starts before I came to realize that only by letting go of important truths from my life, could I hope to achieve the kind of semblance to reality I was seeking for the story. Ironically, getting rid of the truth made the narrative more real because it stopped drawing attention to irrelevant clutter and allowed me to focus on the essential elements within the story.

Fear shields innocence from all sorts of worldy wear and tear. But once the rot sets in….

"Corrosive Agents" appears here for the first time.

Corrosive Agents

In grade seven Ben moved twice. The first move took him from an idyllic wooded hillside on the west coast – which, in his memories, was all but enchanted – to a town full of ranchers and bullies where he got body-checked into the lockers all winter. His only friends were the two other kids in school who couldn't skate.

While the latest move had kept them in the prairies, they at least went to a city. The bigger the school, the less he would be noticed. Ben had cultivated invisibility, had practiced it almost every day of his life. Remaining anonymous was so much easier here than it had been in Fort McCleod.

Having towed his family through half a dozen starkly different realities in as many years, Ben's dad was, once again, living a step and a half ahead of the rest of his family. He'd finally brought them north on the promise of a shiny salary from Family Services. But working with police to rescue abused children turned out to be soul destroying, so he quickly got a new job with the municipal government of a city another few hundred miles north – leaving Ben and his mom on their own again, in a strange city again.

He was thrilled about the better TV reception, which allowed them to watch *Star Trek*, *My Favourite Martian* and *Stampede Wrestling*.

Being completely invisible was lonely, and Ben's challenge as always, was to find somebody in the fringes who was as invisible as he was. Other new kids were initially the easiest to make friends with because they were grateful for company. But the nerds were better because they were often dreamers like him.

Percy Ratzlaff was both new and nerdy – a tall, frail-looking kid whose hooked nose and big round ears stuck out from his head like the triple fins of an old-fashioned rocket-ship. After his mom died, Percy moved with his Dad into a ritzy split level house on a suburban crescent out near Northgate Mall. The combination of money in his pocket and adventure in his heart made Percy the most exciting friend Ben had made in years. Maybe ever.

That summer, they built a raft and explored an abandoned farmhouse in the middle of a swamp at the edge of town. Percy pointed out muskrats. Some guy had told him you could kill them with a whack on the head with your paddle. Said you could get twenty bucks for a muskrat pelt. They tried, with Ben poling the raft and Percy playing the executioner, but never managed to nail one. Their headquarters for the summer had been an abandoned house in the middle of the swamp where nobody without a raft dared to come.

Summer's passing and the disappearance of the raft pushed them indoors. Percy's dad worked irregular hours, and it was important not to wake him up, by accident or for any other reason. When they got to his house after school, Percy would sneak up the hall, avoiding the spots with squeaky boards. After confirming his father's absence, he'd take Ben to his impeccably tidy room and lock the door softly behind them. Then they'd settle down cross-legged on the world's plushest carpet, and Percy would slide a box of UFO magazines out from under the bed. There were more than a dozen different titles on the newsstands and Percy had them all – including an issue of *LIFE* with a flying saucer on the cover.

They got into drawing schematics for mother ships. The last set of Percy's made no sense. It had no doorways. Percy explained that his aliens weren't humanoid, they travelled through holes in the wall into different chambers. He pointed out that it was ridiculous to draw schematics if you don't even know what the aliens look like.

Reaching back under the bed, he pulled out a separate box. James Bond movies, *Dangerman* and *The Man from Uncle* were all hot properties and the spy comedies were just gaining steam, so spies were popping up everywhere. The box was filled with *Man from Uncle* comic books; magazines dedicated to *I Spy* and *The Saint*; and trading cards picturing James Bond, Moneypenny, Oddjob, Jaws and an old woman with knives in the toes of her shoes.

You could hear the admiration and longing in Percy's voice when he said, "Their lives are secrets. Imagine that. I think that's why my dad never talks about his work. It's top secret."

"Your dad's a spy?"

"He won't tell me. That's suspicious in itself, don't you think?"

"Does he carry a gun?" Ben asked.

Percy's silent smile went straight across his face like a zipper with a tiny upward twist at each end.

The idea of surveillance thrilled him – of watching someone, without them being aware of his existence. He told Ben once that the ability to be invisible was what had made him a desirable friend.

Percy once showed Ben how spies avoid making noise. They walk differently than most people – stepping onto their toes before settling down onto their heels. It made him bob up and down when he walked. Percy was always practicing, even down the hallways at school. The cool kids laughed at him, the girls shied away. Ben thought at first that silence was pointless if it required you to make a quiet spectacle of yourself. But Percy got better at it. After awhile Ben was the only one who noticed anymore.

They saw less of each other, Ben often sitting out on the front steps of his house staring into the night sky with indefinable longing. If anyone had asked him outright, he could only have explained that the stars proved there was more to life than what we could see.

Seeing her son stare into the sky every night made Ben's mom think he was interested in astronomy, when in fact he was just looking for UFOs. For his birthday, she bought him a telescope. Seeing stars at eight-times magnification didn't enhance them much, turning Saturn from a fuzzy dot into a fuzzy disc, but revealing nothing remotely like rings. Mars looked white, and just twinkled red. And it was almost impossible to point and lock on anything moving, so it actually reduced the chances of seeing a UFO.

The little telescope would have stayed on his dresser gathering dust if Percy had not decided to explore its espionage potential.

Ben had to admit that big rectangles of light were easier to get a bead on than fuzzy discs, and potentially more fun to watch. From his second floor bedroom, they could see a dozen different windows in the apartment building across the back alley. A red-headed girl from St. Mary's lived there. Percy pointed out a silhouette moving behind a frosted window and suggested it might be the Catholic girl toweling off after a bath.

Ben pretended to be unimpressed, but for the next week in the bathtub, he imagined her in the bath with him. Then he started imagining it was Charmaine Wickend.

Charmaine was in Ben's science class. Her friend, Nancy, sat at Ben's lab table – the end without the sink. While neither of the girls ever really looked at him; they talked constantly and Ben's vantage point afforded him an unobstructed view of Charmaine's face. In the course of a single class, he fell in love with her porcelain skin, her curving lips, her hazel eyes that flashed like golden coins in sunlight.

Over the summer the boys started taking the telescope to vacant lots throughout the neighbourhood, seeing what they could see through living room windows across busy streets. They weren't exactly inconspicuous, a fact that discouraged Ben but challenged Percy. They got good at staying in the shadows.

But ultimately, spying on people took incredible patience and offered little reward. Ben mostly just watched the sky while Percy did reconnaissance. Within a week, they were going back to Percy's place, bored again.

One day, Ben stood in the hall of Percy's house watching Percy approach his father's door. It swung open and a big jowly slab of a man with an expressionless face and sallow, flaky complexion stepped out. His robe was royal blue and the lapels were paisley. The shoulders were white with dandruff.

The way Percy jumped back from him reminded Ben of a mongoose he'd seen on *The Wonderful World of Disney* – as did the way the two stood staring wordlessly at one another.

His dad pulled the bedroom door shut behind him the same way his son always did, and looked at Ben. "You're Percy's friend?"

His voice was very soft, almost a mumble. What appeared to be bubbles formed at the corners of his mouth, which he wiped with his sleeve. He didn't look at all the way he imagined a spy would look. His accented voice lacked any cadence. "Glad to see he has friends."

Was it possible he was a Russian spy?

Percy said nothing, so his father kept talking to Ben. "Percy should introduce us."

Percy turned and stammered, "Ben, this is my father."

Mr. Ratzlaff's handshake was brusque and loose and moist. He wore some sort of cologne, which couldn't hide an underlying sour scent. That afternoon, Percy wouldn't meet his father's gaze as the older man said, "Don't make too much noise."

As soon as the door snicked shut behind him, the boys ducked into Percy's room. But he didn't go diving for his stuff the way he usually did, just sat on the bed with his hands clasped in his lap. After another long, silent moment Ben asked, "So. We gonna do something?"

Percy shrugged.

"I can go home if you want," Ben said, getting up and reaching for the door handle.

Percy beat him to the door and blocked his exit. Putting his ear to the white surface and his finger to his lips, the taller boy stood mannequin-still.

They could hear a woman's voice and then a man's, much quieter. A moment later, the front door closed so softly that you could feel the change in air pressure more than actually hear it.

Percy turned and opened the top drawer of his dresser. He pulled something out and dropped it in Ben's lap.

"Guess what these are."

Ben looked down at a pair of cheap plastic eyeglasses. Instead of lenses the frames held hypno-discs. He laughed out loud, "X-Ray glasses! They look just like they do in the ads."

"They don't work," Percy said, unnecessarily. "The stuff from the comic books is crap. But I got these from the *True Detective* magazine." He held up a pocket protector containing two pens. "This one writes in disappearing ink and this one is a microphone. The tape recorder is in here."

From the closet, he retrieved a briefcase that contained a tiny tape recorder with reels no bigger around than silver dollars and a cord that plugged into the pen. The pocket on the lid of the briefcase contained a booklet that said "CIA Manual." It also contained a birth certificate from New Mexico that said Percy was twenty-one.

Ben went to the bathroom and when he came back, Percy was playing a tape he had made in the East Mall Coffee Shop. He explained how he had pushed his briefcase under his chair so he could record what took place in the next booth, where a couple of high school guys were teasing their girlfriends.

First came a girl's voice, her words too faint to discern. One of the guys said something about beavers, which drew drifts of laughter. The girl said something back to him that must have been funny because everyone laughed again.

"I can almost figure out what she said," said Percy as he rewound the tape and turned the volume louder. He pressed his thumbs on the speaker cover to reduce the vibration.

To Ben, it was still incomprehensible babble, but Percy shouted, "There, did you hear it? 'I'm going to a different...' something. "

They rewound and listened to it several more times before Percy revealed that the speaker was Charmaine Wickend.

"After you told me about her, I followed her a couple times," Percy explained.

A week later, Percy cut a hole in the briefcase and installed a white plastic camera that was almost as small as a deck of cards and not a great deal bigger than the square lens. He clipped the pen into the pocket of the briefcase so that no-one could see the cord and taped the remote shutter button to the handle of the briefcase. They planned to locate Charmaine in the courtyard at lunchtime and he would stand with his back to her so Percy could take covert shots. Though it sounded simple, the actual mission took more than a week.

In the downstairs bathroom they developed the tiny square prints. Percy's dad had either allowed him to convert the bathroom off the poolroom in the basement into a darkroom or else he didn't notice. Soon they were looking at fuzzy photos as well as listening to muddy tape recordings.

Percy didn't have an enlarger. In most of the pictures, Charmaine looked more like a thumbprint, but even in the dim red light, you could make out a skirted figure in a white coat in several of the pictures.

When Ben got up, his pantleg stuck to the edge of the bathtub. "Ew."

Percy explained, "I think I did that with the developing chemicals. If I don't clean it up my dad will kill me."

When Ben worried aloud that it would leave a stain, Percy told him to get it into the wash. The next day when his mom was hanging clothes out to dry she asked, "Did you try to iron your brown pants?"

When he shook his head, she said, "I don't know what you got on them then. They have some sort of shiny spots."

That day at school, Percy sidled up to Ben in the lunch line-up. When he was sure no-one was listening, he said, "I can show you where she lives. We should bring the telescope."

That Friday, they walked past Charmaine's house and circled back through the alley. Percy showed Ben a vantage point on top of the garbage can shelter in the driveway from which you could see right into Charmaine's bedroom.

Ben was equal parts jealous and repulsed. "Have you seen her, like, undressed?"

"Not yet. Maybe tonight."

Charmaine was an only child and her mom worked at night. Her dad came and went after work, but that night they saw no sign of their 'target' as Percy called her.

At ten, he suggested, "Let's at least look through their garbage."

"That's sick."

"Standard ops."

"You're such a dork."

"I'll prove it to you. Bet you ten bucks we learn at least five new things about her, five important things."

Ben shook his head. "I don't have that kind of money."

Percy said, "You can owe me."

Percy dug into the first bag and held up a Chinese food container. "Now you know what she likes to eat – where to take her out for supper."

"What if it wasn't her that ate it?"

"She ate some of it, there's a bunch of these containers."

"Hmm," Ben half-conceded, not wanting to get into an argument about whether she actually liked Chinese Food.

From the second bag Percy extracted looseleaf sheets from Charmaine's math binder, filled with calculations and formulae and doodles of clouds and flying hearts. With a palm-sized flashlight partly concealed in the sleeve of his coat, Percy pointed out the initials CW and CB with the Cs interlocked. In some, the Ws morphed into butterflies and carried the Bs into the clouds. "Chris Boychuk," Percy hissed. "What a retard!"

Opening the next bag, he pulled out and explained the significance of several items: a small heart-shaped box of chocolates filled with nuts that had been liberated of their chocolate coating; a plastic Hudson's Bay bag stuffed with used sanitary napkins; some bad poetry about the futility of life crumpled into little balls; and half a dozen envelopes addressed to her from Thelma Wickend in Calgary.

When it came to covert operations, Ben was a rookie, so he didn't argue when Percy claimed he'd lost the bet.

After school the next day, Ben went with Percy, following Charmaine and Nancy until they turned down a side street. Percy informed him. "Nancy lives in those row houses. Second building. Third unit. Her sister, Beth is in grade ten at Queen E."

Ben was impressed. Unaware that Canada had a separate secret service agency, he imagined Percy passing the CIA entrance tests someday.

On the third day, he was assigned to follow Charmaine home by himself, again returning via the alley. By the time he turned the corner at the end of the block, he saw Charmaine's white coat half a block away. She and a woman who was probably her mom were getting into a big blue Impala convertible that was idling in the alley. Ben waited in the empty driveway behind the darkened house until Percy arrived.

Percy pushed open the back gate.

"Where you going?" Ben whispered, horrified at the prospect of being caught in their yard.

"Maybe they left a door or window unlocked. C'mon."

Ben shook his head. "I'll stand lookout."

"So they'll catch you creeping around in their driveway instead? That's real normal. Come into the yard. Then at least you can choose which way to run."

The basement and side doors were both locked and after Ben gave Percy a boost to check the kitchen window, they left.

"Wanna go to my place?" Percy asked.

"Isn't your dad home?"

"He said he had to go out of town."

When they got there, Percy wanted to go through the pictures of Charmaine and her friends but Ben was fed up with the spy stuff and paced back and forth. "You're going to wear out the carpet. After a while, he said, "You want to go downstairs?"

"To the darkroom?" Ben asked.

Percy shrugged and left the room. Ben followed him to the basement. The billiard room was better illuminated by the bright hall light than either the red light in the bathroom or the low hanging fixture over the big table. Ben wouldn't have seen the stack of cardboard boxes in the corner if Percy hadn't pointed them out.

"My dad works with a guy who's trying to stop drinking. Emptied his whole bar. Dad said he doesn't even know what's in here."

Placing the top box on the floor he opened the lid and took out a bottle of clear stuff. The label said it was gin. Percy went to the bar and came back with some glasses. They sat on the floor and put some in each glass. It tasted like what Ben imagined shoe polish would taste like only this stuff burned on the way down. They each had little sips and tried not to make faces or comments. When Percy doctored his with maraschino cherry liqueur, Ben joined him, but that didn't improve it much.

Percy emptied his and nodded at Ben. "Just swallow fast."

They emptied those in a swallow and Ben gagged as it went down. He had never been drunk before and he didn't like it so far. Head spinning and stomach roiling, he wanted to pour out his drink in the darkroom sink.

"That's like pouring a dollar down the sink," said Percy. But even he was down to tiny sips interspersed with a lot of wincing.

Something loomed in the doorway, blocking off the light from the hall.

Heart stuttering and stomach clenching, Ben stood up and set his glass on the pool table.

"Not there!" said a voice behind him. It had barely touched the felt before Percy scooped it up.

Ben marveled at how Mr Ratzlaff seemed a hundred pounds heavier. His face was grey and he glared at the boys with tiny, red, pig-eyes.

Dark stains glistened on the sleeves and lapels of his deep-blue, satin bathrobe.

Just before he reached the boys, he stopped.

In his almost inaudible mumble, he said, "You shouldn't drink that shit." Then he reached behind the bar and pulled out a square-bellied bottle made of cut crystal.

Taking the glasses from Percy, he emptied them into the bar sink that no-one was ever allowed to use, then filled the glasses with a liquid so black and thick that it made the navy rum look like lemonade.

The whole time he did this, Mr. Ratzlaff was making some sort of noise. A deep-throated gurgling sound that reminded Ben of an outboard motor. A step nearer, he could identify the sound as laughter – a chuckle on slow broil. He gave one glass to Percy and pushed the other into Ben's hand. "Drink. Now."

Percy did what he was told, then nodded at Ben, expressionless.

Ben lifted his but it smelled like vomit, and when he gazed into it he saw that the liquid was somehow alive, teeming with little snakes and centipedes. "I've gotta go," he said, looking for someplace to set the glass down. Mr. Ratzlaff took it from him.

Until the moment he clamped his arm around the back of Ben's head and grabbed his jaw, Ben wasn't aware that his skinny friend had been working out in anticipation of becoming a spy. But he pulled Ben back as though he were a small child. Arched backward, Ben looked up at Percy in mounting desperation, but there was no sign of friendship in the boy's eyes. No humour, camaraderie, patience. Nothing.

Ben managed not to open his lips as Percy tried to pry his mouth open, so Mr. Ratzlaff poured it under his nose. Ben could feel tendrils of liquid slithering up his nostril toward his brain and he snorted and yelled, whereupon the rest of the glass was poured down his throat.

He started choking and retching so they released him and Ben looked at the two of them through teary, blurry eyes. At first he thought Percy was crying too, but then he saw that the streaks down his face were chalky white. Looking at Percy's father, Ben saw thick white foam at the corners of his mouth and a sulphurous smell in the air. It dripped down his chin and Ben realized that his lapels weren't glistening with grease, they were actually eaten away and you could see his flaking white skin right through the holes. A piece of his forehead peeled off and landed on the floor like a wet potato chip. The skin beneath it was translucent and white and some sort of cream oozed out where its surface was cracked.

Panic surged up inside of Ben, along with the entire contents of his stomach.

Percy's dad stepped back to the other side of the doorway, very quickly for a man his size and condition.

Feeling woozy and empty, bewildered and alone, Ben lurched past them both, running straight up the stairs, gathering his coat and shoes at the door. He was halfway home before he even slowed down enough to put them on.

He didn't see Percy much after, except for fleeting glimpses in the schoolyard or in the distance after school, bobbing off down the long curving road to the mall. It never occurred to Ben that Percy would keep stalking Charmaine with him gone, until she stopped coming to class shortly after the first snowfall of the winter. A week after he'd first noticed her absence, Ben approached Nancy and explained that he had borrowed some notes from Charmaine, but couldn't find her to return them.

Nancy shrugged, "You can probably keep them. Her parents are splitting up and she moved to Calgary to live with her aunt."

He would have let it go without another thought if he hadn't seen Charmaine while he was walking home from school. It's like she had been waiting for him at the corner of the street where she lived, walking with her head down and her collar pulled up. As Ben approached, Charmaine turned her head and looked directly at him. Ben couldn't recall ever looking right into her eyes before and his breath caught in his throat. She smiled, put her head back down and walked away.

That evening, Ben poked at his dinner, eating very little, then told his mom he was going over to Percy's to study. She sounded pleased. "I didn't think you two were getting along anymore!"

Ben simply shrugged.

The walkway at the back of Charmaine's house hadn't been shoveled. Ben was conscious of his feet crunching through a several layers of snow and of the trail of footprints he was leaving up to the back gate. Seemed that no one had even taken out the garbage in the past week.

Sure it was Charmaine he had seen, Ben went into the yard. Lights were on in the dining room, kitchen and basement. He felt relieved.

As he stood on his tiptoes to peek in the side window, he was so startled by a voice behind him that he almost cried out.

"I thought you might come round here tonight," said Percy.

Ben stood with his back against the wall of the house and hissed, "What are you doing here?"

When Percy shrugged his familiar full-body shrug, Ben almost missed him for a moment. Then he remembered the betrayal and his warm pang of regret was replaced with a chill.

"I've talked to her, you know?" he said. "She invited me over tonight."

Ben's immediate reaction was to laugh and say something like, "yeah, sure." But Percy rang the doorbell. And before anybody had a chance to run, the door opened.

Charmaine was framed by warm incandescent light. From this close up she seemed more beautiful than ever.

"You brought Ben," she said to him without inflection.

Ben didn't really know Charmaine, or at least, she didn't know him, so nothing could have surprised or alarmed him more than his dream girl knowing his name.

She pushed open the storm door and Percy held it and motioned for Ben to precede him.

"I'll take your coat," Charmaine's sweet voice murmured and Ben almost let her do it, before Percy crowded onto the landing behind him and nudged him toward the stairs.

Charmaine now stood one step up, her eyes even with Ben's. But they had lost their sheen. They were a lifeless turquoise, verging on grey. She put her hand on Ben's shoulder, pulling him toward her so Percy could close the door.

Ben noticed Charmaine's fingernails, not just chewed, but almost blackened beneath a chipped coat of pink polish. She kissed him with lips so hot they burned like that liquor. She wore perfume, but Ben recognized the same bitter, sour smell that had stung his nose in Percy's basement. Reeling in sudden panic, Ben almost pushed Percy down the stairs, as he burst out through the storm door, jarring the metal frame off its hinges in his rush to get down the front walkway to the street.

No-one followed Ben.

Neither Percy nor Charmaine was at school the next day. Percy went home for lunch detouring past Charmaine's house. The windows were all dark. Seeing no curtains or pictures on the wall, he surmised that the place was empty.

When he looked down, he was surprised to see only one set of footprints coming down the sidewalk to the side of the house, where the storm door hung on one hinge.

He wondered if Percy and Charmaine were still in the house. He thought about ringing the doorbell and running if someone came, but what would be the point?

He took deep breaths, trying to figure out what was going on, what the right course of action would be. The cold winter air carried no scent it all, but if it had, Ben imagined it would smell like someone trying to jumpstart a battery – a flat metallic scent with a sharp, burnt edge. The smell of corrosion was growing familiar.

Ben looked down at the shoulder of his suede parka. There was a flat spot in the nap, he could make out the individual fingers where the material had thinned as though touched by a hot iron.

Ben put his hand on top of where Charmaine's hand had left its mark and it was like holding hands with a ghost.

"If I led him to you, I'm sorry," he whispered, before turning and heading home through the icy but thawing streets.

Exposure

Preamble – Exposure

In 1998, when my story "At Fort Assumption" (now "Exposure") was published in *Northern Frights 4*, I was pretty pleased with myself.

It was the most technically challenging story I'd ever written in the way it shifts back and forth between reality and several layers of "dream," and according to more than one reviewer, I had written it "quite expertly."

It was by far my most autobiographical story and I had dredged up some very vivid memories of the summer I'd lived in the town of High Level. I remember when my sister read it and said to me, "There is no flying saucer landing pad in High Level you know."

I should have just told her, "Well that's why they call this fiction." After all, my Mom was still alive and it was my Dad who had died when I was a teenager – and the narrator of the story didn't even have a sister.

But what I actually said was, "How can that be? I remember it clearly."

Our house was less than a block away from Centennial Park. I could draw a street map.

But it turns out I had misremembered it completely. The landing pad was actually in another town where my Dad had lived and worked (St. Paul, Alberta). The memories had melded together in my brain over the years – something that almost certainly happens to everyone. We transpose tiny snippets of memory into more familiar surroundings because they are so fragmentary we don't have the context to mentally file them where they belong.

And we all have incidents or people we think we remember because we've seen photographs or people have told us stories. I went for years actually believing a story that I myself had made up because I wanted so badly to believe it. I had told it so many time that it had actually seemed true.

However true something might seem, it almost never is.

Which has me wondering, how much truth must something contain to support the statement "based on a true story?"

Exposure

In daylight, the flying saucer landing pad looked cartoonish against the bleak brown landscape. But in the eternal twilight of the northern summer, it looked frighteningly alien and Theo loved it. The only thing in High Level he could ever love.

Sitting in the centre of the paint-worn, concrete disc, Theo blinked his eyes, which stung from bug repellent splashed on too thickly. The air should be fresh in the middle of nowhere but instead smelled like dust filtered through an oily sheet. At least the sky was filled with stars. He took a deep breath and lay back in spread-eagled surrender to the vastness.

"Come and get me."

■

Betty at the Esso Restaurant told all the tourists it was famous but Father knew the truth and bequeathed it to his son. The local Rotary Club had built this landing pad as a Canadian Centennial monument in 1967, only to find that it was one of half a dozen such artifacts built by prairie communities vying for media attention. The publicity furor began and ended with a single line in the AMA Guidebooks. "Things to see in High Level: Flying Saucer Landing Pad in Centennial Park."

Now the saucer was just the centrepiece of a huge, weedy park in a town on a mudflat in the centre of the muskeg. When dry, the white mud filled the air like filthy talcum powder; when wet it turned to soft slime that painted fences, trees, vehicles and buildings up to human eye-level in a fine spray. It was August in High Level. Nights were crisp and the mosquitoes moved in small thunderheads through the empty streets.

Father should have returned from Fort Assumption hours ago. Probably went straight to the Legion Hall after the long drive back; presidential responsibilities and the magnetism of the liquor more imperative than the love of a son he'd barely seen in nine years. Theo was supposed to be on this trip, his last chance to spend time with his father before going back to school in Edmonton.

■

"Entertainment Options in High Level," said the *Klondike Guidebook*, "Seven Pines Motel, on highway – featuring Lounge(which refused to serve Theo), Restaurant (where all the kids from the trailer park hung out) and Satellite TV; Legion Hall – Members & Guests Only (his father would not be thrilled to see him); Esso Restaurant, on highway; High Level Movie Theatre – Main Street, downtown (a ten minute walk from his father's house on the far corner of a tiny patch of suburbia in the wilderness)."

■

The only movie theatre for five hundred miles in any direction had a blue tiled facade. On the night his father didn't come home, the poster display box was empty, so there was no indication of what was playing.

"What's the movie?" Theo shouted through a metal grate.

A plump man with a fringe of wiry gray hair shrugged, "This is a replacement for *The Omen*. Can't remember what it's called, "*Timeslip* or *Bedslip* or something."

"Can I get some service in here?" shouted a voice from the lobby. Through the open door, Theo saw a thin man with a beige and white plaid shirt and a straw cowboy hat standing at the snack counter as though in a saloon, a young Métis girl standing quietly at his side.

"Bedlam? There's no poster. I dunno. You buying a ticket or not?" the fringed man asked Theo.

"Yeah, sorry." Theo paid and as he entered, the man bustled past him to the snack counter. "I remember. It's called *Timelapse*." The popcorn machine was an empty glass monolith on one side. On the other, stood a rack with two bags of chips and some peanuts. Lying flat on the counter was a large box of Goodies.

"What does it matter? He already paid." said the cowboy. "Gimme some spits."

"We don't allow them. No spitting, no smoking even in the washroom. Got peanuts."

"These aren't peanuts they're fucking gopher nuts. Probably like chewing pea gravel. How old is this candy?"

"Whattdya mean."

"The packaging looks yellow. Could probably sell it as fossil fuel." The cowboy laughed.

Fringe guy sighed. "You gonna buy it? Or not?

While this was happening, the girl stared at Theo with a defiant gaze. Her date was still laughing as her date turned away from the snack counter with a can of cola and grabbed her around the waist. With a smirk, she whispered into the cowboy's ear and giggled.

Contemptuously, the thin man looked Theo up and down, then turned and walked the girl into the theatre.

The choice was between warm, generic-brand cola or orange soda. He took the cola, but when he went to slide into the back row, the cowboy's date waved at him and Theo recalibrated and continued down the aisle to the front. They were the only other patrons. From his threadbare seat near the centre, Theo could hear them snickering and murmuring behind him.

They shut up briefly when the opening credits came on.

"*EXPOSURE*," said bone white letters on a black field.

"*Exposure*! What the fuck?" The fringed man's voice came from the projection room. "That's not what it says on the cans."

As Theo sat, he glanced back to see the cowboy sitting alone. The girl giggled again, invisible. The cowboy smiled. The music swelled and when Theo looked back up at the screen, a subtitle had appeared. "*The Theo Richards Story.*"

Sitting slack-jawed with wonder, his memory filled in the sensory details that went with the visual images on screen.

He watched himself arrive for his mother's funeral wearing mirrored sunglasses and a black tuxedo. His father grabbed his arm and steered him through a doorway into a cool, dark room, tearing the glasses from his son's face.

"Ow, that hurt my ear."

"Is that the suit I gave you the money for? You rented a tuxedo for a hundred and thirty dollars?" His father's complexion looked florid even in the dim electric candlelight. "I guess I'll be getting some money back."

Theo smelled beer.

"You're drunk?"

"Not drunk. I had a drink. There's a difference."

"You promised."

"Where did you get the tux, Ted? You rent it?"

"Well kind of." But before Theo could go on to explain, it occurred to him that there was an open coffin in the room. "Is that Mom?"

"What do you mean, kind of?" Father said. "How do you *kind of* rent a tuxedo?"

"Let's not talk about this in front of Mom, okay?"

"That's not your mother any more. It's just a place she once lived. She's gone, I'm your reality now and I'm telling you that you are not going to wear this monkeysuit to her funeral."

Theo turned his head toward the casket, to look at whatever had, in his peripheral vision, just sat up. But when he looked directly at her, his mother lay still and silent in her forever bed of blue silk and mahogany.

Organ music droned from the chapel. Wasn't everyone depressed enough already?

Mom's eyelids flickered infinitesimally. Was that the suggestion of a smile? He stepped closer, she became more real than ever, as though she would sit up at any moment in her crisp white dress and ask him if he'd finished his homework, quiz him in her usual gentle way until he confessed that he was lying to his father.

Her lipstick was the wrong shade.

"Did you hear me, Ted?" Father said.

"It's Theo now. Mom calls...used to...call me Theo." Past tense. In a few days, he'd be living with Father in High Level. Spending the next month with a man he hardly knew anymore.

"Now take off this fucking monkey suit." Grabbing the collar and one of the lapels, Father pulled the garment roughly off Theo's shoulders. "Where's the receipt for the tux rental?"

"Must have lost it." He actually rented the tux for forty through the Ballroom Dancing Association that his friend Ben's parents belonged to. He and his friends had blown the rest of the money at the arcade. "I'm sorry, I should have been more careful about the receipt."

"I'll go to the rental place with you tomorrow and look at their copy."

Theo nodded because he couldn't think of anything else to do. Besides, his father wouldn't come with him to return the tux. He never followed through with anything.

As his father folded the jacket and tucked it under his arm, the music stopped.

His father said. "We'd better get in there."

Theo reached out and touched his mom's cheek, recoiling at first from the powdery marshmallow texture of her flesh and the second time from its coolness. The third time, he slid his fingertips lightly across her skin to the corners of her mouth. Wondering if there was some chance it would make her smile and call off the joke, he pushed up the corners of her mouth as though they were made of modelling clay.

"What are you doing?" Father stepped up behind him, face full of anger, gaze locked on Theo's face. "Don't do that."

Looking at Father, Theo suddenly realized the man couldn't even bring himself to look at the corpse of his ex-wife. The iron man of his childhood didn't live there anymore.

"Give me the jacket. I'll hang it up," Theo said.

As his father extended the folded garment, the collar slipped from his fingers and the jacket dangled like the Hanged Man from the Tarot, arms dancing madly.

Even as Theo took the jacket his father was walking unsteadily away.

"It's about to start," his words melted into the light. The man Theo saw occasionally on Christmases and birthdays left him with his Mom for the final time.

She didn't look like someone who had died in a car accident. Didn't look like his mother anymore either. This time when he touched her lips, she moaned. A very sexual sound. Theo jerked his hand away but discovered the voice wasn't coming from the casket, it was coming from behind him in the movie theatre.

Peering back into the darkness, he saw a woman's naked shoulders rising and falling. He averted his eyes, back to the screen, where the Métis girl was lying naked in the coffin staring at him like she'd done in the lobby. The giggle from the back row had turned into his mother's rich, familiar laughter. Theo swivelled in his seat.

The scene onscreen pulled back for a full length two-shot of boy and coffin, then slowly faded to black.

In the diminishing light from the screen, Theo could see nothing. He'd look like a total perv going back for a better look at the lovers, so he forced his attention back to the movie, where the scene had changed dramatically.

A white DC-5 banked across a cloudy sky above a monotonous low forest, dissected less and less frequently by the grey ribbons of roadways.

Cut to an interior of the passenger cabin, where Theo pressed his head against the airplane window, watching intently for the occasional black and yellow squares of farmland or glistening blue amoeba-shaped lakes.

"Everything is going bad all at once," said his father. "Julia left me. Your mother died. And you know what started it all? My teeth."

The man in the airplane seat next to Theo, his father, looked impossibly distant, as though seen through the wide end of a telescope.

"Never had a cavity in my life. Then six months ago, the dentist in Peace River told me that they've been rotting from the inside out. They all have to be pulled." As remote and indecipherable as the landscape below them, his father's voice crackled and trailed off into a tinny blur. Covering his face with both hands, his father wept.

At the funeral, all he talked about was money. Now it was teeth.

Theo put his forehead against the window again and let the vibration take him away from this chattering and weeping about petty things and into the forest far below where the trees grew smaller and sparser and less full, like twigs reaching up like skeletal fingers out of a lime green sea.

Wondering if his mother was eavesdropping from whatever dimension or time warp she was in, he looked at the streaky, distant clouds, perhaps hoping to glimpse her there, but instead he saw a light, darting and dodging through layers of sky.

"Hey, what is that?" Theo said. But when he turned back, his father was looking smaller and more faded than ever. Still talking about government dental plans, his voice disappearing into swirls of static. He seemed unaware that Theo had spoken.

The object outside was clearly visible now, less a saucer than a giant hubcap. Coloured lights flashed randomly around the rim.

"Don't you see it?" Theo asked aloud. But the seat beside him was empty. And when he looked back outside, the saucer too was gone. All that was left was the drone of the plane and the music soundtrack.

Theo normally just had some toast for breakfast but his father had been making a deal out of breakfast. Not that he was complaining. As he decapitated the second soft boiled egg of the fifth morning of his northern exile, Theo scowled at his father who unexpectedly looked up from his newspaper.

"Something wrong with the egg?"

"No. Good egg. I'm just bored. You're never home and I don't know anybody."

"I could get you a job."

"There's less than three weeks before school. I'd hardly start before I'd have to quit."

"A lot of casual jobs come through my office. Perfect for the Indians. Work two days, get drunk for a week then come back for a couple more days work. Only way to keep them at something longer term is withhold their paycheque until the project's finished. Most are good workers when they're sober. Trick is, keeping them away from the bottle."

Theo knew not to mention Father's drinking problem, however relevant to this conversation it might seem. "Yeah, but...this hasn't been much of a summer holiday, with Mom dying and all. I want to do something interesting for a few days. I mean I think that's cool about the casual jobs and all. I'm definitely interested. I was just kind of hoping to do something...you know...fun?"

Theo's father grinned. "You want to see what I do for a living? I'm flying out to John D'Or Prairie for a meeting this afternoon. Why don't you come along?"

On the plane, his father's shouted commentary filled the air as warmly as the sunshine slanting in the cockpit window. After a week without company, Theo found his father's redneck philosophies not only palatable but almost profound. "This is a model reserve. The Band Council outlawed drinking. With the money they would have otherwise spent on booze, they built a sawmill. They keep their lawns neat, houses painted. This is what the other reserves have the potential to become."

When they landed, a fat first nations man was waiting to pick them up.

"This is my translator, Raymond Cardinal, from Fort Vermilion. Nobody at John D'Or speaks English."

Theo's father went into a meeting. The only person left in the office was a secretary who spoke Cree and French. There was no visible English language reading material, so Theo went outside.

Strolling aimlessly down the dusty road, he listened for the absent shouts of children. Occasionally, a saw whined in the distance. The field around him was freshly turned, brown clumps of dirt bristling with yellow stubble. The earth here in the river valley was richer, less dusty than in High Level.

There were no birds chirping, just grasshoppers buzzing up at him from the roadside like little rudderless helicopters, dragonflies whirring past constantly. A chain saw chortled to life nearby, but before Theo could determine which direction it was coming from, it stopped and didn't start back up again. There was no wind. No traffic. No livestock, although the smell of manure hung faintly in the air. Houses were tiny white dots, barely visible at the end of the road he was standing on. But Theo couldn't go anywhere in case the meeting ended. Knowing Father would be pissed if he was gone, he went nowhere. The sun continued to shine. The wind didn't rise.

That was the first hour. The next three were much longer.

When the doors to the meeting room finally opened, they were back on the airplane within five minutes.

"What did you talk about in there?" Theo asked.

"Oh, the meeting? Nothing interesting. Look, I've got to write a report before this all goes out of my head. Sorry, Ted."

"It's okay," Theo said. "Look, Dad, could you please call me Theo?"

"I'll try to remember," his father mumbled, going back to his work, which he didn't manage to finish before getting back to the airport. Dropping Theo at the Esso, he gave him ten dollars and said, "Pick up something to eat while I check in at the office. I'll come round and pick you up."

"Should I get something for you too?"

"No, I'll grab something later at the Legion. It was nice having you along today, Ted. We'll do it again before you leave, when I won't be stuck all day in a meeting."

At first, Theo dreaded the day, but by week's end, he was begging Father to go along with him again before school started.

"The only trip on my calendar is Fort Assumption."

"Couldn't I come with you?"

"I dunno. It's not as nice out there. When I give them their welfare cheques on Monday, it'll all be gone by the end of the week. Spent on potato chips, cigarettes and booze. It's hard to break out of this life, when you came into the world as a baby sitting in its own shit and your Dad committed suicide before you were born and your Mom is passed out drunk all the time. Sometimes there's a brother or sister to take care of you, but there's no store on the reserve and there's only one car in the whole town anyway. They drink cola instead of milk because that's all their brother or sister could find to feed them. The kids fend for themselves until the parents sober up. There's lots of abuse. The reserve is squalid. And it's not accessible by plane. Schoolbus only gets up there when the road's passable, a couple months a year. But there's no airport, so I'll be driving, four hours there and four back. There for about an hour, that's all. And there's nothing to see."

"It's better than being cooped up here."

"Well, okay, but we have to be up at the crack of dawn."

■

The conversation on screen was almost identical to the one they had a few nights earlier, only with a different outcome. In real life, his father received a Sunday night phone call and returned to the table apologetically, explaining that there had been another suicide on the reserve.

"Under the circumstances, I shouldn't have you along with me. Sorry, son."

"But you promised, Dad."

"It's out of my hands. I'm sorry."

In the movie it all played out quite differently. The father was going out simply because it was welfare day and his job to hand out the cheques. The movie-Theo got to go along.

In the theatre, Theo's mouth hung open as he watched himself and his father and son climb into the four-by-four. From the driver's seat, his father smiled at him, pulling the flat black rifle clip from his coat pocket and sliding it under the seat cover, between his legs.

"Never know when you're going to hit a deer or run into a bear. Had a showdown with a moose last time."

"You killed it?"

He shook his head. "Naw, but it charged the truck."

"You're kidding."

"That's why I got that big grill put on. They do that sometimes."

"Wow."

The enthusiasm on Theo's face wore off as the drive rumbled on and his father wouldn't let him take the wheel despite his learner's licence.

"Mom always let me drive."

Father explained that the "Texas pea gravel" on the highway often shattered windshields and if something like that happened, he'd rather be at the wheel. His declaration proved prophetic because, an hour later, the driver's side window of the four-by-four was hit by a knuckle-sized rock thrown by an oilfield truck that roared past them out of the tundra. A sheet of shattered glass avalanched into their laps. His father managed to steer the vehicle to the side of the road. He pounded on the horn and shook his fist out the window, but the truck didn't stop.

They cleaned out the broken glass with some hunting magazines from under his father's seat, but had no way to patch the window. All that was under the seat were empty motor oil bottles and seatbelts that had been pushed down behind the seat cushions and hung, coated in oil and dust, to the floor.

"What now?" asked Theo.

"We're half an hour from the turnoff. Then there's no more gravel."

"Can we get it fixed out there?"

Dad shook his head. "There's no service station. No stores on the reserve."

They kept an eye on the carpet of forest and twice before the turnoff, they saw rooster plumes of dust coming toward them on an intersect courses. When the two highways trucks actually passed, the air grew so thick in the truck cab it made Theo gag. The twenty minutes to the turnoff into the forest seemed more like an hour.

In the movie theatre, Theo experienced the entire passage of time onscreen. He vividly remembered a trip like this, one that had never taken place. With the windshield missing, the trip had grown many times louder, so Theo was forced to sit silently in the machine gun rattle and roar of rocks against the undercarriage pondering what life would be like living in this vast nowhere. Theo's mouth felt gummy with mud. He remembered it sucking the moisture out of his mouth. And rolling down the side window to spit. And seeing wolves at the edge of the forest.

"Coyotes," his father yelled. "Lots of them around here."

A decrepit VW van went past sounding like an eggbeater inside a cowbell. Theo repressed a laugh.

As his father stepped on the brakes he yelled, "That's one of the three working vehicles on the reserve!"

Just as they turned off the so called highway, Theo sucked in an entire lungful of dust.

Theo put his face in his hands and coughed until his throat hurt.

"Shuttup," said a distant voice behind him and Theo looked over his shoulder at the couple in the back row. It was hard to tell in the dim light, but her sweater seemed to be rucked up under her chin and her small breasts seemed so perky they were pointing upward.

The cowboy threw a soda can towards him and Theo turned back around as it clattered to the floor. He was sucked straight back into the movie. The air even seemed colder as he lifted his eyes back to the screen.

"Forest" was a generous description of the countryside. The trees were thin as tentpoles, holding aloft airy webworks of leaves beneath an empty grey sky. "Road" didn't begin to describe the rutted, muddy pathway they were driving on. The worst parts had bridges of freshly felled trees which hammered like angry demons at the four-by-four's undercarriage. It might have been exhilarating at a greater speed than his father was driving. At least he was forced to pick up the pace a bit by the mosquitoes which filled the cab whenever they went too slow.

"How do people get out here when the road's not passable?" asked the Theo on the screen.

His father shrugged. "This is actually the worst time to drive. They take a bulldozer up here every winter to level the road. By the end of the summer, it's always like this, half sunk back into the muskeg. There's a helicopter for medical emergencies and food drops."

The trees along the roadside were grey with mud. Theo said, "Why would anybody live in a place like this?"

"Because that's where they put the reserve. Stay there and they get a welfare cheque every month. Hardly any living expenses. Family all around. The minute they go off the reserve, they're on their own. But they have to move to town if they're gonna have any chance of keeping the job. I can find jobs and apprenticeships for them and they'll do great for a month or two. Then they'll get homesick or get drunk to blow off some steam and wake up in their own bed with a hangover a week later. No job. Nothing left of their paycheque cause they've been buying rounds for everybody."

Just then they hit a bump that almost put Theo through the roof of the cab. He clutched his head.

"You alright?"

The truck was standing still. Mosquitoes almost literally poured in through the space where the windshield was supposed to be.

Theo worked up a grin. "I'm fine, let's just get going before we're eaten alive."

A nod. They took off again. Once braced for it, Theo managed not to hurt himself again.

It was well after noon by the time they got there. Unpainted, ramshackle houses rimmed a big field of mud. A crowd was gathered in front of the church that stood in the centre of the open space, its austere black steeple aimed into the sky.

His father climbed out of the truck with his briefcase in one hand. He slipped the bullet clip into his pocket with the other. "You can get out and walk around if you like."

Slamming the driver's door, his father went into the church, leaving Theo alone among the crowd of villagers grunting strange monosyllables among themselves. A couple of them looked in the broken window.

"Cheques here?" asked an emaciated looking man with a businessman's haircut, casually brushing mosquitoes from his face and neck.

"Yeah, I think so," said Theo.

The man nodded and turned, his announcement in Cree eliciting scattered cheers.

A moment later, his father came back out on the steps, calling names. It reminded Theo of Thursday nights when his father called Bingo at the Legion.

Only the winners didn't react as enthusiastically.

"Rene Lefevre...Pierre Lefevre..Yves Lefevre....Wilfred Cardinal...Alice Cardinal...Leopold Sauvage...Anne Sauvage... Jean Sauvage..."

People streamed past, cheques in hand and grim purpose in their downcast eyes.

When he was done, Theo's father went back into the church and closed the door behind him.

When he didn't emerge a few minutes later, Theo rattled the church doors. But they were locked.

The gaunt man walked back past the church with his arm over another man's shoulder. Seeing Theo at the door, the gaunt man said, "They're in the basement having a drink. Church had no wine last spring. Somebody stole it. So he always locks the doors now."

"The priest locks you out of church?"

"No. God locks us out, 'cept on Sundays, eh?"

"Is there any other way in?" Theo asked.

"Course not," said the man, "Then what would be the point of locking it?" He walked away laughing, leaving the other man at the door beside Theo.

"Is there a doorbell or anything?" Theo asked. But all Theo got back was a goofy smile and a handshake. The man's ears stuck out on both sides and his head actually got narrower toward the crown. He had buck teeth and no chin.

"Lefou," said the ugly man pointing at himself.

"What?" Theo asked. He was pretty sure LeFou meant "the Fool" which didn't seem like something someone would call themselves.

"Charlie LeFou!" The man drooled as he kept pumping Theo's hand. He wasn't strong, his grip spidery and light. His other hand patted Theo's shoulder. "Je suis un bon homme, n'est-ce pas? Un bon homme! Je m'appel Charlie. Charlie Lefou."

Perhaps Charlie the Fool was his actual name.

Charlie wouldn't let go of his hand.

"No, I don't want to shake anymore." Theo tried to pull away, but Charlie treated it like a game, laughing and shaking almost violently.

What was the French word for 'stop'? "Arret. Arret!"

Theo pushed Lefou away and ran for the church doors, which were locked. He pounded on them but no one answered.

As he walked around the side of the building, he looked over his shoulder and saw the pinhead wandering away.

Behind the church, the ground was mossy and wet. There was no back door. If there was a basement, the room had no windows. Theo kicked the soncrete foundation, producing no audible sound beyond a scuff. Mud dropped in clumps from his shoes, which were clearly getting ruined.

Mom would be furious. Stopping and thinking about that made him want to hit something but there was nothing to hit but the wall of the church. There was a ditch on the other side filled with muddy water, and there was nothing to climb so he could look into the stained glass window. It wasn't as translucent as it seemed anyway. Theo backed up, but could see nothing through yellow, green or red. There didn't seem to be a light on inside.

Theo briefly considered putting a rock through the window, then looked out at the now distant Lafou. Theo pounded on the door once more before turning and running after the only human being in sight, following him into the woods.

Tree trunks no bigger around than broomsticks created an effect like a vertical slat curtain. Through them, Theo saw a blur of movement.

"Charlie! Wait."

The mud path ended a few steps into the woods, the ground underfoot turning into small hills of thick moss. Spindly pines and birch trees poked up like sidewalk weeds between them.

Why was Charlie walking away from the houses? Maybe he was so pathetic that even his own people didn't accept him. Maybe he lived out here. Or maybe he just had a bad habit of wandering off.

When Charlie flickered briefly into sight again, Theo forged a bit deeper into the forest. The tussocks of moss grew smaller, the gaps between them bigger. The crevices weren't wet or muddy but were very deep. When he missed his footing, he occasionally sank in past his knees.

Realizing Charlie wasn't going to wait for him, Theo turned and began threading his way back the way he'd come. When the village and church steeple remained invisible after several minutes, he curved to the left. Was it possible to get turned around in such a short space? Obviously it was. He stopped and thought hard about any unconscious turns he might have taken.

Movement again.

"Charlie?"

Wearing six-pointed antlers and a startled expression, a mule-deer buck fled the instant it saw him, bounding deftly through the bog.

The sky was an even, dull grey, shading toward black. Theo couldn't even hazard a guess where the sun was. It couldn't possibly be as late as it looked. Almost evening.

Picking a direction at random, he walked. The first time he paused, mosquitoes settled on his skin in living sheets. Frantically brushing and swatting at them, he hurried through the woods shouting, "Charlie! Dad! Somebody!" After awhile, his shout turned to, "Help!"

As long as he kept moving, running his hands frequently over his face and the back of his neck, which of course, left them to land on the back of his hand but there wasn't much he could do about that. His progress slowed as the terrain grew more uneven. Moss hung from the lower tree branches and the ground grew squishy underfoot. He was heading deeper into the muskeg rather than back toward the village, but whenever he turned to retrace his steps, the landscape became more severe. There were no landmarks.

Sweat irritated the bug bites. Beginning to panic, Theo ran and his foot slipped into a crevice. If he had been wearing regular shoes, he'd have lost one, but the running shoe was tied on tightly. He was trapped. Above him a shifting black cloud of mosquitos formed and grew bigger and blacker in the darkening sky. Trying to shield his face, Theo sobbed into the crook of his arm.

He heard Charlie Lefou's voice but could see no one. Subtitles appeared on screen. "Everybody gives up out here. There's no choice. But you didn't last long at all."

"Can you help me out?" said Theo aloud. "Where are you."

Charlie spoke again. "You saw me just a moment ago," said the subtitles. "The one with the antlers."

The onscreen Theo scratched his head, clearly unable to understand.

Theo consulted his internal library of high school French and came up with, "Um, assiste moi, s'il vous plait." Just as he thought the words, his onscreen counterpart said them aloud.

"Help me, please," said the subtitles.

"You have to help yourself," Charlie's voice said in English. "That's what your father always tells my people,"

"Please."

"Climb up. Climb up he tells us. He doesn't know."

"Wait!"

As Theo finally managed to free his foot, Charlie spoke again. "You don't know. But you're learning. Gotta learn fast out here. Not many options. All of them, shitty."

And Theo realized that the dialogue was no longer in subtitles and in fact, it wasn't even spoken. He had simply understood as though he was thinking it rather than hearing it.

As Theo peered through the accumulating darkness, the trees now brightly visible, like bars encircling him, trapping him in the bog.

The next time his foot slipped off a tussock of moss, it didn't sink in very deep at all. As Theo pulled his foot out, he peered down and saw a human arm, part of a torso, white skin crusted with mud. Resisting his instinct to scream and run, he reached in queasily, checked for a pulse. It was a dead woman, skin puffy and bloodless.

Dangerously close to vomiting, Theo stood up, unable to walk away. Finally, with a grimace, he bent back down, took hold of the hand and pulled, praying that her arm wouldn't separate from her body or something equally obscene.

As he pulled the body out, Theo saw his mothers face and released her with a squawk. He scrambled away, tripped, then lay there hyperventilating, suddenly oblivious to the mosquitoes.

After several minutes, she hadn't vanished. Edging toward her, he reached out and ran his fingertips over the familiar contours of her face. Finding the mole on her collarbone and the vaccination scar on her arm, he wrapped his arms around her and began to cry.

This had to be some sort of hallucination.

No. Now he remembered! It was a movie.

It just didn't feel like a fucking movie.

The screen faded to black.

Theo turned in his seat and looked toward the back of the theatre but where there should have been empty seats, were only more tussocks of moss. Trees jutted up between them like long, thin bones.

He heard loon cries and saw the wings of huge white birds climbing into the twilit sky.

The space between the tussocks had filled with ice cold water. The first few missteps were just ankle deep; on the third one he sank to midthigh. The ground slurped hungrily as he pulled himself back out.

Darker, colder, the night swirled in around Theo, alive and thirsty for his blood. In the pale moonlight, he could see that the trees had thinned to almost nothing. Everywhere he stepped was moss or muck, sucking at him, pulling him down.

He fell face first. When he submerged, the cold water soothed his burning skin and kept the mosquitoes away. He lay there for a moment, enjoying the momentary relief, then swallowed some water, rising up and spitting out the foul tasting stuff.

His face itched horribly, but when he scratched his cheek, he found something wet and tissue-like, clinging to his skin. He pulled at it, but it oozed out between his fingers. Black streamers hung from his wrists and the backs of his hands. Running his fingers over his face and neck, he felt dozens of leeches on his face and neck. Inside of his clothes too he knew. But he could do nothing to get them off. Couldn't even try!

Managing to crawl to more solid ground, Theo curled into a foetal position covering his head with his arms and crying until his throat was raw. He rolled onto his back, staring into the sky, no longer noticing the thousands of mosquitoes coming down to feed. And through those open eyes he saw a light; a flashlight? A search party come looking for him? But no. It was coming from the wrong direction, out over the lake.

As the light came closer, he recognized the flying hubcap shape. Despite the fear that roiled through his insides like a thunderstorm, he sat up, waving his arms and shouting.

The object zig-zagged toward him across the darkened sky, held aloft by a cylinder of light, illuminating the oily water which rippled beneath it in shattered rainbows.

Theo stood up, walking toward the warm yellow light issuing from its belly. Before he got there, it shot back into the sky like a meteor freed from Earth's gravity, leaving Theo weeping, slowly sinking into the wet moss.

"Some forms of escape work better than others out here," said the voice of Lefou, gently from behind him. "Making babies is good when you're young, but my personal salvation came in one of these."

The fool gave him a glass bottle in a familiar shape. Theo had seen one just like it in the cupboard before coming to the theatre. He didn't even like whiskey, but he drank deeply and it made him feel better. So he drank the rest.

The police found the empty bottle beside Theo's body which was sprawled across several theatre seats.

"The movie didn't arrive," the theatre owner explained. "So I wasn't open last night."

"Did you find him?"

"No, they did," the theatre owner pointed at the cowboy and his very young "date" who were being questioned up at the snack bar.

"I don't allow booze, so I dunno how he came in with that."

"I don't think he did," said the cop, rolling the boy over. "It must have come in with whoever brought the body in here."

"You think he was dead already?"

"Must have been," said the cop, rolling the boy over.

A few leeches still clung to a face that was lumpy and as swollen as a soccer ball.

"I'm no CSI, but he sure didn't die in here."

Razorwings

Preamble – Razorwings

Faerie meets *Conan the Barbarian*? Really? Well, yes. With a bit of *Buffy the Vampire Slayer* thrown in for good measure. And if it's ever made into a movie, I want either Quentin Tarantino, Joss Whedon or Guillermo del Toro to direct.

The "Razorwings" idea began at *Pulphouse*. One of the assistant editors there told me a story about how they had come up with a new genre that would marry the always popular epic fantasy with the hottest genre of that time – splatterpunk. They jokingly called it "splatterfairy" and actually began batting around the idea of putting together a splatterfairy anthology.

Enthused by the opportunity to become one of the seminal "splatterfairy" writers, I immediately started writing. Although the anthology never materialized, my ideas and characters stuck with me. The following novella was published in a magazine called *Terminal Frights* and well-reviewed by Brian McNaughton - writer of the brilliant *Throne of Bones*. Intrigued about Jaynie's origins, I have been working on a "Razorwings" novel, called *Out of the Nether*, ever since.

Those weren't the only "Razorwings" projects. In the mid-1990s I was on a mission to become the first writer of fantastic fiction in my circle to have a website of any kind. It was going to be dark fantasy and I did the story and the photo-illustrations and laid it out in html – which I was teaching myself out of Dummies books. I used a single frame rotoscope style that looked great on the page but in those days even static pictures were so large they were slow to load onto most computers. The project stalled just as my personal life underwent some upheavals. I became an entrepreneur and published a mainstream publication that got some respect and made me a living. My new partner, Laura, saw the need for a creative outlet bubbling up in me and encouraged my explorations in sculpture. Once back in the creative groove, I started writing and ultimately creating websites again.

So now, I need to rescue Jaynie from obscurity once again, try not to cut myself dusting her off and hope that the world is finally ready for the first heroine of splatterfairy...

Here she is, in the bloody red corner – the slicer and dicer of dark monarchs, the immortal champion of the uncared-for and disenfranchised – it's Jaynie Razorwings!

Razorwings

"Rats-ass, rats-ass...chew on my bone," sang a male voice from the other side of the front door.

A male? This was different.

"Bonewolf?" I grinned. "You bitch."

I opened the door to find a young man shuffling restlessly in my entryway. His bald head wore a helmet of tattoos. He was dressed in camouflage pants and a black raincoat. No shirt.

Giving me a broken-toothed grin, he walked straight past me and flopped down in one of my living-room's two plush leather sofas. I leaned over the brass railing, grinning down at him, despite my exhaustion from walking all the way from the bedroom.

His left ear wore more than a dozen earrings. The other side was unpierced.

A huge, framed photograph of my Brandon Sutter husk filled the wall behind him. The gleaming, naked body bore little resemblance to the husk I was now inhabiting. I clenched my hands into bony fists and stared at the bruises blotching my skin like smudges on parchment. Sutter would be dead by now if I hadn't moved in.

Bonewolf had taken a young one. Six months from now, his new body might still not have reached the state of decay my Sutter had reached in less than two months.

"I've found the perfect hunting grounds," said Bonewolf. "You're coming with me tonight."

"I can't go..."

"Don't you dare give up on me at a time like this."

I shook my head, swallowing thickly. "A time like what?"

"With all that's going on at the barrow." He cocked his head in apparent wonderment. "You really don't know, do you?"

"Know what?" I felt dizzy and confused. "Why are you talking in riddles?"

Bonewolf stared into his lap. "I promised not to tell."

"Doesn't matter anyway. I'm not going hunting," I said, sitting down on the step and leaning my forehead against the wooden bars of the railing. "Just get out of here."

"Don't be so pathetic. I worry about you because I need you."

That made me feel a bit better. "But I'm still pissed off about you talking in code," I said. "Tell me, or I won't go."

Rolling his eyes, Bonewolf said, "Alimatheon made me promise not to tell you."

"Tell me what?"

"How annoyed he is that you don't...bring him more husks. He's ready to banish you to the Nether, Ratman. You've got to come hunting tonight. For me. I really do need you."

"Where's this hunting ground?" I asked with a smile. I was surprised that those facial muscles still worked.

"Dance at the OAP Hall."

When I didn't respond, Bonewolf shook his head. "I admit, you won't be doing any waltzing tonight. The husk I'm in belonged to a singer. David Greenbaum. Guitarist. Great band. Call themselves Sir Cum Size. But between the drugs and attempted suicides, Greenbaum wouldn't have lasted another week."

"Me at a dance? I'd drop dead on the spot."

"If you don't come, you'll die here alone."

"How young is that husk?" I asked, pointing my finger at him. With Bonewolf, attack was the best way to change the subject.

Bonewolf ran his hands over the skin of his belly and chest. "Nineteen. He really would have OD'd within the week. Be a shame to let this one go to waste."

He got eagerly off the couch and took my hand. Instead of shaking it, he kissed it. I pulled away from him.

"What's the matter?"

"I have AIDS."

"I know. It's only been weeks, Gallowrat." His use of my real name brought me to attention.

"Five weeks. Almost the whole time I've been in this body."

"Whatever. Doesn't compare to half a century."

"Thirty-eight years. And I've been back for thirteen."

Bonewolf nodded. "Numbers are important to you. Here's a number. Two hundred. I lived almost two hundred lifetimes without you. I thought you were gone forever."

"I'm sorry. I..."

As Bonewolf waved away my apologies, I shuddered at the memory of cold nothingness, my soul trapped inside the corpse as nature slowly consumed the flesh. I balked at the memory of years spent working my way up through the ground into the Nether and then discovering that my barrow was no longer where I thought it was. If the location of something changes on Earth, it changes in the Nether. And after two hundred years in Romania, King Alimatheon had suddenly decided to move the barrow halfway around the world.

During the early months of my Death, Alimatheon had been recruited by one of the Ancient Ones to kill the Laird Auldearne, the man who drove the barrows from our ancestral home on the Scottish coast. Back then, the humans called us changelings and we were almost as common as they were. Now, thanks to the Laird, we barrow-imps were rare creatures. Only a few dozen left on the whole planet.

I got back to the barrow just in time to witness the Laird's entrapment by a group of dark monarchs working together. I watched as they killed him.

How could I not feel good in the knowledge that barrows would continue to thrive? Bonewolf and I would live on, probably for many more centuries. How could I not be happy? But somehow I wasn't.

Bonewolf took my hand again, gently. "We have hours before the dance."

I pulled back, leaning against the wall as I stared at Bonewolf's new face through the wooden banisters. Life was as much of a prison as death.

"I can't get it up anymore," I said.

"So what? I can."

"It's too painful."

"What is?"

"Everything."

"You've waited too long. I shouldn't have left you alone. Should have known what would happen." Bonewolf turned away from me.

"A punk dance?" I said.

Turning back with a smug grin, Bonewolf shrugged, energy seeming to pour back into him. "They don't call it punk anymore. But it's the same sort of gig. Might even be some groupies. Maybe I can find a new husk for you. At the very least, you'll hear me play."

"This is assuming I make it that far."

"I have drugs. Bennies to get you there. Heroin to blot the pain. Whatever you need."

"Nothing works against the pain anymore. Give me the speed, though. Might get me through the night."

He dropped three of the capsules into my hand. "Take it now. I want to be here when you get some of that energy back."

"We take our hits of happy where we find them, eh, Gallowrat?" Bonewolf pronounced with a shit-eating grin. "I'll do a song for you."

"A song?"

"Tonight. We'll go early. I'll prop you up on a chair near the stage. Tie you to the chairback if I have to! Hunting will be good at the dance, Ratman. I promise."

"If I looked like you, maybe," I said, holding out my arms; bones wrapped in a white parchment. "But I looked like death warmed over."

We both laughed at that and I coughed so hard I thought I'd die before ever making it out the door. He picked me up off the floor, carried me to the couch and made love to me gently.

It turned out that Bonewolf was right about good hunting at the dance. I found a perfect prospective husk. Problem was, I didn't realize at the time that I wasn't the hunter.

Empty, the hall had been warm, but crowded, the place was sticky with heat and reeking of beer and smoke. A hundred small, round tables had been jammed around the perimeter of the dance floor. Most of the kids at that dance were visitors to the edge of darkness, with loving homes and hopeful futures. No one appeared hopeless enough for my feeble husk to seduce.

When Sir Cum Size came on, Bonewolf didn't even introduce the band. He just looked at me and muttered, "This is for you, Gallowrat," then played a raunchy cover of "Parasite Waltz" by the Dioxides – the punk band he had played in so recently. The more I thought about it, the more I appreciated how long ago that had actually been, the mid-eighties or even earlier. Dozens of incarnations ago. Just after I came back from my long death.

The stumbling of the bass guitarist told me that my friend had never bothered to teach the band the song before he started playing it. I shook my head with a smile. This opportunity to release some of the angry, discordant music inside him would give Bonewolf enough pleasure to make up for fifty of the usual brief, squalid lifetimes.

Buoyed by the energy that Bonewolf's gesture had injected into my veins, I got up to cruise the crowd. The smoky air seemed to grow solid in my throat and I barely managed to hold down a gag. I stared at the bodies leaping and colliding on the dance floor, edging nervously away from the centre of activity. A husky young man pushed past me, knocking me off my feet. I lay there, feeling insignificant for an instant before the guy came back.

"Jeez, I'm sorry man. Lemme help you."

Shaking my head, I climbed slowly back to my feet. I walked unsteadily back to my table to find that a group of people had taken up residence there. My leather coat was in a heap on the floor. As I bent to retrieve it, someone tore it from my fingers.

I looked up to see my coat draped over the shoulders of the most tragically beautiful waif I'd ever laid eyes on. Her skin was Mary Shelley white. Even her hair was white. Shaved up the sides and hanging to her waist in back, it was tied into a ponytail by a huge black lace bow. The same swathe of lace that held her hair trailed down to wind loosely around her thin body; a garment of obedient smoke. At her waist, the lace was tied off into a belt. And from beneath those billows of diaphanous fabric, a black skirt flowed down to her shoeless feet. Through the haze of lace I could see gold hoops piercing the nipples of her tiny breasts. Barefoot in December and obviously more bent than any bedbug, Jaynie drew me to her like a piranha to babies' flesh.

I gazed into eyes that looked neither brightly manic nor vacant and depressed. She didn't have the unnervingly distant and unfocused stare of a schizophrenic, but rather a gaze so intense it was almost primal.

"This yours?" she shouted over the twin wails of Bonewolf's guitar and voice.

"You can wear it if you like."

"Seriously?"

I didn't have a chance to nod before she was kissing me. She must be charged up with Ecstacy, I thought. It was too easy.

"Why don't we go someplace," I said.

Part of me hoped that the white-haired girl would push me away. But most of me wanted her. Wanted to become her. It was usually Bonewolf who had the female body and me the male. The switch would be fun.

"Sure."

Sliding my hand under the layers of lace, I inserted a finger into one of the nipple-rings and tugged on it sharply. She moaned and kissed me harder, confirming the impression I wanted to believe. She was zoned out.

Firmly grasping her arm I led her toward the door.

"Wait," she said, suddenly tense.

Letting go of her reluctantly, I watched her weave away through the dancers. I hoped my anxiety hadn't sent inadvertent vibes of the nightmare awaiting her.

Bonewolf was right about giving up. It was pitiful. Foolish. Life is meant to be lived.

So, why was I feeling so jumpy?

Stopping at a table on the far side of the dim, low-ceilinged room, she wormed her bare feet into a pair of black workboots. Slinging a knapsack over one shoulder, she returned to me with a sigh.

We exited the dancehall into a corridor that led to administrative offices and turned left toward the lobby.

"So, where're we going?"

"Friend of mine has an apartment near here."

"Yeah?"

"No. But if I told you I was gonna take you under the bridge, you probably wouldn't come."

"I always come," she murmured. "Sometimes two or three times, depending how long you last."

I stopped and stared into those piercing eyes. I preferred my victims to be almost dead. But it was no time to get picky. I might never get another chance. And at that moment, I desperately wanted another chance.

"I don't even know your name yet," I said.

"Does that bother you?" She sounded surprised.

"I'm...Brandon," I volunteered.

We paused in front of the big windows that looked out to the street. It was pouring outside.

"I'm Jaynie," she shouted too loudly as the door closed behind us, replacing the pounding grunge of the dancehall with the splatter of hard, icy rain.

"Are you for real?" I asked.

"Do you believe in the tooth fairy?"

"What do you mean by that?"

"Just wondering."

The hall was less than six blocks from the barrow, but we didn't get far past the first intersection when I saw Horsefly and Catbreath come steaming around the corner toward us.

They'd come to steal the husk I'd found, knowing that the barrow-king didn't give a fuck who brought in the bodies. Eighty years ago, my old friend Catbreath had joined up with Alimatheon's ring-wearers, Horsefly and Toadwart, and started stealing bodies from other imps on the way to the barrow. He was no longer a friend.

"C'mere," I whispered, pulling Jaynie around the corner into a narrow alleyway. The facades of the buildings in Old Town had been dolled up for tourists, but the back walls of the brick and stone buildings glistened blackly with filth. The smell of garbage was strong even in the cleansing rain. Wordlessly, I hustled her deeper into the darkness. She resisted, but I chugged on, finally dragging her into the archway behind Plover's Restaurant.

"What's your problem?" she shouted.

"I didn't want to run into those dudes who were coming toward us."

"The blind ones?"

"What?"

"If they didn't see us come in here, they must be blind or dead or both."

"They were under a streetlight. We weren't. Maybe they didn't see us."

"You really think so, Brandon?"

I nodded.

As though my hands were suddenly coated in grease, she pulled effortlessly away from me and danced several steps into the middle of the alley. "Then I'd better make sure they don't miss out on the fun."

"No wait..." I whispered, feeling puzzled and desperate all at once. "What the fuck you doing?"

"In here!" she shouted, clearly audible over the splattering rainfall and the hiss of passing cars. She threw off my leather jacket and unravelled the lacy fabric of her dress with the grace and speed of a rhythmic gymnast. Then, she swept her arms out in the grand gesture of a magician unveiling a surprise.

With a sound that was a cross between the ringing of bells and the clashing of sheet metal, Jaynie's great metal wings rose up, slicing through the remaining cloth, which fell away from her in tatters. A blade touched the sodden sleeve of my shirt and a thin line of blood became visible. I pulled apart the clean edges of fabric to find a deep incision in the flesh of my arm. Instead of pain, my flesh felt cold and numb. My attention shifted jaggedly upward, observing Catbreath and Horsefly rounding the corner at a run, Jaynie's wings flashing strobe-like in the reflected yellow and red of nearby neons and streetlights and blood spraying in all directions – painting the brick walls with the graffiti of death.

"Sorry you had to find out this way," she said, turning back toward me.

My mouth went dry and I tried not to think about that eyeflash of mutilation I had just witnessed, tried not to let panic destroy my concentration as I dug through my memory for some sort of spell to either ward Jaynie off or get me the hell outta there. Unable to squirm deeper into the corner, I muttered, "Where Alimatheon's magic walks..."

"No wait!" Jaynie shouted.

"...motion stops like an unwound clock." I threw my hands into the air. "Now stop!" Feeling the spell settle around me, I scampered up the alley like a roach running from the light, not glancing back until I reached the sidewalk.

Jaynie was frozen like a statue. I gaped like a moron. That was the most significant magic I'd loosed in over least eighty years. And it had worked!

The soles of my shoes slid in a puddle of blood. The last thing I saw before I turned the corner and ran was Catbreath's headless, limbless torse. With the ribcage collapsed, the corpse was almost unrecognizable. Having no idea how long the spell would bind her, I hoped to be several blocks away before Jaynie snapped out of her trance. But before I reached Government Street, I was sliding down a wall onto the sidewalk, sucking in desperate whooping breaths between fits of phlegmy coughing. AIDS was such a drag.

I was sure Jaynie would hear me from blocks away. And I remember nervously peering through the glare of the streetlights in case Jaynie's wings were good for more than slicing and gutting.

Suddenly, I realized that my wallet and ID were in the inside pocket of the blood-soaked jacket that I'd left in the alley. All I had now was a thin wad of twenties. If I didn't go back and fetch the wallet, Brandon Sutter's townhouse would soon be crawling with police. Leaving me without a home.

I had to go to Alimatheon.

But what if he blamed me for almost leading the razor-winged woman to the barrow?

What if Jaynie was somehow watching me? My magic spell had worked too well. It would be more prudent to wait.

I had to find a new husk.

I wandered the streets for an hour, before I was approached by a hooker. She didn't seem disturbed by the bloodstains on my clothes, in fact, she was too stoned to notice. I reached into my pant pocket for the moonstone moneyclip Bonewolf had given me last New Year's. He was the only one in the whole barrow I still exchanged gifts with.

"What's your name, honey?" I asked.

"Madonna."

"Madonna?"

"Riches. It was my stage name. I was a big draw. An "A" list dancer."

"Madonna Riches," I sighed. "I think we may be in business."

Her room at the Fort Hotel wasn't much bigger than her sagging double-bed. I couldn't tell if her sheets were grey with grime or just looked that way because of the piss-yellow light seeping through the plastic shade of the room's single lamp.

"What'd you come here for if you don't wanna fuck?" she demanded.

"You don't want what I've got," I said.

With a dismissive handwave she said, "When I got into this, I thought I could stay clean by refusing to make it with any client who wouldn't wear a rubber. You wouldn't believe how many johns consider rape to be part of the package. Whatever you've got, so do I."

I tried a different tack. "As long as I pay, why should you care whether we screw or not?"

After thinking about it for a moment, she shrugged. "Have it your way."

Not knowing whether it was the drugs or the adrenaline rush that was keeping me awake, three times I staggered down the hall to the shared bathroom before I slept.

Toadwart opened the door with a pass key at five am.

"Willy?" said Madonna, "I have a client."

"He's the one I came to see, Sweetie. Remind me to take you to dinner tomorrow to thank you for finding him for me."

"Oh, that's..." Madonna tapped me on the shoulder, "What *is* your name, anyway?"

"Alimatheon wants you," said the pimp to me rather than his employee.

"How'd you know I was here?" I asked.

"The barrow-king knows everything, asshole! Now get your diseased little dick out of my next husk's bed and get over there." He backhanded me across the side of my face, tearing open the skin on my cheek with the sharp-edged embossing on a gaudy ring he was wearing. Only two imps in the barrow wore the rings of the most faithful. And Horsefly was dead. As

Toadwart turned to leave, he looked at me suspiciously, "And don't think about taking her with you."

"It never occurred to me," I lied.

Toadwart waited outside the door and escorted me out through the hotel lobby. I hurried down deserted streets to the old bunker-like building on the harbour where the barrow of the soul-eater Alimatheon occupied half the basement.

A breaching spell opened the iron gates at the back of the building and transformed the mossy, concrete wall of the foundation into the earthen entranceway to the barrow.

The briny odour grew musty and bitter, as I threaded through unlit corridors, a route so familiar that I seldom even needed to reach out and touch the walls. The inner chambers reeked like sewage – only apt, this being a repository of a different kind of human waste.

The air grew hotter and thicker than usual when I entered the barrow-king's chamber. Alimatheon's tongues slid over me. Tasting me. I trembled as I always do in his presence.

I could see quite clearly, as though by bright moonlight, although there was no apparent source of this light. He wanted me to see whatever was about to happen.

"I understand that you left the dance hall with a warm new bod. Where is she, Gallowrat?" said the barrow-king in a sexy yet asexual voice.

I was scared to admit my failure. "She got away."

"Slashing your jacket in the process?"

"Slashing?"

"Letting Horsefly and Catbreath bleed all over it!" One of his many tongues snaked out of the wall of flesh that was Alimatheon and wrapped itself around my waist.

"Why didn't you come to me right away?" A hundred slits broke the surface of his softly glistening skin. Each was a mouth full of teeth which snapped at me hungrily as the tongue pulled me closer.

"Dint wanna lead the killer teyahhhh..." My words turned into a jumble as I watched all of Alimatheon's little mouths meld together into one huge set of choppers.

"I can take care of myself," he said. Soft and slimy as it was, the tongue was wrapped around me tightly enough to lift me off my feet. I worked desperately to breathe.

"I'm surprised you survived, Gallowrat. How did you escape when the killer did such a thorough job on the other two? Who are you working for?" The barrow-king's voice came from all around me as he slid my whole body between the rows of teeth into the furnace of his mouth.

If he genuinely suspected my loyalty, he might leave me in the spirit state. I imagined an eternity of consciousness without presence. Loneliness and boredom so relentless that they turn to madness. I screamed, more afraid that I had been in centuries, perhaps ever. "I work for you. Only for you! I used magic to escape. A freezing spell!"

Alimatheon spat me out, laughing. I landed on my shoulder, feeling muscles tear, and pain enveloped me again.

The soul-eater's voice boomed. "You used a parlour trick on this queen of swords? How could your magic be stronger than Horsefly's when he was wearing my ring?"

I lifted my face from the soft, sticky floor and rolled over to face my king. "Not swords," I coughed, "wings."

"Wings?"

"Metal wings. Sharp as razors. Horsefly and Catbreath walked into them. Never had a chance to cast spells. Hardly even think about it 'fore Jaynie cut them to pieces. She threatened to kill me unless I took her to you. That's when I used the freezing spell."

"Jaynie?"

"That's what she called herself."

"She wanted you to lead her to me?"

I nodded. "I swear."

"Why didn't you kill her when she was frozen?"

I shook my head. "Dunno. Trying to get away. I...I was scared. Never thought of it."

"Never thought of it!" The walls glowed as the king's fire-sprites melted through his flesh into the chamber. They danced around me, too many to count, maybe even all thirteen. Although they were only aspects of the king, each had its own personality. The one we call Rage lashed out, catching me across the face with a firewhip. Like streams of hot oil, whips slapped across my back and arms and legs and groin, turning the skin to mush and flaying it off in strips as wide as a fingertip. The Nether began to pull me into it. Instead of howling with pain, I barely had the physical wherewithal to groan or whimper. I couldn't hear anything but the snapping of whips, the delighted squeals of my torturers and the pounding of my own pulse in my ear. Despite my intention of dying nobly, I found myself clinging pitifully to my last vestiges of life.

"Who is she?" The barrow-king's true voice cut through the din.

"I don't know," I croaked desperately.

"It couldn't be the Laird. We killed the Laird. Who is the one with the razored wings?"

"I don't..."

The firewhips stopped.

"You really don't know, do you?" said his voice tentatively. Another tongue protruded from the wall, proffering a gift; a single human finger that was still wearing a ring identical to the one Toadwart had just cut me with. "You're to wear Horsefly's ring. Your magic will be stronger. And I'll be there to make sure you don't fuck up on me again."

My breath came in shallow gasps. I could barely lift my arm to accept his offering. Trying to separate the ring from the severed digit was like pulling the cork from a wine bottle. I thought I was getting it, then realized that the finger was merely separating at the knuckle, coming apart like a chicken wing.

I gagged and dropped the thing, but Alimatheon scooped it up and thrust it back up at me.

"Push out the previous finger with one of your own," he instructed.

I held up my hand. "Which finger?"

"It doesn't matter," he snapped. "Just push your finger in. The ring can tell when you intend to put it on, even better than you can."

I poked gingerly at the bloody little stump of flesh inside, knowing that he wouldn't permit me to leave without it.

Wincing apologetically, I pushed my own finger through. The ring tightened excruciatingly below my knuckle and the barrow-king's presence flowed into the husk of Brandon Sutter with me. The pain from my many wounds faded. Energy flowed through me. Without my consent, my limbs began to move. I began to shuffle toward the door. But Alimatheon himself could barely keep my husk animated.

"Had I realized your condition was this poor, I wouldn't have punished you so harshly," said a voice inside my head. "But what's done is done. Toadwart should be here soon with your little giftie. Wait here."

"Giftie?" I asked, in an incredulous swoon, falling backwards.

The next few minutes or hours was like a blur of light and sound, where the only thing I could distinguish from roar was a woman's slurred voice saying, "What's going on you sick bastard. S'no bed in here? Feels like walking on a bed."

I heard her screaming then licked my lips and touched the bare flesh of my heavy breasts spilling out of the top of my dress; Madonna Riches' dress.

"Here's the ring," a voice boomed all around me. Alimatheon lifted Brandon Sutter's arm with a tongue-like tentacle and waved the corpse's hand in my face. The soul-eater tore off the empty husk's finger and dropped it in my lap.

"Put it on."

Toadwart stood over me, looking righteously pissed off. He saw me looking at him and gave me a crooked sneer, a familiar symptom of an imp losing control of its husk. The muscles on half of his face paralysed. Gradual loss of motor control. The pimp's body was nearly used up. No more than a week left before he'd have to vacate, and Alimatheon had just given me the vessel my barrow-mate had been nurturing for months, loosening Madonna's grip on life with drugs and beatings and humiliations. Now I'd stolen his prize from under his nose.

I felt good about that.

Just a few lifetimes earlier, Toadwart had lectured me about humans, while in the act of stealing a husk from me. "I was once like you. Until I reasoned, that humans don't value life enough. I treasure it. So I deserve it more than they do. More than you do too, Gallowrat."

"What are you standing there for?" said Madonna's voice. It took a moment to even realize I was speaking. Alimatheon was under complete control of my new husk. "You'd better get out and start looking for a new one."

Toadwart nodded unenthusiastically. "Gallowrat should have to find me one."

"I agree, Toadwart. Together, you'll find a new one in no time."

As my barrow-mate sullenly left the chamber, Alimatheon's voice swelled up around me, "when I'm not inside you, you're to do exactly what Toadwart tells you."

"Why did you...?"

"Don't question me."

"...beat me to death and then save me?"

"You failed me."

"Why have you given me your ring? It's always been a reward for the faithful, not a punishment for failure."

"Quiet."

The king took over my body and I stared down in amazement as the limbs of the husk I occupied began moving of their own accord. Madonna left the inner chamber, marched through the labyrinth and up to the street. As we walked out the door into the cold, wet night, Alimatheon gradually relinquished control of my new husk's body and I walked of my own accord.

"Why have you given me your ring?" I asked but it felt as though I was alone in my head. Controlling me now would be a strain on the king's resources. Even communicating with me was obviously an effort for him. "I'll let this husk die, unless you answer my questions. I might even walk in front of this bus."

"You really would do that, wouldn't you Gallowrat?" Alimatheon said, shaping the sounds of the wind and rain into words. "I gave you the ring so I could keep an eye on you. I don't want to give you a chance to betray me again."

"Why didn't you simply weed me out? Condemn me to an eternity in the Nether? Isn't that what you've always done with bad imps?"

"I have very few imps left. The way they were dismembered should have freed their souls at once. They should have found their way back to the barrow. But instead, I sensed their deaths, as surely as if they had been burned."

"Jaynie actually destroyed them?"

"And even if you aren't collaborating with her, you're the only imp who's ever returned from a confrontation with her. You may be of some use to me."

Then he was silent. I walked through the rain, too self-absorbed to realize how my makeup was smearing. I stopped and stared at my reflection in a shop mirror; a grotesque old whore. If I had a true face, this was probably as good a representation as I'd ever seen. Rain trickled down my cleavage, tickling my belly. First cold, then warm.

At least I was alive.

As the joy and relief of that realization suddenly overtook me I began to laugh. A throaty sound gurgling up from me.

I was alive.

After all the pain I'd suffered, I was amazed at the thing that pleased me most about my new husk. Madonna Riches didn't wear contact lenses. Sutter's had been a constant source of irritation to me.

I checked my purse, found twenty dollars and decided to find a pub and get as drunk as I could. Halfway through the night, I was hit on by a sleepy-looking middle aged man, who wanted to take me to his apartment. At first I turned him down, and then realized it would be better than throwing myself at the mercy of Toadwart, and putting up with his anger about losing the husk.

Old Jimmy lived in a single room, a meticulously neat downtown hotel apartment. As he started taking off his clothes, I pointed at a picture on the wall. A nun.

"Who's that?"

"My sister."

"Doesn't it bother you to have her watching?"

He shrugged and lifted the photograph off its hook, laying it gently, face-down on top of his dresser.

In the middle of lovemaking, Alimatheon entered my head again. And I watched helplessly as my husk grabbed the guy by the balls, squeezing until he screamed. My hand tightened, wringing him out as the man croaked and slobbered and swung impotently with both fists. With the other hand, my husk grabbed a brass bedside lamp and began clubbing him until he stopped moving. After taking the money out of his wallet and finding another cache in his sock drawer, the king got my husk dressed and walked me back downtown.

I could feel his power waning as I stumbled down the street. But despite his exhaustion, he somehow kept me moving, back into Toadwart's sphere of influence.

"Gallowrat must be punished," Alimatheon said to my barrow-mate. "Take care of it." And then he was gone.

Toadwart slapped me and I reeled away. He wasn't expecting me to retaliate. Kicking and punching him, I hissed, "I can outlast you. Are you ready to die for our king?"

He feinted a swing, then pulled back abruptly. "You took my husk."

"As if you've never stolen any of mine."

"You have to help me find a new one."

"No I don't."

"We're the only ones left, Gallowrat."

"What about Bonewolf?"

Toadwart shook his head.

"What do you mean?"

"Bonewolf is...gone."

"Dead?"

"They're all dead."

"No. Alimatheon doesn't know for sure. He just thinks they're dead."

"They're all dead."

"Not Bonewolf. Last night. The new husk. The music," I protested.

"They're all dead. The razorwinged woman went back to the club last night."

"No." All of my rebelliousness drained out of me. All my joy. The earth under my feet and the air I breathed turned fluid and I was suddenly drowning in a sea of fatigue. I sank to the bed, covering my face with my hands. Rolled onto my stomach and cried. The functioning of tear ducts is one of the first autonomic functions to go. In my hundreds and hundreds of incarnations, I had never actually cried before.

"We have to stay alive. Save the barrow," Toadwart said.

I felt real tears on my fingertips as I lay on the bed. I tasted them. They were salty.

And then I slept. The next time I looked up, daylight was filtering into the room. I was still in my dress which was wrinkled and bloodstained from the poor human, Jimmy.

And Bonewolf. Gone forever? His fierce joy turned to dust in the Nether.

Vaguely I could remember Toadwart leaving but it was if I had always been alone in the room.

I had never felt more alone.

Looking down at the ring I was wearing, I spun it idly around. The band wasn't made of metal, it was woven of tiny human arms, grasping one another by wrists and elbows. To the touch, they seemed like tiny fragile things made of real flesh and bone. The mount consisted of two perfectly formed human hands holding up the amber stone. I wondered if the stone could be smashed and what would happen to me if I tried and failed.

First I thought I should see what would happen if I tried to pull it off. I grasped it and tugged violently.

Not only didn't it move, it ignited a fire that spread through my whole hand. I tried not to scream as my fingers burned. Then the pain crawled over my wrist, as if I was dipping my arm into boiling oil. My pulse sounded like waves pounding inside my head as pain enveloped me. Slowly as fog, it lifted.

The barrow-king's voice penetrated the haze, lecturing me on how absolute obedience assured me of life and warned me how Jaynie wasn't the only one who could shred even my spirit so that I would be trapped in the Nether forever. I was glad I hadn't tried to smash the stone.

That was three days before Christmas.

The newspapers didn't mention any of the murders. I wondered how Jaynie had concealed the evidence. She had to be awfully damned powerful, maybe even stronger than Alimatheon.

On Christmas Day, Toadwart and I found a new husk for him at a local shooting gallery. A skinny boy of anywhere between fifteen and twenty-five; another casualty from the new shipment of super-pure Asian heroin that had all the city's junkies living on tightropes, dying in droves. It was easy to pluck a human being from that environment without anyone noticing. Especially on a night when most of the social workers were home with their families.

Toadwart's new husk wasn't big or strong enough to beat on me, although its health actually improved slightly after my barrow-mate went through a horrible, feverish Boxing Day. I cruised in and out of the hotel, deliberately irritating him with jokes about how the best thing about Christmas was the cold turkey afterwards.

We survived New Year's with no sign of Jaynie. Toadwart actually came out on the roof of the hotel with me to watch the fireworks. I offered to share my blanket, but my barrow-mate just shook his head and stood farther away from me, arms wrapped around his skinny body, trembling as we watched the colours blossom across the sky.

At night, Alimatheon had us both working the street. The bedroom was first come, first served. During the daytime, the barrow-king made us put on conservative clothes and search the libraries and records offices for some local history on the Laird Auldearne.

"Only the Laird could command enough magic to threaten a barrow-king," Alimatheon mused aloud while I sat in the library staring into a michofiche view screen for hours on end. "Perhaps he tricked us. Maybe he trained some sort of doppleganger to take his place. Maybe it was a trap all along, and we fell right into it."

A 1912 society photo showed the Laird helping an unidentified young woman from a train. The caption announced the arrival in Vancouver of Scotland's Lord of Auldearne, Abraham Melin. A 1948 photograph showed Melin at a retirement dinner for Canadian Prime Minister William Lyon McKenzie King. A 1974 newspaper photo showed a man identified as Abraham Melin III at a corporate party in Las Vegas, looking exactly as he had sixty years earlier. In each of these photographs he was with a different young woman. When I looked at their faces with my intuition rather than my eyes, I saw Jaynie staring out at me from every page. Something inside me instinctively knew she was all of these women.

What was this Jaynie Razorwings? Some sort of faerie employed by our most ancient enemy? Or was she human like the Laird was; a magician; another immortal?

In the time of the Picts, when we imps first started hearing stories about the Laird, it was said that he was born with the ability to distinguish changelings from real human beings and had been charged with a sacred mission to drive us out of our ancient hills, hunt us down and destroy us.

When the whispered legends had turned out to be true, Alimatheon had been one of the few dozen kings to escape. But Auldearne had tracked us, first to Ireland, then Eastern Europe, where suddenly, he'd disappeared.

Having encountered no sign of him for two hundred years, Alimatheon had hoped he'd finally been defeated.

According to Bonewolf, our king found out differently when Belial, one of the ancient ones, sought him out to take part in the assassination of Melin.

It happened during...in fact, it was the cause of my long death.

Since kings could only communicate through imp messengers, the whole barrow knew the story. Belial said that the Laird had gained his immortality by stealing the power of every king he defeated. All four kings he'd recruited for the task had been skeptical.

"If Melin has killed dozens of kings," Alimatheon had reasoned, "shouldn't he be as powerful as all of them combined?"

"No," Belial had explained. "The necromancy the Laird employs to keep himself alive has been slowly using up his powers. He is weak."

Belial hadn't said how he came to possess such information, but even one as brash as Alimatheon didn't have the temerity to raise the ire of an Ancient One.

The assassination squad closed in on their prey over the course of decades. But the actual confrontation had all ended in minutes. The Laird's elimination had been easier than any of them had dreamed.

And maybe it had been a dream, or at least, an illusion. Because, now Alimatheon suspected that the Laird was still alive.

I wasn't about to share my observation that Auldearne had merely taken an apprentice.

One thing I knew for sure was that Alimatheon wouldn't tell me what he knew or didn't know. I was lucky he was keeping me alive.

A chill went down my spine at the sudden notion that wearing the ring might enable Alimatheon to read my mind.

I gazed back up at the screen, moving the viewer to discover that the front page of the 1974 newspaper contained a story hinting that Jaynie had been a weapon in the Laird's arsenal for a long time. In July of that year, a man named Bryce Patterson had been sliced to ribbons in his bathtub. It was one of three similar murders. "One of the most gruesome murders in British Columbia history," the article called it.

That evening, I was working the uptown side of Government Street when I saw a new babe in a tiny red miniskirt posing like a fashion model in front of Bastion Square.

"Do it," Alimatheon's sudden command made me jump. I hadn't even felt his presence.

Crossing the street to intercept the blonde newcomer, I came up behind her and said nervously, "This is my territory, bitch." She turned. With her pretty face still wearing a layer of babyfat, she looked like a cheerleader gone bad. But those cold emerald eyes were pure Jaynie.

"You," she said. I trembled under her scrutiny, then sprang back like a mongoose from a cobra's strike. Nimble. Until I tripped on my high heels. As I kicked them off and began to run, I felt Alimatheon's power pouring into me.

"Wait, I want to talk to you!" Jaynie shouted.

"Stop," Alimatheon's voice rang inside my head.

"Forget it," I gasped as Alimatheon's rage filled me, feeling sure he would just push my spirit aside and take over my husk.

"I told you to stop." I felt a moment of hope at the notion that maybe he no longer had the strength to take over anymore.

As I went to turn away, I realized that my body was doing something completely different from what I had intended. Now I was simply along for the ride.

I heard my voice casting spells, saw Jaynie somehow block them and come twirling towards be through the air, which was so filled with magic, it was looking through heat waves in the desert. Then everything went black.

After what seemed like no time at all, a voice probed the murky ache that filled my head and I opened my eyes to see someone bending over me, sliding a hand under my dress.

"Fuck off," I muttered and to my surprise, my assailant stumbled backward. It wasn't Jaynie. It was an old man, who stood and shook his head.

"I thought you was dead."

"So you were checking my pussy for a pulse? How fucking humanitarian." I tried to rise to a sitting position, finally managing to prop myself against a tiled entranceway like a drunk.

Across the street was an antique store with a black and white tudor facade. Just as my mind was slowly giving me a fix on where I was, the old man grabbed my arm and I fired him a dirty look.

"Just trying to help."

"Do it again and you'll get a knife in your throat," I growled. He disappeared.

The cops were usually pretty diligent when cruising Antique Row. Not wanting to be hauled in for vagrancy, I staggered to my feet and started walking. Sore all over and covered with dozens of tiny cuts, I realized that I probably just looked drunk. A pitiful old whore. How true. The irony hurt almost as badly as the bruises. And it felt like a truck had run over my chest. It hurt to breathe. Forcing myself to keep walking, I finally reached the barrow.

Alimatheon remained silent even as I entered his chamber. I began to wonder if Jaynie had somehow destroyed him.

"What happened?" I asked.

"Even with the strength from the ring, I couldn't defeat her while I was in human form," Alimatheon said. "I had to use a dislocation spell to save your miserable husk."

"Well I...uh..." He must have had a reason for saving me but I couldn't imagine what it was. "Thanks."

"She has the strength to challenge me. She should have been able to fend off your freezing spell with the blink of an eye."

"So, you still think I'm working with her?" I asked.

"No. I would have found that lie inside you. But if she didn't have you in mind for something other than mutilation, she'd have done you in already. She'll try for you again. I want you to bring her to me. Start working the park toilets with Toadwart. As often as she seems to change husks, this Razorwings creature seems restricted to female form. If she shows up in the park as a woman, she'll stand out like a circus clown at a convent."

"And I won't?" I said, gesturing at the sagging body I was wearing.

"Toadwart will fix that. He'll bring you a new husk later tonight."

"But this one still has plenty of life left in it. It's not right to take another one yet."

The pain from the ring spread through my hand again, stopping when I finally began to cringe.

"Don't question me," Alimatheon said.

"I won't. Just stop the pain."

"You need another lesson."

"Please..."

"And since you won't need this husk for much longer, I won't have to worry about damaging it."

Two fire sprites poked their faces from the king's flesh.

"No, please..." I saw what he was intending. Using the ring and the sprites to torture me again.

"No," I clenched my fist. "I refuse."

I stared at the unbroken wall of glowing flesh that surrounded me and incanted a breaching spell.

Emerging only partway out of the flesh of the king, one of the sprites began lashing at me frantically. The ring-pain crawled up my arm to my shoulder.

Alimatheon emitted a long, peircing shriek as a doorway opened like a cut in his flesh, beyond was a dark, empty passageway to freedom. I took a step toward it and the king's presence flowed through me, pulling me back. But he didn't have the strength to take over my body again.

Had the fight against Jaynie exhausted him? Or had the diminished diet of human souls depleted his strength?

I took several more steps, actually staggering out of the door, before the king's will took control and threw me back into his chamber. The pain finally filled me completely and I began to writhe. Four fire sprites had materialized by now and they surrounded me, swinging madly. And I screamed as I lay there with my arms straight out to my sides. Alimatheon may have had trouble moving me but preventing me from moving was easy. All I could do was writhe. And scream. And writhe some more.

I woke up in the husk of a boy barely in his teens.

I checked his pockets for ID as Toadwart led me back up to the street, but they were empty. Even though my new husk had experienced none of Madonna's torture, my hands shook with residual trauma.

Throughout the weekend, I hung out in Beacon Hill Park with Toadwart, selling favours to any number of gay men who were afraid to go public with their proclivities. The square yellow brick washroom building in the centre of the big urban park was illuminated. We'd line up along the walls so that our middle class, middle aged tricks could get a good look at us before taking us into the bushes, over to the playground or into a washroom stall.

One of Toadwart's regulars was a pathetic little masochist named Gordon Taylor, who always carried a pouch full of his favourite sharp instruments. To him pain and life were synonymous. What scared me was the feeling that I understood him. I turned to watch them walk into the stucco building together. They went into the women's side, where there were twice as many stalls.

"You charge for blowjobs?" said a gruff alto voice behind me.

I spun around, ready to dive to the ground. But I could tell instantly that it wasn't Jaynie in male guise. It was a mortal, a tall, white-haired man in dark suitpants and open-collared dress shirt. Might it be the Laird? Determined not to let my fear show, I decided to give him an attitude. "No, I just hang around here because I'm a fucking satyr."

"A what?" he asked astonished.

I obviously owed him a retort more typical of a seventeen year old street kid. "Just wondering how long I fucking sat here. Got a problem with that?"

"That's not what you said."

"What'd I say then, asshole?"

He shook his head.

"What you want from me, Gramps? Want me to introduce your face to the bottom of my boot? You wanna suck some sole?"

He backed off another few steps.

"No. Just some...oral sex."

"Let's see your money."

"After the services are rendered," he said, looking suddenly self-righteous.

It's not the Laird, I breathed to myself. To him, I sneered, "That's what the last guy said. But he didn't even give me a smoke afterwards. Just pushed me out of the car. From now on it's payment up front, Gramps. If you don't like the terms, find yourself another boy."

"I think I will," the man said indignantly as he strode to the driver's side of his white Coupe de Ville. He squealed in reverse and then again as he accelerated down the service road and out of the park.

"You forgot to say thank you," I muttered.

As I waited for Toadwart, I was suddenly aware of the silence. Gordon was usually noisy, squealing like a banshee when Toadwart administered his punishment. Yet I hadn't heard a sound from the little man in five minutes.

Time to go in and check the place out.

As my eyes adjusted to the anemic light from the single fluorescent tube that flickered overhead, I saw that it was standing in a huge puddle of some sort. My feet slid on the smooth tile floor.

Blood — a lake of it spread from under the doorway of stall number three, threading into tributaries which meandered between the tiles. Under the door of the stall, I could see that someone was sitting on the floor. As I bent down, I realized it was Gordon's fat, middle aged butt. Had Toadwart killed another human?

Barely audible muttering, was punctuated by occasional sharp squawks from the peacocks which inhabited the park. It grew louder as I approached the door of the stall, but I still couldn't make out any words.

I pounded on the door with the heel of my hand. "What's going on in there?"

I pounded again. "Toadwart?"

Pushing open the door of the stall next door, I carefully climbed up on the rim of the toilet to stare over the partition.

Clutching an ice pick in one hand and a small knife in the other, Gordon sat in the puddle of blood repeating the Lord's Prayer over and over. Toadwart's mutilated body peered up at me from the throne. His eyes were the only parts of his face left unsliced.

Shaking my head, I got down from my perch, wondering what to do.

"Get the ring from Toadwart," Alimatheon instructed me.

I tiptoed through the sticky mess and shouted, "Open the door, Gordon."

"Kick it in!" Alimatheon commanded, but then there was a rattle and the door swung inward. Gordon stared at me.

"I didn't kill him," he said. "It was the Angel of Death, I swear. Wasn't me. Really, it wasn't."

Snatching the knife from Gordon's bloody hand, I used it to slice off Toadwart's ring finger. Gordon stared up at me with some sort of awe.

As I turned to leave, Alimatheon told me, "Kill the witness."

"It's not necessary," I said out loud to the voice in my skull. "Noone will ever believe him. If he goes to the police, they'll arrest him for the murder."

"Do as I tell you."

"Find some other imp to do it," I said.

"You are *mine* and you will do as I tell you!"

"I haven't been your imp since before my long death. You know that."

My right hand, clutching the severed finger, moved toward my left hand, where the stone of my ring slowly brightened. The index finger extended as I looked down in dismay. I struggled against the king and managed to throw off his coordination so that the effort to put the ring on my finger was like trying to stick together identical poles of two giant magnets.

"Run, Gordon!" I shouted, but the stupid man just stood watching me fight myself. Inevitably, I lost control to the soul-eater.

My hands came together and manoeuvred into position, with one finger poking out the stump of flesh, then suddenly the second ring slid into place.

Alimatheon wrenched my husk completely out of my grasp. Unable to shut my eyes, I had to watch as my hands directed the scalpel that dissected the poor bewildered masochist. He actually smiled as I slit his throat, as if he'd been jealous of Toadwart's mutilation and was pleased when someone finally turned their blade on him.

I stumbled spastically out of the park, occasionally wrenching control back from Alimatheon, swinging my arms and yelling things like, "I'm not going back to the barrow" or "Call the police!" But no one did.

So I stepped out in front of a car.

Headlights flared, a horn honked frantically, tires screamed, and with a rush of cold air, an early model Hyundai Elantra rocketed past me, crammed full of teenaged boys. Car windows opened, profanities were shouted. And I found myself back on the sidewalk.

Perhaps nervous that I might succeed in my impromptu suicide, Alimatheon walked me down the steps to the Inner Harbour causeway. The cold, dark tang of the sea filled the air. When I heard the soft lap of the water, I realized that Alimatheon was losing his grip on my husk. But before I was able to move an inch, the king seized control again and I could only watch my body march with a purposeful step, back up the stairs to the street. At least a dozen people heard me yell and watched, uncomprehendingly as Alimatheon reined me in.

"You'll go wherever I tell you," he said, to me alone. This time, the pain shot electrically up my arm.

"Augghh," I roared, my arms flailing out to each side. My walk slowed to a lurch. Most of me kept trying to flee but my legs locked with one foot in the air and the momentum toppled me face first onto the grass that bordered the sidewalk.

My forehead glanced off concrete while the rest of me landed on the grass at the very edge of the sidewalk. It felt as hard as the concrete itself. My husk almost lost consciousness but, a moment after my world turned into a thumping, roaring, chattering abstraction, my senses flooded back and I recognized the thumping of car doors, roaring of traffic, chattering of voices. "...a seizure...some kind of drug thing...OD'd or something...if the cops...friends or something...out of here. I opened my eyes and stared down at the cold, wet grass that tickled my nose and lips. I wanted to lift my head, but couldn't. Alimatheon wouldn't let me.

I couldn't turn my head, either.

As the sound of footsteps receded, I wanted to shout to them for help, but Alimatheon held my tongue. Then, there was just the cold hum of the streetlight and the swish of distant traffic.

I waited for the barrow-king to rematerialize inside me, but nothing more happened.

Still, no matter how hard I tried, I could neither lift my head nor turn it. So, I pushed with my arm, hard enough to roll over.

And I kept rolling. As I turned, I caught dizzy glimpses of a steep hillside and the gleam of glass and metal from a parking lot far below. The top edge of a concrete retaining wall was little more than a flat spot at the bottom of the incline. It was enough to stop me from tumbling over the precipice. My legs dangled over the edge, churning helplessly in the air. I dug my fingers between blades of grass, unsure I could conjure any magic powerful enough to save me from the impending fall.

Directly below me was a blood red Corvette. I turned my gaze up-hill and managed to swing one leg back up onto the ledge. I pulled myself into a kneeling position but my battles with Alimatheon for control of the husk were taking a toll. I barely had the strength to get my feet under me, then the soles of my shoes couldn't gain any purchase on the slippery grass. I kicked them off and one shoe bounced and flipped over the ledge, landing on the Corvette with a dull thump. A car alarm began whooping shrilly.

Pulling my socks off, I managed to scramble barefoot, back up the hill. By the time I reached the sidewalk, my wet feet were so cold they hurt. A car sailed past, its rigid, middle-aged male driver carefully ignoring me.

Noone had yet reacted to the alarm.

I walked as quickly as I could, given the meagre strength I was able to muster. The big blue drawbridge loomed ahead. I'd spent years living among the drunks who inhabited the honeycombed brush that grew under the bridge, but I'd had to leave when I started caring about them as individuals. It became too damned difficult to accept their friendship one day, then steal their husk the next. And feed their eternal souls to the barrow-king.

Besides, I told myself, it was a good place to hide from Jaynie, since good looking young women were as rare as troll's teeth (the last of which rotted away a millennium ago) under the bridge. Jaynie would have a tough time sneaking up on me.

I recognized it as the same strategy which had just failed Alimatheon in the park.

But it had one advantage; I knew the bums well enough to be certain they'd take care of me. It was less than two years since I had dwelt among them, so I'd still know many of them by name.

It was the closest thing to home on the mortal side of the barrow.

None of the people who lived under the bridge would recognize me of course, except maybe as some premonition of death, a shadow underneath the eyes, a pallor; or perhaps just an uneasy feeling, an obtuse suspicion of something wrong.

Despite the drizzle which should have sent everyone under cover, there was noone sleeping under the concrete bridge abutments, in the bushes, or between the pilings underneath the marine repair shop. The smells of oil and ocean were overwhelmingly strong. There was no sound except from the odd car or truck humming over the metal bridge deck above me. I felt more than a little bit tense. I needed the safety of familiar faces, of other lives; real lives.

On cue, Black Charlie came hobbling down the path toward me with a skinny native woman. Unable to see much more than her silhouette in the fading light, I jumped to my feet, ready to run.

The old Indian stopped and peered at me suspiciously.

"Who're you?"

"Paul," I said, picking a name out of the air.

"Why aren't you up at the youth shelter?"

I shrugged. "Too late for curfew. Who're you?"

"Charlie. This is Henrietta." Charlie said, kicking an empty brandy bottle out of his path then stopping and regarding it hopefully after hearing it slosh.

"It's fulla piss," I told him. "I already checked." I wasn't lying.

"Glad to meet you, Henrietta," I said, extending my hand.

Instead, she didn't even acknowledge my presence except to say, "yup," under her breath. She had no front teeth. She kept her head down without actually hiding her face. Part of me recognized the type, told me not to worry because she was completely typical of women in that run-down fringe of society – complete non-people, as if their own lives were plays written by someone who hadn't bothered to tell them their lines.

Charlie laughed, shook his head and led Henrietta down the path to the clearing in the blackberry thicket. He spread out his blanket on top of the thin layer of wet soil. On top of that, he put a big green sleeping bag, and I suddenly realized that this was to be their bedroom, so I looked away.

After making the "bed", Charlie walked up to me with two cans of creamed corn, "You cook this for us, you can have some."

Then he gave me one of those knife-can-openers you can pick it up for two bits at the Goodwill. "One can's hers though."

While I rounded up kindling and damp newspaper, Charlie grinned. "You got some wine or something, Henrietta might give you something else too, eh."

So involved in building the fire and cooking the food, I nearly jumped out of my shoes when Charlie tapped me on the shoulder a few minutes later. "She says she'll give you a free sample," he said, crouching down beside me.

"This Henrietta, she's alright, eh?" I said with a passable pretence of enthusiasm. "You known her long?"

"Henrietta? Shit, yeah. She's from the Pacheenaht Reserve. My friend Stan's known her since they were kids."

I sighed with relief. I knew Stan. But I had no desire to take Henrietta up on her offer.

"No," I said, shaking my head. I was going to tell him I had AIDS but then I remembered what a homophobe old Charlie was. "I got the clap."

He pulled a wad of condoms out of his pocket. "They were giving these out down at the clinic."

He gave one to me.

I sighed, realized it would be as much trouble to keep arguing with these people as it would be to get it over with. I ducked through the archway of brambles, where the woman lay in the shadows like a dried up old piggie in a blanket. I saw Charlie peeking as I pulled my pants down and crawled in with her.

I felt her wings curl around me at the same instant as she fixed me with those electric eyes.

"Hi, Gallowrat," she whispered.

"Oh, shit," I gasped and waited for Alimatheon to come storming into my head but instead I experienced a different pain when all of the fingers on my left hand were severed as though by garden shears. Both rings went with them.

Closing my eyes, I screamed and howled as loudly as I could but Charlie didn't come running. Panic surged through me and I thrashed madly again for a moment before grasping the significance of being not only helpless, but still alive. Through tear-filled eyes I saw the old man standing at the end of the blanket staring down at me.

"Help!" I said to him weakly, hoping that Jaynie wouldn't destroy me in full view of the human. To my astonishment, she released me. I leaped to my feet, clutching the stubs of my fingers to stop the blood from spouting out. Wordlessly, Black Charlie grabbed my arm and wrapped a makeshift bandage tightly around my hand.

Jaynie sat up, saying, "You need not die when I destroy Alimatheon."

I heard her words but through the trauma of my severed fingers, it was hard to translate them into anything meaningful.

"Listen to what she's saying," said Black Charlie. "Rats-ass, we need you."

The word 'Rats-ass' penetrated my haze, its meaning following shortly after.

"Bonewolf?" I croaked.

"In another year and a half, we could be human." My friend said, hugging me.

"If you last that long," said Jaynie. "After Alimatheon, we take on Belial himself."

I was simultaneously so zoned out, excited, scared and confused that Bonewolf could have dragged out me of my husk with an Abracadabra.

Then my hard-earned cynicism took over. "How do you know she's on the level?" I said, forming my words carefully as I clutched the stumps of my fingers through the sodden handkerchief. My mouth was so damned dry it was hard to talk.

"How do you know she's not?"

"What's this all about? Why didn't you kill me?"

"He wouldn't let me," said Jaynie. "It's part of our deal. Besides, we'll need all the help we can get."

"I'm...sorry. I don't have the strength to help you." I stared down at the damaged hand I was cradling against my chest. "It's hard enough remaining conscious."

"Would you if you could?" asked Jaynie, or was it Bonewolf?

And did it matter?

As I nodded, the two of them put their hands on me and I felt their strength flow into me. The throbbing pain of bloody stumps where my fingers had been turned electric and I looked down to see new fingers forming.

"The sooner we get moving," Jaynie said, "the better our odds of catching Alimatheon by surprise. Are you up for it?"

"Catching Alimatheon?"

Bonewolf nodded. "We can consider it reparation for all the human lives we've stolen."

"What? We're going to...I mean...she...keeps us alive. If we destroy him, we'll die. It's suicide."

Bonewolf shook his head again. "I've been with Jaynie for months. This husk is as strong as ever. And Charlie's soul is still alive, in here with me. I'll never need another husk. And Jaynie can do this for you too."

"It's not quite as good as it sounds," Jaynie corrected. "Keeping Bonewolf and myself alive is already a strain on the Laird's resources. All we can offer you is mortality. You'll live forty, maybe fifty more years. You'll never have to destroy another human again."

"This is the gift you're offering me for helping you destroy the barrow-king?"

Jaynie turned to Bonewolf. "Are you absolutely sure about this one?"

"Yes. Just give me five minutes with him."

After Jaynie and I got dressed, she walked back up the embankment.

"I'm sorry I didn't disobey her and tell you all this before the dance," Bonewolf said. "But Jaynie...and the Laird were afraid they couldn't trust you, no matter how hard I argued. If we destroy Alimatheon, we can be together forever. No more thirty-seven year gaps. I've always known who and what you are. But when I look at you, I want to see the person I love. Sometimes, I don't even learn to love you again before you're stolen away and I have to fall in love with a new Gallowrat."

"A new husk. I'm always the same."

"You know what I mean. Intellectually I know it's you, but emotionally... it feels different. I don't adjust as quickly as I once did. I want to know your look, your smell, your touch."

"If you were taking up permanent residence in a husk, why didn't you choose a woman?"

"Because it would have meant hunting again. The Laird wants to stop the hunt forever. I want to help him."

I felt amazed and betrayed and afraid by what was happening. How had things swung so far out of control? "What about our own kind? You hunt for us, now."

"Jaynie does all the killing. I'm just here to help her face off against Alimatheon. And then, you and I are free to go. We'll have a long lifetime together." He took my hand.

"But the Nether will claim us back eventually, Bonewolf."

Bonewolf shook his head. "That's the best part. We won't be imps anymore. We'll be humans or close enough anyway. We'll have the right to die."

"Die?"

"Permanently."

"But...what if it's like the Nether, an eternity of loneliness?"

"I thought it was only me who wished for that."

"Y'know, during your long sleep, the first few years without you were bearable. Then I began to think you'd never find your way back to the barrow," said Bonewolf, staring into my eyes. "And after a while I became certain."

"You've told me that before. A few hundred times."

We hugged and Bonewolf said, "But there are things I've never told you. It was hard to accept that you were gone. It was easier to take when I thought of the good that had come of your death; how many humans got to live out their lives because you weren't there to take it from them. Two hundred and six in thirty-seven years."

"I thought I was the only one who cared about numbers."

Bonewolf looked me in the eyes again. "Belial was right about the Laird being weak. The dark monarchs injured him badly in their trap. He may not have the strength to beat even a single barrow-king. But with our help, he thinks it's possible. If we kill all the dark monarchs, we can end the hunt forever, Gallowrat."

Eventually the Laird will get his strength back. Until then, he's depending on us and Jaynie."

"To beat Alimatheon?"

"Jaynie's strong."

"Come on. I put her under a freezing spell. I was never at the top of my necromancy class."

"You caught her by surprise. If she'd been trying to kill you she would have."

"Maybe, but did it occur to you that we could lose? Alimatheon could banish us to the Nether permanently. And we might never be together again."

"If our battle takes us closer to the end of the hunt, then at least we'll have accomplished something. Our king was about to give birth. We had to prevent it."

"Give birth? What are you talking about?"

"You've noticed how ringbearers disappear over the centuries? Do you know what happens to them?

I shook my head.

"They become kings."

I kept shaking my head.

"If the Laird dies, the barrows will multiply exponentially. Soon, they won't be preying on the weak and confused anymore. They'll go after anybody. Until there are no husks left to take."

"That would take thousands of years. Won't happen."

"Are you coming?" shouted a woman's voice.

"One more minute," shouted Bonewolf.

"What happens if you don't convert me?" I asked.

"I don't know."

"You think Jaynie would destroy me?"

"She might do that anyways. Your strength could be enough to give Alimatheon the edge. But you'd destroy me in the process. And you'd be Alimatheon's only imp for who knows how long. He'd make you wear his ring. You might become a king yourself and feed on human souls. I promised Jaynie that you'd be on our side. I believe in you Gallowrat."

After a long, wistful kiss, Bonewolf headed up the path toward Jaynie.

I was angry. What kind of choice was this?

The amber rings glowed and I hurriedly bent down and picked up the two bloody digits. I didn't know why but I felt certain that it was important to take the rings with me. I shoved them into the side pocket of my jeans, then stopped with a jolt of paranoia. What if Jaynie saw the bloodstain on my pocket? I might not have time to explain before she turned me into mincemeat.

I looked down and laughed out loud. My pants were already covered with blood. As was my shirt.

I hurried up the hill after Bonewolf.

As I reached the sidewalk, a small crowd of derelicts scampered past me on their way down the hill.

Bonewolf grinned. "The Laird's magic has been keeping them out."

"Where IS the Laird?" I peered along the sidewalks in every direction and looked for faces in parked cars.

"Out of harm's way," Jaynie smiled sadly.

"He can employ enough magic long distance to defeat Alimatheon?"

Bonewolf grimaced at me. Jaynie nodded.

"Through me," she said. "And if we really need him, the Laird can actually materialize."

Jaynie turned and led Bonewolf and me past the cluster of restaurants between us and the barrow, which was only a few blocks down the street along the same shoreline. I crossed my arms in front of my chest as I walked so the blood on my shirt would be less obvious to any pedestrians we passed. I worried for nothing, because most people did their best to ignore the downtrodden. The stones of Alimathea's rings pulsed with heat and I wondered why I'd felt so compelled to bring them with me. Was I still under the king's influence? It seemed likely.

The key wouldn't work in the gate and the usual breaching spell didn't uncover the door.

But nevertheless, Alimatheon made no more than a token effort to defend the barrow from us. Was this his full strength now that his usual intake of "nourishment" had abated? Or was that what he wanted us to believe? There had once been thirty-one imps harvesting souls for Alimatheon. Now there were two. And we were fighting for the other side.

Jaynie chanted, "By the Hammer of Boleskine and the Tome of Auldearne, we shatter barriers before us and their benefactors burn."

When the wall was gone, Bonewolf looked at me and shook his head.

Now there was no going back.

I followed Jaynie and Bonewolf through the familiar maze of corridors – our home in Alimathea's barrow where we were reborn every few months since the beginning of time.

Firesprites filled the corridor behind us. Walls of Alimatheon's flesh flowed in front of us, around us.

As though suspended in glass, I couldn't move my arms or legs. The feeling of helplessness was almost as profound as those times I'd been trapped inside lifeless husks.

A lash of flame sliced across my back and I somehow clenched my teeth against the pain, refusing to cry out. Something was reaching into my pocket for the rings. Something else was pummelling and pawing at my face, my lips.

I heard a scream and as I gasped, a tendril of darkness wormed its way into my mouth. I tried desperately to spit it out, or at least block its path, but the tendril flowed onward, curving down my throat. Then suddenly the wall of flesh that encased me seemed to pull itself apart! The tendril, unable to hook itself on anything, slid painfully back out of my mouth.

Another sprite hurtled toward me, arms out to embrace me.

Through an aperture in the darkness, I saw the face of Jaynie glowing – not the hapless little crone from under the bridge, but the white haired woman-child from the OAP dance so long ago.

I heard Jaynie chanting spell after spell.

The sprite who was coming toward me literally froze; flames turned to motionless swirls and gleaming spires of ice, lit from within. Then the fire began to flicker again. A halo of flames formed above its head, gradually growing brighter and more fierce. The sprite seemed to perceive what was happening at the same time I did; its own heat was destroying it. Eyes widened with helpless terror, became liquid, and flowed down the melting face. Liquid flames poured down the frozen torso to the floor. The headless thing toppled and was soon just a burning, shapeless puddle.

"Where's Bonewolf?" Jaynie asked me.

I shook my head, feeling half-asphyxiated. Then saw Bonewolf lying motionless on the tile floor.

Jaynie turned and shouted a jumble of nonsense words, which I only partially understood. "Thrimondel and Palexi Doras le compte abra-melin de maleficarum dies mutatus."

I interpreted it to mean that she was summoning the Laird to help us, inviting him to materialize through her. Jaynie grew brighter and taller and broader across the shoulders, moaning and chanting as her voice deepened. Within seconds, she was gone and the Laird Auldearne himself stood in her place. He glowed like a thousand watt bulb and the sounds that came out of his mouth seemed physically impossible for a human to produce – all thrums and strange pops and hisses. I shrunk back from the power of the magic in them.

The black walls of the king's flesh which had closed in around me, now turned to tatters in my hands. Suddenly there was no sign of Alimatheon.

Was the great soul-eater dead? I didn't think so but couldn't imagine where he might be hiding.

I ran to Bonewolf, slid a hand behind my lover's head and sobbed tearlessly. The lashes of the sprites had done much more damage to Bonewolf than they had to me. Bonewolf's eye on the ruined side was blistered shut in a sloppy weld.

Bonewolf reached up, gripping my shoulder with surprising strength. "Al...mathe...eon's..." he said with a cough and something that looked like motor oil bubbled from inside him. It smelled like shit. "...magic inside me. Don't let him winnnn...help Jaynie," Bonewolf's voice became a cross between a gurgle and a scream. Lifted a hand from my shoulder, my lover pointed straight up, eyes widening. I glanced upward, seeing nothing; and looked back down to see the oily substance rising out of Bonewolf's mouth like a tentacle. In a blur of blackness moving, the rest of Alimatheon rose up out of Bonewolf's body like smoke, seeping from all orifices and pores. It curled and spread out to wrap itself around me.

As I leaped to my feet, the Laird sang out, "Guarder del Illuminates, antessra."

Before the Laird's protecting spell could enclose me, the dark cloud which was the barrow-king's new incarnation became fluid, then solid, closing in around my face, squirming between my lips, seeping between my teeth. I grabbed at Alimatheon desperately with my hands, but his flesh seeped through my fingers like molten wax, hardening, then just as suddenly, evaporating. The barrow-king became a swirling cloud of darkness.

I felt cold and smelled the dead air of the Nether as the ancient realm opened in front of me like a vast, sucking pit.

The Laird's cocoon of magic, which encased me, began to glow. The rings in my pocket heated up, suddenly welding themselves onto the flesh of my leg. From their point of contact, I felt the king's still formidable will flowing into me. Alimatheon's mind pushed mine aside, taking over my husk's tongue, my voice.

"Thank, you. That was close," I heard myself say.

The Laird now standing beside me, reached out a hand.

"Back away from the portal slowly," the he said. But his voice sounded different. His fingers felt small, almost child-like. The Laird was gone. This was Jaynie beside me.

I wanted to scream a warning, that I wasn't really me, but couldn't.

With all my concentration, I took control of my free hand and groped into my pocket for the rings. It was like closing my fingers around burning coals. I somehow managed to retain control and not black out from the pain. With a curse, I smashed the objects down onto the pavement. And drove my heel down on one of them. Predictably, the stone remained intact.

The air moaned around me, brightening as it became a wind rushing up out of the broken stone and I stumbled back, somehow keeping my eye on the other ring. I leaned forward, lifting my foot. The darkness formed itself into a great black hand, which grabbed me and crushed me.

Between the fingers I saw a blurry image of metal wings slashing down. The air began to moan again and I saw Jaynie being enveloped in the darkness along with me. All the remaining light in the chamber had coalesced into a tiny sun, which was growing dimmer and dimmer. Then that dimming light shattered into thousands of infinitesimal stars which each began to go out like the embers of spent fireworks. The last remnants of light were being extinguished.

"No," I screamed, as I tried desperately to remember the words of even the most rudimentary illumination spell.

"In fieri, inferverato, inferno! Burn ye now, ye wicks of Mithras. Twixt waxen lips where candles come. Make my flesh light to show the way," I shouted, realizing almost instantly that I had left the spell unfinished. "I give myself to fire!"

I lifted my hands into the air and they began to glow, growing bright as a streetlamp. The stars all rushed toward my light, each of them adding to its intensity. The room flared to a blue incandescence.

This time, I recognized Alimatheon's voice screaming. And I smiled, despite the intense pain of the real flames consuming my hands. Then another light joined with mine, and another, until I could longer see.

"It is done," I heard the Laird (or was it Jaynie, or was it the wind?) say as I crumpled to the floor.

When hands touched my mine, I screamed in agony. And those hands became pillows of healing air. I opened my eyes and saw small hands, glowing red on top of mine. Looked up into Jaynie's face as it contorted with the pain she was drawing out of me. This wasn't the most recent version of Jaynie, but the white-haired razorwinged waif I'd met at Bonewolf's dance.

"Wait," I said.

Jaynie opened her eyes, smiled and released my hands. While they felt as though they should be charred and black, they looked merely pink and tender.

"*We* defeated Alimatheon." Jaynie crowed, her wings sliced up through the air as she pirouetted across the vast empty room. Glowing, just as the Laird had glowed.

"Where's the Laird?" I asked.

"The party here is over. So he's gone back to more important things."

I shook my head. "The Laird Auldearne is dead, isn't he?"

"He was just here. You saw for yourself."

"Alimatheon and I saw what you wanted us to see, interpreted it the way you knew we would. Why did you pretend to be the Laird?"

Jaynie shrugged. "Alimatheon was afraid of him. Not of an ex-barrow-imp like me."

The outrage inside of me was drowned out by sheer awe.

"An imp? Defeated a barrow-king?"

"Two ex-barrow-imps," she corrected me.

Then the anger came pouring out of me. "You kill your own kind?"

"You just killed your own God."

"That's different. He deserved it. But how can you kill imps?"

"You kill the humans whose husks you steal."

"That's not the same…it's not fair. You killed humans once too."

"But I don't anymore. Nor imps, if I don't have to."

"Why do you have to kill anything? Why don't you just teach us all the magic we need to break free from the dark monarchs? Let the soul-eaters starve."

"Don't think the Laird never tried. He risked his own life countless times, giving chances to imps who turned out to be pathologically devoted to their kings and queens. Imps who would never trade their eternal lives – no matter how miserable – for mortality. No matter how much it has to offer."

"Because they don't know what it has to offer. They've never experienced anything like love or compassion," I said sadly.

"They don't want to know. They're too preoccupied with staying alive, hunting for new husks," Jaynie said, sounding suddenly defensive. "Learning to care about anything other than themselves and their king is not only unlikely and difficult, it's self-destructive. An imp who develops a conscience will inevitably question the morality of the things it has to do in order to simply stay alive. No worse than humans, I guess? Eating animals, subjugating one another. We're no lesser species than they are."

"Who's side are you on, anyway?" I asked her.

She shrugged. "I just want you to know, I like killing imps even less than I enjoy killing humans."

"But you do it anyway. Very human of you."

"Bonewolf said something like that about you. How you seemed more human than imp."

"I wasn't like that when our…in the beginning. Bonewolf knows what I was like then."

"How long ago?"

"A few hundred years. Right after our barrow moved to Romania. Bonewolf was in the husk of a dark-haired woman. We were trying to move in on the same husk. And we became lovers for two months. Her husk collapsed first, so I gave her the new one. And we started hunting as a team." My voiced cracked and clearing my throat, turned into a sob.

"You're sure Bonewolf is gone?" I managed to say. "There's nothing you can do?"

Jaynie shook her head. "Bonewolf no longer exists, in this world or the Nether."

Wait a minute, I said to myself. "Alimatheon told me the same thing once. He was wrong. With all the things I saw tonight, how should I know what's real or what's possible? And why should I believe what you tell me?"

"I'm the Laird's apprentice, Gallowrat. He taught me to see and function in both realms at once. I saw Alimatheon destroy Bonewolf the same way I destroy imps. He released his soul from his body, pulled it into the Nether with him and then immolated it."

"And you didn't do anything to stop it?"

"There wasn't time. Alimatheon would have beaten us." Jaynie stared down at the floor, her luminosity dimming as she spoke. "Destroying other imps is the most difficult thing you'll ever do. But watching the deaths of imps you care about is worse. I had hoped Bonewolf would become my apprentice."

My perfect grief was shattered by a streak of jealousy. I stared into Jaynie's eyes. "Did you love Bonewolf?"

Jaynie Razorwings shook her head. "No. But I have been in love."

"With another imp."

"Now's not the time to talk."

"Why not? When is the right time."

I had an insight. "It was the Laird, wasn't it? You fell in love with the Laird himself."

Wordlessly, Jaynie walked away. As the darkness congealed around me, I wondered what would happen if Alimatheon was still alive, lying in wait. I found it hard to care.

"You were the only thing that kept me alive for the last few years," I said to Bonewolf's empty husk. "We should have shared this too. This chance... to live..." My voice cracked and faded to a soft, keening wail.

I pushed him into a sitting position and wrapped my arms around him, clasping my hands against his chest.

No breath. No heartbeat.

I stared into the gloomy depths of the barrow with my eyes, my mind and my magic but found no trace of Bonewolf's vagrant soul. The husk's eyes were like dull marbles, devoid of depth.

When I thought of Bonewolf, was this the face I'd see? Or would it be the Romanian woman?

My love had a thousand faces. Now all of them were gone.

I closed my eyes and wished for tears again. After a long time, I got up and hurried toward the light.

White on White

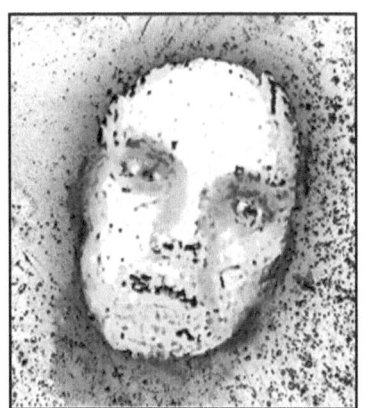

Preamble – White on White

I had no intention of including this story in this collection. But when I re-read it and I found it such a delightful metaphor for the latest part of my life – and for the societal roles of all us over-fifty caucasian guys – I simply couldn't resist.

The voice is naive-colonial. The ending is inevitable tragedy.

White on White

When Joe Steen arrived at the hangar, a thick-bodied Malaysian woman with oily black hair gave him coffee in an insulated cup and a choice of sandwiches.

He declined but she insisted. "Flight to mountain take five hours. You are very late. My only passenger today. You get hungry. We not stopping for pizza or burger with cheese." Her laughter was a deep chuckle, simultaneously real and processed.

She led him to a small black heli-jet with a green and blue Xanadu logo. "Take any seat. Enjoy your flight please, Mr. Steen." She made her way to the cockpit and sat down in the pilot's seat but before Joe could determine whether there was anyone sitting next to her, she latched the door between the cockpit and passenger area and the blades began to spin.

Shel's words kept coming back to him. "Of course you have no choice." What had she meant by that?

He finally distracted himself by reading *Marketing Magazine* down to the employment classifieds.

He'd worked overtime every night last week so he could take this week off for his anniversary cruise with Shelley. He knew it was important to her and he didn't want this marriage to go the way of the first two.

At eight pm Friday night, that little queer from Progressive Consulting, Dennis, caught him in his office and told him to make new plans. He said that the entire management team was being sent to an important seminar at Xanadu Resort. His boss, Dylan Pearson was already there. Waiting.

When he got home, Joe told Shel how he had protested. And he wasn't exaggerating. He had argued, ranted and tried to bargain, but all to no avail. Dennis made it very clear his job was at stake.

When Joe finally said 'yes' the sanctimonious prick gave him a satisfied smirk, checked something off on his clipboard and minced out of the office.

It surprised him when Shel didn't lose her temper at the news. "What else could you do?"

Maybe she didn't care anymore.

Maybe he couldn't blame her.

The slowing of the aircraft woke him up, its rhythmic roar reverberating off a mountainside. Joe opened the blind and couldn't see anything for a long time, then he realized he should have been looking up rather than down. They were climbing toward a cluster of lights in a patch of darkness on a blue mountainside. The plateau where the chopper set down was lined with scrawny, brown trees. There were patches of snow on the rocks all around them. In a second, smaller clearing was a four-by-four which drove him the rest of the way up the mountainside.

Dylan Pearson met Joe at the door with a shit-eating grin and a hearty back-slap. Hair no longer the colour of a lawn starved for water, it now glowed with the robust blondness of youth. A recent face-lift had restored his strong-jawed, cleft-chin perfection – where he had once been an aging Dudley Do-Right, he was now a shiny new one. "Glad you made it Joe. Let's get a drink and a bite to eat."

"My suitcase..."

"Your girl will take care of that."

"My girl?" Joe winced. "I don't think...."

"They come with the rooms. Yours has a degree in psychology. And she paints," Dylan pointed out. "You like that creativity stuff."

"I'm just not interested in that sort of room service. It's my anniversary, for crissake."

"She isn't necessarily a bed partner. It's her job to look after you, like a butler. This is what she's getting paid for, buddy. Don't sweat it."

"Look, I don't want her."

"Tell her to keep a low profile and she'll fade into the wallpaper. Now, before we start talking business, we have to work some of that tension out of you. You're jammed up, jelly tight, pal." Dylan talked continuously, frequently patting Joe on the shoulder to lead him down through a series of corridors and through an archway of palm trees to the balcony of a large and busy lounge.

The vast room was filled with middle-aged men sitting at wooden tables of all sizes that glowed in the light of hundreds of floor-standing and wall mounted glass lamps. Huge, big-leafed plants filled the spaces between the tables. Dark, muscular men walked between the tables with huge rattan fans, and ornate tapestries and ancient flintlocks adorned the walls. At least there were no animal heads. The drone of hundreds of male voices sounded like gargantuan machinery.

Wrapping his hand around an ornately carved wooden banister, Joe followed his boss down the steps. The domed ceiling was like that of a small stadium. They arrived at a long table near the fire. The instant he was seated, a turbaned man in a belted robe brought him a Southern Comfort and a mug containing some sort of hot mead. It was delicious.

"How did they...." Even though Joe spoke quite loudly, he was barely audible through the din.

"They know what you like," Dylan shouted, "if you know what I mean."

Joe sat down beside his boss, across the table from a white-haired giant with a fastidiously trimmed orange beard who introduced himself as Bill Olafson. A thin, deeply tanned man with a old-fashioned pencil moustache sat beside Olafson. Standing, he presented Joe with an open hand. "Kipling."

Joe grinned. "Rudyard, I suppose."

"I beg your pardon?"

"Rudyard! I-suppose!"

The man smiled slyly back at him. "Have we already met, sir?"

Joe laughed. Everyone joined in and after that, they laughed about everything. Their server returned, lifting a sterling silver plate-cover to reveal three lines of blow. "Thai, Colombian and finest Peruvian."

It was tempting, but Joe shook his head. He said to Dylan, "You said you had something important to tell me."

"No. I just said it was important that you come."

"But you implied...."

"Big changes on the way. Patience is part of the gig here. Learning to chill in high stress situations is a big advantage in business . . . in using power effectively." Nodding happily, Dylan offered the straw again and Joe took it. "The Colombian is bliss."

They didn't mention business again that night.

Late in the evening, Olafson showed off his plastics company's newest novelties – one was an almost life-like plastic businessman inside a jar with holes punched in the lid. 'WASP in a Jar' read the label. A second one, called 'White on White', was one of those dome-shaped plastic paperweights that snows inside when you shake it. A plump white man sat naked and uncomfortable on a snowdrift. When the snow fell, the little man was lost against the whiteness all around him. The objects were passed around the table to the merriment of all, but by the time Joe had it in his hands, it made him uneasy, somehow. When he turned it upside down and the man disappeared, Joe passed it immediately to Dylan.

"I can't believe how real they look," said Joe. "Did you shrink people and put them in there?" From the reaction of his newfound friends, it was the funniest thing said that night. Relieved to be rid of the object, Joe found himself laughing too.

The blow-tray came back and his paranoia evaporated in a rush of self-confidence and braggadocio. Late that night, when it seemed to Joe that he could see the shape of the chair back, right through Kipling's chest, he got Dylan to guide him to his room.

He kept trying to talk but nothing sensible was coming out of his mouth. Dylan laughed at him several times.

Joe's 'girl' met them at the door and introduced herself as Desirée. Her profile looked Incan. Even with the almost beak-like curve to her nose, she was beautiful and nut-brown and exotic, in a wispy nightgown, the colour of leaves in the rainforest. She led him to the bed and began undoing the buttons of his shirt. He touched her hand to push it away and her fingers intertwined with his, pulling him toward her, rubbing the back of his hand against her thick, firm nipple.

"I just want to go to sleep, okay?"

"I'll be here in the morning. Or if you wake up in the night." She pulled off his pants, leaving him on the bed in his underwear. She made him stand up and she pulled back the covers.

She kissed him and crawled into bed with him.

"It's my anniversary," he explained.

"Happy anniversary," she said as she kissed him, the nightgown drifting like a shed skin to the floor. She was the most completely sexual creature he had ever encountered. Joe cupped her naked breast like a globe of molten wax in his hand.

Pulling away, Joe said, "You're so hot."

"And you're so cold," Desirée responded with a smile.

She took Joe's hand in fingers like stove elements and placed his hand against his own cheek. It was like ice.

"I am cold."

"Everything's relative."

He touched her gingerly.

"Don't worry," she said. "You won't melt."

And then she kissed him and made love to him and Joe felt as though he was melting the whole time, but as he drifted to sleep he touched himself and smiling, confirmed he was all still there.

He felt even colder in the morning, when Desirée woke him by laying his clothes out on the bed while he was still in it.

"Hurry up, sleepyhead," she said. "The orientation seminar starts in twenty minutes."

He cracked open his eyes – saw her looking like she'd been up for hours – and closed them again.

What had he done? This was his wedding anniversary! He shouldn't have come, but it was too late to do anything about that. On the other hand, he didn't have to stay. All the guilt he was feeling coalesced into a firm resolve. He had to go home, to make things right with Shel. At the first opportunity, he would tell Dylan he was leaving.

When Desirée reappeared it was with a cup of coffe and a slice of toast. "You missed breakfast."

"It's fine. I'm not staying," Joe said. "I just need to talk with Dylan Pearson."

"He's not at the lodge this morning."

"Where is there to go?"

"If you had gone to breakfast, you'd know. He's at a different stage of the program. Almost the end. Your schedules won't intersect for several days."

"You don't understand. I need to talk to him today."

"No. You do not understand. Mr. Pearson is not currently in residence at the lodge. It is not possible for you or anyone else to talk to him."

"Then where the hell is he?"

"He must have mentioned the hunt last night."

Vaguely he remembered something about a hunt, and that reminded him of the disappearing man in the paperweight blizzard. He shuddered. "I could lose my job if I leave without telling him."

"I'm sorry, Joe. You have to go through the program and earn your way into the hunt. Your company has paid for it all."

Joe shook his head. "I'll just leave him a letter then, explaining why I had to go home. Do the heli-jets come on a regular schedule?"

"Twice a day, usually. But right now, they're grounded in a snowstorm. And the phone lines are down. For the moment at least, we're totally out of touch with the rest of the world."

They were standing right beside a window into a clear blue sky. "Snowstorm?"

"At the base of the mountain they got thirty centimetres in the past four hours and it hasn't slowed down."

"Come on, it's the 21st century. Some form of communication must be possible."

He demanded to see the resort manager.

"This happens a couple times a season," said the whippet-thin, middle-aged black woman who had finally shown up. "White-outs don't usually last more than a day or two. Lots of the time, we don't get any of the snow up here. We'll let you know the minute we've re-established contact."

"My boss brought me to this resort. It's imperative that I speak with him immediately. Desirée says he's 'in the hunt'. But I was with him last night, so I know he can't be too far away. I need to talk to Mr. Pearson. My career and my marriage may depend it."

"Are you always this melodramatic, Mr. Steen?"

With hundreds of guests, it amazed him that the hotel manager knew his name. When her words sunk in, Joe's indignance overwhelmed his paranoia. But neither emotion caused a ripple or a stammer, as he licked his lips and carried on. "Look, I've tried to be polite, but not going to take any crap. Either you help me in any way you can, or I swear to God I'll get my lawyers on your ass."

The manager laughed. "This resort has benefactors you couldn't imagine, Mr. Steen. I want you to understand that we're doing this out of compassion, not because of your threat."

The woman spoke to Desirée. "Take him to his friends, but remember the first rule."

■

"The first rule – no outsiders at the hunt, so we have to make sure you don't look like one." Desirée told him as she helped prepare for the elaborately costumed trip. "Seeing you in street clothes would make them self-conscious. So you have to wear the same costumes they're wearing."

"This is ridiculous."

"Don't complain, Joe. I'm amazed management is allowing you to speak to Mr. Pearson at this point in the program."

"What is the program all about anyway?"

"You should have gone to the breakfast seminar." She smiled and offered a tiny, apologetic post-script. "It's about self-discovery."

Joe chuckled dishonestly. "Discovering one's male-essence, I suppose."

"Oh? Were they talking about it last night in the lounge?"

Though the subject had a fuzzy familiarity, Joe shook his head. "I don't think so."

Desirée dipped her fingers into a beaten silver bowl of green-brown goo and ran her fingers down his cheeks giving him camouflage, war paint and a lecture in one long, sensuous, stroke. "If you join the Hunt, you have to be ready to participate. It often takes twenty or thirty spears to bring down a mammoth. It is dangerous for someone who is not prepared. You could get killed."

"Mammoth?"

"It's not a real mammoth. It takes teamwork to kill it. It has a built-in sensor to judge who scored the most lethal shots."

■

The costume she dressed him in was elaborate. First, there was a furry loincloth-belt affair. His feet were wrapped in coarse brown cloth, tied on with cords of supple deer-hide. She criss-crossed them around his shins and calves, and tied them behind his knees. Then she wrapped rectangular furs around his legs and knotted them into place with rawhide thongs. Around his torso, he wore a coarse dress. His arms were covered in the same fashion as his legs, his hands wrapped in cloth and inserted into clumsy fur mittens.

Once he was fully clad, Desirée stripped naked, enjoying his stare as she pulled on long underwear, followed by a white snowmobile suit.

Returning from the closet with an armload of thick blankets, Desirée dumped them in his arms.

"What are these for?"

Ignoring his question, Desirée took his arm and guided him out the back way through a corridor that grew colder as they reached the door at the end; which turned out to be the middle, because then they were in a longer, brighter, even colder corridor. The next door took them outside, where the air was so crisp that Joe was immediately able to pinpoint every centimetre of exposed flesh. Desirée kept walking when he paused to adjust his leggings and he had to hurry to catch up. As he jogged along a well-lit passageway between the outbuildings the concrete became more icy underfoot. He slipped and would have fallen if he hadn't caught a window ledge.

"You really aren't ready for this," said Desirée.

"The boss-lady said it wasn't snowing up here."

Desirée shook her fur-hooded head. "It's not. We haven't had any new snow since last winter. You're walking on a glacier. "

When they reached the last outbuilding, he followed Desirée through a corrugated metal door into an open-sided shelter, filled with snowmobiles in various states of disrepair. She beckoned to him from a black vehicle in the middle of the room, bigger and sleeker than any snowmobile he'd ever seen before.

The instant Joe's ass touched the frozen seat, he knew why she had insisted he bring those extra blankets. He saddled the machine with them..

"Keep a couple to cover your legs," Desirée shouted as she started the engine.

They went over several hills and made a couple of unnervingly steep descents before reaching a large grassy plateau that was suspended in an immense crevasse in the mountainside.

"If they hear the machine, it will break the spell, so you're going to have to walk from here. They've probably just made camp in the cave. They'll be going out in hunting parties. Be careful as you approach them, that they don't mistake you for prey."

As he dismounted, she handed him two wooden spears. "The short one is for throwing, the long one for thrusting."

The first group of seven men was visible from quite a distance. He approached them waving his arms and shouting. Bill Olafson was among them. Icicles hung from his beard and his skin was turning so blue he should have been dying from hypothermia rather than out here acting like a schoolboy on an adventure.

Several men were angry at Joe for scaring away their prey.

"If there was a mammoth out here, it would have already seen you, just like I did," said Joe.

Olafson scowled at him. "Dylan is in the next group over. Try not to spook the wildlife when you approach them."

A short while later, a spear came sailing out of the sky, clattering against the rocks at his feet. If these businessmen-in-disguise were better shots, he would have got a spear in the guts as he approached.

But before Joe could utter any protest, the mammoth came rumbling out of nowhere and charged straight at him.

It looked for all the world like a real mammoth. Joe stumbled back, mentally deconstructing the beast. Shaggy, matted grey fur hung down almost to the ground, striated with blood and filth. The torso beneath was probably made of fibreglass, stretched over a sturdy frame and mounted on an ATV or even a small truck.

When it lifted its trunk and trumpeted, Joe was so transfixed by the special effect that he almost waited too long to jump out of its way when it thundered toward him. He landed on his shoulder in a patch of dirt, jarring both spears from his suddenly numb-fingered grasp. One of the mammoth's huge feet slammed down inches from Joe's outstretched arm.

No, that couldn't be right. It didn't have legs.

Peering up through a cloud of dust, he saw the animal's muscles working. The pain from his shoulder was overwhelmed by the pounding of his heart and the deep rasp of his breathing.

Hunters ran in from all sides. Twenty minutes ago, these men had looked to Joe like pathetic rejects from a Flintstones movie, with their animal skins, skinny legs, pasty flesh and potbellies. Now they looked almost heroic as they drove long spears into the 'animal's' side. A skinny little man ran past waving his short spear and whooping with excitement as he threw it. The mammoth came to a standstill, tossing its great head and bellowing. It stumbled backwards, almost toppling as it turned, and then it charged again.

Joe groped for the spears he had dropped, finding only the short one. He looked up into tiny eyes that glowed like molten ingots. Shouting excitedly, Joe ran toward it, dodging out of the way of a tusk at the last moment and planting his spear deep in the animal's eye socket. Someone threw a spear that missed his shoulder by inches.

The mammoth shuddered and stopped.

"It's dead!" shouted the expedition leader.

Men were plunging knives deeply into the mammoth's flank, peeling off strips of steaming flesh. A cheer came from the crowd of men behind him – a roar of victory and affirmation.

It's real, he thought, even in the face of all the evidence to the contrary. I killed it!

His heart was hammering. He found himself hyperventilating. He'd never experienced this sort of excitement, not even when he was robbed at gunpoint when he'd worked at a pizzeria during high school. The air around Joe seemed to vibrate and he held up his hand, half-expecting to see blue sparks crackling from his fingertips. His nerves were jangling and blood roared through his veins. He looked out upon the men gathering around him.

A square-bodied man thrust a wineskin into Joe's hands. "You're the champion, man! That took guts and timing like I've never seen before. Have a drink!"

He took a long unsteady draught of the ambrosia, splashing it onto his chin before feeling it burn deliciously down his throat.

Someone else said, "A literal bulls eye. Amazing!"

Tilting his head back for a long drink, Joe peered into a sky that was turning the dull violet of a fresh bruise. The long grass glowed more and more dimly as the luminous disc of sun was covered completely by clouds.

Someone whooped with exhilaration, and Joe looked around to see hunters gathering around him. Dylan wasn't among them. A goateed man passed Joe a jug filled with a thick sweet ale that tasted of musty apples and rich, pure honey. When two men in the crowd lifted him to their shoulders. Their flesh of their hands and shoulders was so cold that Joe shouted, "Holy shit, you guys should put on some more clothes."

They all laughed. Cradling the bottle in the crook of his arm like an old hand, Joe took another draught of the mead. Twenty minutes later, as the men walked up a slow incline toward a cave entrance he was holding another wineskin and much of the whooping and hollering was coming out of his own mouth.

Snow had started to fall.

Even as drunk as he was, Joe was starting to shiver from the cold.

As they lowered him to the ground, Dylan came up behind him. "What are you doing here. Today was supposed to be your orientation." Then he turned and walked away.

"Hey, where you going, buddy? I came all the way out here to talk to you," Joe said, breaking away from his fellow revellers and running ran after him. "Hey wait up!"

He caught Dylan at the cave mouth and grabbed his boss's naked forearms.

Dylan stood stiffly. "You shouldn't be here. You're not ready."

Dylan's skin was so cold.

"We should find the fire," Joe said. "We can talk there."

"Far as I'm concerned," Dylan declared, "you're not here."

"I don't wanna be here. That's what I wanna talk to you about!" Joe shouted as Dylan disappeared around a corner.

Joe drunkenly tried to follow his boss through a network of caverns and passages. He had two realizations; he was alone and he was about to pass out.

Putting his back against the wall, he slid down onto his ass and closed his eyes.

▪

He awoke in darkness, submerged in furs, so cold and so bruised and sore from the battle with the mammoth that he could barely raise his hand.

Even through the wrapping on his feet, the icy floor was jagged and too cold to tolerate. But there was no choice. What else could he do?

So he groped his way gingerly down a narrow corridor, toward a barely visible glow in the distance. Joe followed that faint hope through six tunnels and six chambers, and the light grew brighter so gradually that he didn't realize he could see until he found what appeared to be a man, seated against the wall of the seventh chamber. Frowning at the seeming translucence of the skin, he came close enough to see that it was Dylan – no, it wasn't – it was an ice sculpture that looked exactly like him, so detailed Joe could see the scar on his boss's chin where he'd had a small melanoma removed.

Then he saw an impression of his own hand melted into Dylan's forearm.

Feeling like he was going to be sick, Joe hurried out of that chamber and into a larger one. In the distance, he could see the looming brightness of the main cavern. But in order to reach it, he had to navigate through an immense domed chamber, the same size and shape as the lounge back at the lodge. There appeared to be a crowd gathered at the far side of the room, but they were eerily silent. As he approached the fringes of the throng, he saw they were all made of ice, just like that statue of Dylan.

Joe looked back the way he had come and saw dozens of small dark cave mouths. Unable to tell which he had come out of, he knew he would never find his way back. So he had to go forward. The accumulation of icy bodies was densest at the nexus, so he tried to stay toward the perimetre of the room. The cold would overcome him before he got more than a tiny portion of the way, he realized. If he was going to get out, he had to take a more direct route.

He asked himself why he was still alive when all of them were frozen and remembered Desiree saying, "You're not ready yet."

Maybe there was still some chance! Perhaps they would remember that he had never wanted to be here. Or maybe they would just remember how he had betrayed his wife on their anniversary. Weaving between the frozen figures, Joe couldn't help but notice the looks on their faces – as afraid as he felt. He stumbled around, desperately wanting to run but there was nowhere to go. His feet slipped out from under him and he crashed to the floor. His skin felt as though it was stretched so tight around his face that it hurt. He could no longer feel his hands and feet. Taking the hand of the nearest iceman, he pulled himself up. When the statue's fingers seemed to squeeze his own, Joe tried to pull his hand out of its grasp but found his skin frozen to the ice like a tongue on a chain-link fence.

Until that moment, he had been still somehow able to hold hysteria at bay. There was no way to rationalize what was going on. Panic seized him. When he jerked his hand back, the iceman's hand broke off at the wrist and splintered on the floor. Most of the men he surrounding him now bristled with frost like something left in a freezer too long, icicles hung down from their elbows and the wattles of their arms, so they looked more like snowmen than intricate sculptures.

He began pushing his way through the crowd. Snowmen shattered on the floor and fell against one another like dominoes. It wasn't long before he found himself ascending a mountain of body parts. Just before he reached the summit, the ice under his feet started to shift and crack. Joe looked down to see a man's jaw snap off beneath his toes.

He didn't know how his disappearance would be explained. But he had to admit as he looked around, he was far from the first to be brought here. And somehow, his abductors were still getting away with it. He tried to tell himself that Shel would call the authorities and demand that her husband be found, but he couldn't deny his horrible premonition that maybe she no longer cared. White on white – he and all his kind were vanishing – becoming history. Perhaps only their own self-importance had made them significant in the first place.

Joe looked up, and despite the futility of the struggle, he kept climbing. If he was going to be trapped and preserved here for eternity, there was nothing he could do about it, except make sure that he was on the top of the mountain.

Bad Copies

Preamble – Bad Copies

An original story created expressly for this collection, "Bad Copies" doesn't have as much of a back story as most of the other pieces.

It was inspired by three entirely separate things.

Several years ago, Karl Schroeder told me how the principles of dot matrix printers were being adapted to create 3D objects. He said that during our lifetime they would likely evolve to the point where they could actually print human tissue using stem cells to create organs for transplant. As cool as it sounded, it seemed very far away.

I met a man who prints 3D objects for a living. They're made out of plastic and not particularly versatile, but within a year of that meeting I've discovered that you can buy 3D printers online.

I've met lots of desperate and ingenious entrepreneurs looking for the next big opportunity.

I was out walking at night and when I saw my shadow break into three separate shadows, it all just came together and I ran home and wrote the first draft in about an hour.

Subsequent drafts took me considerably longer. When I was satisfied that the humour, the science fictional aspects and the crime story were all working together nicely, I posted it on Wattpad for feedback and discovered that some people like this story very enthusiastically indeed. So here it is – officially published for the first time.

Bad Copies

In the intersecting light of the three streetlamps, Floyd Sterling glanced at the sidewalk as he closed in on himself from both sides. The instant the three faint shadows merged into a single dark silhouette, Floyd's mind snapped back to the unpleasant task at hand.

He had been waiting across the street for less than an hour when the New Vista Home Renovations truck rumbled out of the long driveway beside the house. It was nine-thirty. He hadn't wanted to believe the clues that his best crew was getting sloppy, but this pretty much confirmed it. Leaving a jobsite this early on a conversion night was downright negligent.

The fresh dupes would still be sticky and couldn't be safely left alone until at least eleven. What if a friend or a relative dropped in unexpectedly? What if the matter wasn't dealt with promptly and thoroughly? And what if the half baked simulacra drew the attention of local law enforcement?

Floyd had hired Josh and Colin after they had stolen three prospective clients in a row with their snappy portfolio and hipster cred. Floyd kept an eye out and watched them go on to bilk each of those clients out of thousands and tens of thousands of dollars before they even needed to change their company name. When he offered them jobs, they weren't interested, until he waved the six figure salaries in their faces.

Josh scored a thirty-five on the PCL (Psychopathy Check List) Scale and Colin got twenty-five, which was barely adequate but he was in Josh's thrall so it worked fine at least for the first five months. But running this scam was a stressful gig. Despite the astronomical pay cheques and the fact that the actual victims were never physically harmed, the persuasion portion of the operation was truly tortuous for some and the deletion of the dupes at the end of the operation was murder for anybody without a flexible sense of morality. Even the toughest cookies could crack under the stress and Colin was anything but tough.

Floyd shouldn't have ignored the warning signs when the clean-up crew reported a lingering scent of dope in the truck cabin.

He had cut them way too much slack and now it had come to this. Floyd shook his head while he ritualistically (and somewhat sensuously) squeezed the pistol through the satiny fabric of his jacket as he walked up the Henson's walkway. Slipping into the bathroom to put on the silencer would be far less conspicuous than walking in with a gun drawn.

When he rang the bell, Joy Henson answered. "Floyd. What's up? Your guys have already left."

"Yeah, I saw them go." He looked her right in the eye but could see no traces of prematurity – no red eye or strange swellings as a result of being ambulant before her bones had properly set and hardened. Her eyes were pale blue, but he thought he remembered that being their natural colour. "I saw the guys leaving. They were…scheduled to work late tonight."

"Well, they came in really early."

"Yeah?"

"Yeah. With Josh's wife having a baby we thought you'd be okay with that."

"Of course," Floyd scratched his head, utterly failing to hide his bemusement. As far as he knew, Josh didn't even have a girlfriend. This was clearly a premeditated absence! Given that the new Joy was clearly functional, they had at least covered their tracks well. Floyd's worry started to dissipate a bit. Maybe it wasn't as bad as it looked. Maybe he'd have to give the boys a dressing down, but if all they'd done was connived a way to leave early, he might not even have to fire them.

"You want to come in and see what they've done downstairs?" Joy stepped back and allowed Floyd to precede her down the hall. Her voice kept jabbering from behind him, just like the real Joy would have done. "They didn't actually need to stay this late for crying out loud. And we certainly didn't mind them leaving early. Did we Arn?"

Arnie Henson stuck his head out from the kitchen and stuck out his hand. "Hey Floyd! Come to check out the reno?"

Floyd had been forced to buy an insurance policy from Arnie before the Hensons had agreed to hire New Vista for the renovation in the basement. Home based entrepreneurs were usually easy marks but they could be such pains in the ass! Floyd had tired of Arnie's eager beaver attitude about five minutes after meeting him. Tonight, Arnie's handshake seemed forebodingly moist, until he said, "Sorry, just finishing up the dishes. You go on down, I'll be right behind you."

Joy led him downstairs to the rec room, where the windows had been boarded over for the basement upgrade. When she flicked on the light, Floyd jumped back in shock.

There was indeed a pair of melters in the house, but they weren't the ones Floyd was expecting. A skeletal version of Josh stood pointing at the printer.

"It jammed just after lunch. And numbnuts here was so stoned he couldn't fix it himself." He pointed at the gooey foetal version of Colin who was curled up on the floor like a half-eaten sticky bun.

This was typical of dupes that had been removed from the cylinder before the process was complete. Without the injections to gauge and adjust their skin elasticity, they would melt into puddles within hours.

Arnie came through the door behind Floyd and filled in some of the details. "First thing I remember is waking up in that cylinder in a standing position and looking down to see that kid kneeling on the floor with his head between my legs." He absently kicked at Colin, who simply mewled louder and curled tighter.

The thing that resembled Josh spoke in a slur that suggested his tongue was turning to jelly. "I sho…sho…shink…zo problemsh in zha feeder unit, sho I shen Colin to sheck. I din shee he hadj za door open for so long zhey regain consciouzzz…nezz."

"Just had to put my foot on the back of the kid's neck and push down. Smack! Out like a light," Arnie said. "First thing we're going to do when we take over your operation is enroll these boys in self-defence training."

"And rehab," added Joy.

"Well yeah. We don't want them making the same mistakes when they're working for us."

"Hey, i' wazh jush him!" said Josh, waving a three fingered hand at his co-worker. Proto-flesh dripped from it like molten wax.

Floyd slid his hand very slowly into his coat, but before he reached his gun, he heard the pop and felt a three inch spike pierce through the bone and cartilage of his elbow. As he screamed and spun, Joy Henson swung an eighteen inch pry bar up hard under his chin.

By the time Floyd swam back to consciousness, the half baked copies of his crew had melted completely. The real Josh was looking into his eyes, looking larger than life somehow. His face was intact and his voice was clear and crisp. "He's awake!"

Working hard to concentrate despite the pain in his arm, and to talk despite the swelling in his mouth and throat, a question occurred to Floyd, and he struggled to ask it through the lingering effects of the knockout drug, "Who was driving the truck?"

"What?"

"Truck was driving away when I got here." His voice sounded like he'd been sucking on helium. That was an effect he'd never seen before. "If you weren't driving, who was?"

"That was the final set of dupes," said Josh. "There was a bunch of sets. Printer was really jammed."

"You let the preemies drive? What if they got pulled over?"

"I'm sure even my knockoff has some pretty mad motoring skills." Josh sounded offended. "But with the melty fingers they didn't have the manual dexterity to fix the printer." He wiggled his fingers demonstratively.

"They took the truck back to your yard," said Joy, looming into Floyd's blurry field of vision." We worried they might melt down before you encountered them. But even then, we hoped you'd come over here looking for the machine. But we were pretty surprised when you just showed up like that."

Arnie snapped his fingers in her ear and she giggled and snapped hers. "Yeah. Like that!"

As Floyd stared at her, disconcerted by the ongoing distortion, he realized he was looking out through the copier cover.

With the hi-res duplication of brain chemistry that this particular printer model delivered, the dupes hardly ever realized they weren't originals. But this being his operation, Floyd knew from the get-go that he must be a facsimile. His original was probably still in the machine behind him.

Floyd touched his face and despite his injuries from the scuffle, found all of the musculature and skin in place. "You fixed the printer?" he asked Josh.

"Well, it's not fixed yet, "said Josh. "The compound feeder is partially plugged. But as long as I don't print at one hundred per cent, the replication is fine."

"You mean I'm not…"

Josh slid open the cover. "You're at fifty per cent. And you're perfect."

He lifted Floyd out and set him on the floor. He looked up right into the camel toe of Joy's crotch in her tight beige stretch pants.

So much for the plan of surprising Joy and using her as a hostage to get his gun back from Arnie.

"Fifty per cent is not fucking perfect," Floyd mumbled looking up in awe at the giant Joy and Arnie. Now that Arnie had Floyd's pistol, she had the nail gun.

Joy sighed happily, "We thought it might take you days to show up."

"You wanted me here?"

"How else are you going to sign the contract to sell us the printer?" asked Joy.

Aha. The tables were turned. They could do whatever they wanted to him and his original would have no memory of it.

"On very generous terms," Arnie clarified. "You didn't list the printer on your insurance policy, so you'll do much better this way than if it was accidentally damaged or destroyed. If you catch my drift."

"The machine is broken. Why would you buy a machine that only makes fifty per cent copies?"

"Josh says he can have it fixed in an hour."

Josh shrugged when Floyd glared at him. Floyd felt like punching him in the kneecap.

"Printing you at fifty per cent was the test that confirmed what was wrong," Josh explained. "When I explained to the Hensons, they were okay with it. They said you'd be more manageable this way."

"We've been looking for new business opportunities," Joy chirped. "So this was a gift! Now we get to go into the "printing" business, your employees get to stay employed and you get to walk away. Or at least the full size version of you." She nodded at the feeder tube that held the real Floyd. "It's a win-win-win, just like they teach us in business school."

"How do I know you're not gonna kill him…the real me…right after I sign?"

"The deal will seem much more legitimate if you're still kicking. And you'd have a hard time passing for him," laughed Arnie. He handed Floyd a pen as big as a porn stud's junk.

"I'm not signing anything," Floyd said pushing it away. He didn't see Joy coming at him with a yardstick until he heard the swish. "What the fuck!" he screamed.

He turned to see Joy slapping her palm with the thick wooden instrument. "I might just have to put you over my knee," she said.

Anger and pain mixed in equal parts in Floyd's brain. He knew martial arts! He had one good arm! He didn't have to put up with this crap!

Hearing the wooden blade whistling through the air again, Floyd hand shot out just in time for the yardstick to catch him on the back of his knuckles, breaking at least one finger. Floyd screamed and lurched away, tripping over the compressor cord and falling face down. The pain in his left hand fingers and right elbow flared unimaginably as he tried to break his fall. That's when he discovered he was still too embryonic to bleed properly. His nose had snapped right over to the side. Joy grasped it between two fingers and twisted it back into position.

His hosts waited patiently until Floyd stopped squawking. When he was finally able to gather a coherent thought he said, "That wasn't so bright, now how am I going to sign the contract?

Joy put him over her knee and whaled him to within an inch of his life. When she put him back on the floor, he was still simpering so bad he couldn't talk for ten more minutes. Arnie kept talking like nothing had happened. "Your boys were saying this is what you always do to the facsimiles, torture them until they give what you need. Melt them down with a solvent injection and the originals wake up in the morning in their own beds with no idea the dupes had ever been made. But Josh said you never thought of reducing their size."

Floyd muttered, "You wouldn't thought of it either if he hadn't been forced to print me this size. I fell right in your lap." He gaze flickered fearfully to Joy's substantial lap, where he had been sprawled for the past ten minutes. "So to speak."

"You know, Floyd," said Arnie nodding his head amiably," you may be right. Funny how you can miss things that are right in front of your face."

"I pioneered this scam," Floyd muttered.

"Worked out most of the angles," Arnie said admiringly.

"You know I'm never going to sell you the copier," Floyd stated.

"I think you will. Or the new Floyd we're cooking up right now will," said Arnie. "I wanted to go down to twenty-five per cent but Josh said the copies started noticeably degrading at thirty-five."

"At that size, there's a danger of accidentally squashing them," said Joy.

"But that's okay," added Arnie. "They're dry and ready to interrogate in just over two hours so we can do six batches."

Floyd stared at his doll sized replacement as Joy said, "I trust that seeing what we've done to you will convince him to sign."

Floyd's body stiffened as he heard the yardstick switch cut the air again and he surrendered.

As he authenticated his e-sig, he was admiring their business model. You could close a deal three times as fast, using a fraction of the raw materials and leave hardly any mess for the disposal guys. Maybe if he factored this into his next business plan he could get enough of a loan to buy a new machine. That's what he'd do! This would just be a temporary setback! He grinned, looking up just as the syringe plunged into his neck. Or at least that's what he should do, little Floyd realized, if his original had any way of knowing about it. Until then, he'd be just another mark.

Right around the time that fifty per cent Floyd was turning into a puddle, the beep told them that the thirty-five per cent copy was ready.

"Hey honey," said Joy. "We never actually talked about what we're going to do with the original Floyd."

"We're gonna let him go. Just like a regular client."

"Only they have no idea what happened. He does! He'll be dangerous. What if he comes after us?"

Arnie grimaced and ran one hand through his thinning hair. "What else are we gonna do?"

Joy turned to Josh. "What would happen if we enlarged this new copy by three hundred per cent. Would he be the same size as the original?

"Close," Josh agreed. "But there'd be a ton of generation loss. It would be a really crappy copy.

"Would people be able to see it melting?"

"Probably not. He'd just be really porous."

"What would that do?" asked Arnie.

"Make him sweaty, uncoordinated, forgetful. And he might need a diaper."

"Sounds like my uncle after his stroke," said Joy.

"It would be just like that," Josh admitted.

"Perfect," said Joy. "And what would happen if you gave the original a shot of solvent?

"You want me to kill a real person?" said Josh shaking his head.

"You did say you scored a thirty-five on the PCL."

"But this is too risky."

"And the new cost efficiencies will allow us to double your take."

"Oh fine," said Josh ruefully.

∎

After Floyd woke up, he allowed the clients to guide him up the stairs of their house, the man kept pressing the car keys into his hand while the woman said, "He's in no condition to drive. We should call a cab."

Why had he been drinking with them? He couldn't remember.

They poured him a glass of Scotch while they waited for the cab. It tasted wonderful but made him sweat even worse than before. He kept forgetting the woman's name…Grace or Gay or…Joy. That was it, Joy! And he couldn't help but feel that there was something even more important that he was forgetting.

When the driver came to the door they gave him Floyd's home address and voiced their regret about letting him drink so much. Floyd had been too embarrassed to ask if he was the one who left that mess on their new basement carpet. But that concern weighed on him now. While he considered going back to apologise, he saw his shadow on the sidewalk, separating into three shadows before fading away completely. It seemed eerily familiar and somehow profound.

Touching the Screams

Preamble – Touching the Screams

This story grew out of a call for submissions from an anthology I very much wanted to get into.

I was almost 40,000 words into a new novel and didn't want to get distracted from it. So I decided to adapt a chapter into a short story. It seemed like a brilliant idea until my novelist friends all agreed that it was a far more difficult thing to do than creating a stand-alone short story from scratch – precisely because the story must be able to stand alone. You can't include the back story, the many tangential stories or probably even the setting of the novel unless it it relevant and important to what happens in the story.

And that is a very difficult thing to do.

I discovered this for myself during the course of writing "Touching the Screams." While it sprung entirely from my story Avenging Glory, it only shares a bit of the setting, one or two characters and very little else with the parent novel. I pretty much had to re-create the protagonist, Psalma from scratch, because the Psalma in the novel has far too many other things to worry about. So the lead character in the story shares the protagonist's name and sex. Other than that, she's pretty much a brand new character. And after half a dozen intensive drafts I now feel confident that "Touching the Screams" works great as a stand-alone. I also learned that I should pay more attention to the advice of my friends.

Touching the Screams

Micah, where are you?" shouted the sharp-faced clerk. Her voice echoed in the dusty air as she shoved Psalma up the last few steps and steered her into a vast chamber.

Psalma blinked, barely believing she had reached such heights. This eighth floor loft was the geographic hub of the monumental Tomb of the Testator, which was terraced diagonally up Thatcher Mountain toward the Great Spire, eight floors further up.

The windows – filled with mosaics of glass in the old style – were set so high in the slanted stone wall, it was like they were built for a floor above that didn't exist. Multicoloured shafts of sunlight crossed the space like rafters made of rainbows.

One of the six windows was boarded over, with a cavity through which dozens of cables entered and cascaded in a black tumble to the floor. The room itself, with tables, cables, bulbs and boxes buzzing and flickering, formed a horizontal starscape across the floor.

There was no sign of life until a slight man with a trim white mustache and a pronounced pot belly stepped from behind a wall of electronic equipment and reached for the paperwork that the clerk shoved toward him. He almost dropped it when she turned and strode away before he had it properly in hand.

Micah read Psalma's expression and said with a laugh, "Her disposition will improve when we install the elevators."

The Widow's recent "Elevator to Heaven" sermon had not only been the most inspirational thing Psalma had ever heard, it had clearly explained the concept of elevators. Construction was scheduled to start in the spring. This was the biggest news at the tomb since the lights had been strung to the top of the Spire after the Widow had given her famous "Brighter than the Moon" address.

Micah led her through a maze of metal and plastic: stacks of thick plastic cards with bits of metal and plastic lines and cylinders fused to them in interesting patterns; metal canisters filled with screws and bolts; piles of round metallic discs inside broken plastic boxes. More relics than the Hope Museum and, for the most part, what was here was better cleaned and restored. The pathways led to desks and tables along the wall covered in boxes painted with bands of colour. Some boxes were just metal frames containing masses of thin black wires. A few of the boxes were sealed. Some even had tiny blue and red lights that glowed like embers or glinted like ice crystals.

The surface of every desk was illuminated by a single-bulbed electric lamp. On several of the desks were slabs of what looked like streaky window glass, propped upright. Psalma surmised that these were the Holy Windows. She pressed her fingers to the strange luminescent surface of the one in front of her and Micah brushed her hand away like a prissy mother. "Don't touch the screens. It impedes the flow of the crystals and creates dark spots on the images."

"Screams?" she asked. "How do you touch a scream?"

"Screen-n-n," he enunciated. "These things are called screen-n-n-z."

Her laugh was a self-apologetic wheeze. "My art class in Highest School is seven blocks away and we heard the screams from there. My word's better."

"People on the street are still talking about the sermon then?"

"How could they not? I'm sure the names of the Infernal Children and Pinhead and Freddy Cougar are already being whispered far beyond the gates of Hope."

"Those were just the names the Fetchers were told to spread through the crowd. But they aren't the only demons. There are plenty more, waiting to be found," said Micah. "That's why you're here. To put together the video clips for the next sermon."

"What is a viddy old clip?" she asked.

"Like the moving pictures from the sermon."

"I haven't seen a sermon. This is my first chance to look into a holy window."

"Screen!" Micah paused while Psalma's nervous laugh died away. "Looking through a screen is completely different from looking through a window. What you see there is not really happening while you watch. It's recorded."

Psalma shook her. "Recorded? Like a photograph?"

"You know of photographs?"

Psalma nodded. "Our teacher brought a camera into class after they were reinvented last year. We all got to use it and develop our own photographs."

"What if I told you that the ancients could make photographs that move?"

She caught her first glimmer of where the conversation was going. "I've heard that before."

"That's what the sermons are. It's called video. And screens are where you can see the moving photographs."

She stared at the window, trying to make sense of what he was telling her. "So this is some kind of paper?"

"Not really. We'll teach you as you go along. Just watch."

He pushed a button.

Psalma gasped when the screen suddenly brightened. Even through the bruises and shadows that obscured more than half the surface, she could see a bare-legged girl in a very short white dress walking through the darkness. She was glowing like an angel one moment then barely visible the next. She was talking but Psalma couldn't make out what she was saying. Then something round, some sort of a shield, rolled out of the darkness and clattered to the ground. The shadow of a man in a hat transformed into the black silhouette of a man extending impossibly long arms. The girl tried to run but the demon was everywhere, face disfigured, claws extended, laughing eerily. He looked right in her eyes as he cut off his own fingers.

As she stumbled back from the screen, Psalma glanced behind her, half-expecting to see the demon there as well. Nearly tripping and falling backward over a low wall of sharp-edged artifacts, she righted herself in time to see that the demon's attention had turned back to the young woman on the screen, who was now hiding under a blanket. Psalma watched transfixed as the girl was sliced between her breasts by phantom claws and then dragged to the ceiling by an invisible force, where she dangled, dripped and finally plummeted into the quagmire of blood her bed had become.

Any moment, it could turn its attention back to her! Swinging her leg up, she climbed the barrier, trying to figure out which direction to run.

"Stop-right-there-and-look-at-me," Micah instructed. "The demon cannot touch you!" He put his hand up to the screen, then displayed his uninjured palm. "What you see on the screen is not happening right now. Not behind a window or anywhere. Someone else is dreaming about Freddy Cougar and you are watching their dream."

Psalma was just about to take Micah at his word when she looked down to see blood dripping from her own fingertips. The palm of her hand was slashed. She hadn't felt the pain until that instant. Inhalations hitching in her throat, she held it up for her new supervisor to see.

He shook his head. "Climbing on a pile of old motherboards is like climbing on knives," he said. "We'll get that disinfected before getting you to work."

She stood numbly while he walked through the maze of junk to her side. "What is a motherboard?"

"These things." He touched one with his foot. "We couldn't show the videos without them."

Although she didn't really understand, she nodded.

"Your cuts are shallow," Micah reassured as her cleaned and dressed scrapes on her hand and thigh. "You'll survive."

As he led her back to the desk, he sighed. "Can you read old fonts? The ancients sealed instruction manuals inside plastic bags. More than a few survived. I'll get Joel to take you through them. Teach you the lingo and some of the concepts. This will be a big learning curve for you. But the Widow wants a new segment slickedy-quick, so we'd better get a-move-on."

She spent the rest of the day examining instructional manuscripts. Micah and the other members of the "Camera Crew", as they called themselves, were impressed by her ciphering skills. By the end of the day she was talking about splicing and editing, sounding like an old hand, even though she not only had never done it, but never even seen it done.

As darkness fell, Micah said, "You've been assigned a residence on the fourth floor. You should check in now. I'll be here when you arrive tomorrow morning."

Her room was small but comfortable and she didn't have to share it with anyone, which was a blessing given the number of times she woke herself up, crying out, as blades plunged upward through her pillows, or death seized her by the throat with enormous claws, or creatures materialized out of thin air at the foot of her bed.

She climbed the stairs at daybreak and found Micah was still in his nightclothes. He was obviously living somewhere in the shadows.

"You should have had breakfast before coming up here," he mumbled.

"I saved some bread from dinner."

"Then, you should have given me a chance to have breakfast. Don't come tomorrow until after breakfast." Leaving her with a stack of manuals, he stumbled off to dress and eat.

Upon his return, Micah picked up a strange looking device. Although it was black, its shape reminded her of a diagram of a uterus one of her teachers had salvaged from an ancient medical textbook. It had a big silver knob on the left, a quintet of brightly painted buttons on the right and a long wire trailing from the underside. There were rectangular slots where other buttons had evidently once been.

"I'll show you the entire sermon. The digital cameras aren't working right yet, so everything's overexposed and the Widow's a bit blurry at first."

Then he pressed a big green button and they watched the Widow walk toward them, a flickering shadow figure. As she stopped, her round face came into focus, so soft-featured it didn't seem to quite resolve. It was the same visage as in the photos that hung in all the buildings throughout the city, but onscreen, she looked younger and plumper. Her lips were stained red. Her teeth were white and perfect, save for the slight underbite that made her chin seem longer than it was. She wore a red dress. Her golden hair formed a halo of light above her head, despite being tied back. "The camera tech is improving, so we're going to have to get better with the makeup. This was like warpaint, but we had to do that because the Widow says she wants people to know that she's looking at them."

He pushed the green button again and the Widow spoke. Psalma recognized the sermon they'd been playing on the radio all week. She watched the Widow's lips form the now-familiar words. "You…who were left behind," her voice was clipped and clear and not as colourless as it has seemed before there was video to go with the sound. "You who were damned, yet kept the faith without hope of reward…." Micah pushed the pause button again. "Sorry. I'll let it roll in a minute. I just wanted to tell you what it was like looking down at that crowd in the Lobby. We were watching from the rooftop patio on the second floor. The screens were really bright. When I was a child, the Executor used to say that we are "primitives" in comparison to what humanity used to be. That's just what the people looked like when we turned on those screens; primitives in the thrall of our freshly exhumed technology. It was illuminating in ways I never imagined."

Psalma cocked her head, trying to figure out what he was telling her and why.

He saw her confusion and explained, "Just putting everything into context. You now know how the tech works and you know it can't hurt you. That changes everything."

Micah pushed a red button above the green one and the screen went dark. "This key is called 'stop' and the green one is called 'play'," he said. "Push it." No sooner had the picture begun moving and the sound resumed, when her mentor pushed the white button and held it down. "This is called 'pause' and the yellow one is 'rewind'. If you push that you go right back to the start of the video." Releasing the white button, he put his finger on the blue one and grinned, "Rather than make us listen to the whole sermon for a fifteenth time, you can push this one."

"Fast forward," she said, remembering the functions from the day before.

The speakers chirped like angry squirrels and on the screen, the Widow's hands moved up and down faster than before.

The picture pulled back until you could see her from the waist up, then froze. "I want to show you this bit. Our best lighting ever. The Widow's hair hardly shines at all, the camera was working great."

With a jerk, the moving image reverted to real time.

The Widow stood with her hands clasped as if in prayer. "You have grown up believing that you missed your chance to get into the Kingdom of Heaven." She thrust her arms out and up in clear supplication to the skies, and then balled her hands into fists and shook them. "But I have been sent to tell you that this is not true."

Pause.

Micah cut back in. "The Widow said it took months to write the template for these sermons, so she wants to make sure everyone's paying attention when she gets to the good stuff."

He fast-forwarded through what Psalma remembered as a long rapturous description of lost paradise and infinite forgiveness, before segueing back to her main thesis.

When Micah hit play, the Widow was winding up, "… forever wise and giving, He left me as the sole beneficiary of all His earthly chattels and estates and your singular guide back to that realm that you have all… coveted for so long."

At this point, she was completely illuminated from the front in a blinding white spotlight that all but washed out her features.

"Yesterday, there was no hope in the city of Hope," intoned the Widow. "Today, there is nothing but. Claim your due from destiny, not as mere survivors, but as third party beneficiaries of the Testator's eternal wisdom and generosity! Because if you stray from the path...the darkness will swallow you forever."

Micah hit 'pause' and said, "This is where the sermon itself ended and we stopped the audio broadcast. It's where our video clip begins." He hit play.

The widow said emphatically, "...if you stray from the path, you will not know until it is too late. Because the demons may not always be easy to recognize, but they'll always be there."

The next scene was of blonde children standing shoulder to shoulder, their faces like tranquil masks and eyes glowing with interior light.

The screen went black and the widow said, "If you stray from the path, you will face the demons that have been called back from Hell itself to deal with the miscreants and unbelievers."

From out of the darkness stepped a figure in a black robe, his bald head shining like the moon from a distance, but from close up, you could see that his head was bristling with tiny spikes or nails. He was carrying something bright.

That visage was replaced by some strange imagery of flailing chains with big hooks on the ends which were plunged into the torso of a spread-eagled man who was clearly in agony. The colours washed and muted, turning a pool of livid red which faded to black and segued into the Freddy Cougar clip she had seen the day before. "Follow me," intoned the Widow, "and you shall be saved from them."

"Four times we've shown it," said Micah, speaking right over the video this time. "People panic and there are injuries and deaths every time, yet the crowds keep getting bigger."

Even this second time seeing monsters on the screen and even with Micah's narrative, Psalma had to repress the sense of panic. She put her hands behind her back to hide their shaking, closed her eyes and breathed through her nose.

"Who..." She had to pause to retrieve the terms, "edited these videos?"

"Joel," said Micah, pointing at the member of the Camera Crew who'd gone over the manuals with her yesterday. "He thought the project needed a more creative touch but I think he wanted out of the job because his bowels were shaken loose. His mother is a deacon and you know what they say about those born in the shadow of the crypt? "

She shook her head and Micah paused and gave her the side-eye. "You're not from the Hillside, are you?"

Psalma laughed. "A hillside of sorts. I was born out by the Fleshhomes. Barely in the city at all."

That made him smile. He clearly had no idea of the quality of life in the suburbs.

She said, "I'd still be there if I couldn't paint."

Micah nodded. "Your paintings have an amazing sense of composition. And you don't shy away from ugliness. That's why the Widow selected you." Micah pulled over a stool for her. "So that's why you're here. Looking for demons. We've found hundreds of discs with visual data on them. When you find something appropriate push 'pause', then go see Joel. He will show you the editing tools and how to use them."

There were dozens of videos with scenes of people talking or fighting or chasing one another. The sound of gunshots echoing through the mountain passes was becoming familiar, but few had actually seen guns in action since the Widow had reinvented them. Hearing the gunshots on the videos, Psalma watched wounds suddenly blossom on people's chests and the tops of people's heads messily explode. Although horrific, Psalma was inclined not to include these scenes in her clip, because demons didn't seem to be involved. She hunted Joel down to confirm that she'd made the right decision and found him watching a CD that contained no monsters, just people in various states of undress and sexual congress. He turned it off quickly when she came up behind him. When he turned around and couldn't take his eyes off her breasts, she decided to try teaching herself rather than asking for his help. By the end of the day she had figured out how save her edits into a new file. When she finally got to her feet, she was so jittery and rubber-legged that Micah had to walk her to the door.

By the end of the first week, Psalma was experimenting with different cuts, fades and dissolves.

Despite her inexperience and fatigue from lack of sleep, she had spliced together three minutes of horrors. Like Joel before her, she had muted the audio so the clips merged more seamlessly, but unlike him, she devised a way to create new soundtracks from separate clips. Over the next few days, she found screams with no music track and music with no dialogue, enabling her to create her own spooky soundtrack. She too got to sit and watch the crowd react to her handiwork, which was disturbing and gratifying at the same time.

As amazing and hallucination-inducing as the job was, nothing was more surreal than the Widow coming to tell Psalma personally how impressed she was with her work.

Naturally, she descended from above. Psalma was alerted to her approach by the singing of the divas who preceded the Widow down the stairs.

Lightbearers walked all around her, hoisting the four radiant globes that represented the seasons – white, green, yellow and red. The Widow was so awash in light, even in real life, that it was hard to focus on her. The entourage stopped just inside the door and a voice said, "Psalma of Silverbirch, your immediate attendance is requested."

The Widow was actually a small woman but seemed somehow larger and more real than anyone around her. Psalma went down on one knee the way her Maum had taught her and said, "Praise the Bride of the Testator, the Mother of Memory, the Maker of Dreams, the Bringer of Truth. Praise the…"

The Widow held up one hand to stop her and extended the other for Psalma's kiss.

The Widow said, "You enable me to Bring the Truth. And for that, we are grateful. You will be escorted you to your new residence on the ninth floor." She clapped her hands and two women stepped forward.

"Oh," said the Widow, "and get her some decent clothes."

It had never occurred to Psalma to be embarrassed about the simple shifts she wore. Her face burned a bit as the Widow and the rest of her entourage turned as one and went back up the stairs.

The encounter had lasted no more than a minute or two, but they were the most breathtaking minutes of Psalma's life. When she came back down, she was wearing a red dress in a soft shiny fabric unlike anything she had touched before, let alone worn.

The ensuing enthusiasm fuelled her for weeks. In the darkness nightly, while waiting for sleep to claim her and then spit her out again, Psalma found herself thinking about ways she could maintain the effectiveness of the clips even as she was running out of new material. The phenomenon she had noticed inside herself – with sequences that had once terrified her becoming commonplace – was becoming noticeable with the crowds as well. It took more to frighten them.

She had noted that the best clips were those that used suspense and surprise most effectively; when the viewer was waiting for monster to pounce, only to discover that it had snuck up behind them instead.

She was watching Alien 3 for the seventh or eighth time when she stumbled across a way to invert the image. The creature looked just as scary in shades of white as it did in black – scarier perhaps, because it wasn't coming out of the darkness like all the other creatures. It was unexpected.

That night in bed, complete darkness refused to come. Light flashed and rippled across the insides of her eyelids and kept brightening like a snowy

LCD screen. It reminded her of a sunny day. With no darkness to harbor any demons, Psalma began to truly relax for the first time since starting the project…until a bone white alien reached out of the light and gripped her in icy talons. She fell to the frigid stone floor and awoke with her heart pounding like a drum in her chest. Escaping her tangle of sweaty sheets, she scrambled to her feet and started walking around the room, lighting all the candles and starting a fire into which she fed her entire week's wood ration.

The next day at work, she experimented with inverted image, overlaying it on a different background so that the creature convincingly appeared to emerge from the snow.

At the end of the sermon where she'd used it, the crowd in the foyer began to disperse in the sedate manner that was becoming the norm. Only a few seemed to notice that the glow of the screens hadn't completely faded and kept watching, others caught it from the corners of the eyes. There are few things stranger than the sound of a thousand people gasping almost at the same time. As the ice creature seemed to reach out of the wall, someone screamed and the panic seemed to manifest itself in waves as people ran and fell and fell and ran.

The Widow had named the ice creature "Mortis" and the whispered name travelled like wind through the streets. Psalma felt sick about betraying her mandate to deliver the Truth and sent an apologetic confession to the Widow, but she was never taken to task about her invention.

■

Psalma's success had given her much more freedom to explore the capabilities of the software. Both the audio tech and her ability to understand the ancient tongue had improved dramatically. Her new keyboard gave her access to playback settings she had previously been forbidden to use. One menu screen offered the option, "Creature FX". In it, an artist was introduced, followed by a parade of images he'd drawn. He had sketched one of the demons from different angles. Still-images of his drawings were interspersed with footage of a group of people collectively building a corresponding three-dimensional model out of metal and some sort of soft molded material.

At first, Psalma thought they were paying homage to the demon, making icons, perhaps developing plans to build a temple. But the dialogue, though hard to follow, seemed to suggest that the artist and his colleagues were modifying the appearance of the demon as they went along. And sure enough, the monster's head gradually changed shape, gradually transforming into the actual demon from the sequences Psalma used in her clips.

Psalma told herself that these artists had simply seen the creature at every stage of metamorphosis and portrayed it in each. But their dialogue didn't support that interpretation. "We thought it would be scarier if you couldn't see its eyes, so we created these folds in the flesh on its face...."

They'd said it in a dozen different ways. The monster wasn't real. They'd created it. Psalma was in shock. Why would anyone do such a thing?

Then she thought about Mortis, the creature she herself had created, and her gut began to twist. When she'd come up with that segment, her goal was simply to shock people. Because that was her job. And she'd succeeded. Two people had been trampled to death on the day that Mortis debuted.

Realization washed over Psalma. None of the demons in the Widow's sermons were real. These monsters did not exist! The Widow was using lies to control people! Psalma was instrumental in making those lies believable.

Then just as she was nodding off, she jerked herself awake again with the thought that the promise of Heaven might be just another fabrication.

These questions kept her awake more effectively than the usual visions of evil. Psalma couldn't help but wonder if this was evil of a different kind. Perhaps the Widow didn't know that the monsters didn't exist! Psalma wondered if she would be rewarded for bringing the truth to light.

The next day, she approached Micah. "Did you know the demons aren't real?"

After a pause, he replied, "That is a dangerously...heretical...statement."

"I have proof. I need to tell the widow."

He whistled softly. "I'm pretty sure she already knows."

Psalma nodded at the confirmation of her own suspicion. "How can she lie to people like this?"

"The only truth is the one the Widow speaks. She is wiser than we mortals can imagine. She sees where our society needs to go and takes us there using any means at her disposal."

"Scaring people to death with the threat of monsters that don't exist?"

He simply shrugged.

"I'm not sure I can keep doing this!"

"Take the day off," Micah said. "Think it through. Go for a walk in the city and look at everything the Widow has done for us. I'm sure you'll see what needs to be done."

As Psalma walked through the mobs of pilgrims, penitents and job seekers who were already gathering in the vestibule for the evening sermon she saw the looks on their faces, the devotion, the need.

When she got out into the street, the sky was heavy with cloud and the air was wet and cold. She walked down the thoroughfare, taking measure of all the wonders: electric lights illuminating the insides of shops even during the daytime; apartment blocks rising up three, five, even ten stories high with plumbing on every floor; the aromas of cooking food; the happy faces.

When she turned to walk back up the hill, she saw the storm rolling down the valley toward the city. She barely got halfway back up the hill before the snow was swirling madly around her feet. Seeing people milling around in front of her, she realized that she was going to be caught in the queue for the sermon and before long, she was indeed pressing through the crush of bodies.

Not far in, she heard the wind begin to rise and with it, a sussurus of whispered words. People who had been standing still began to mill around.

"It's Mortis," she heard someone say, and she turned to see what he was pointing at. There was nothing but snow swirling out of the darkening sky.

"I see it!" said a woman, and Psalma could tell from the hubbub that similar conversations were taking place all around her.

Psalma tried to take advantage of the distraction to wedge her way more quickly through the crowd. But now, many of the faces around her were contorted in terror. A panicking woman threw her arms around Psalma, squalling, "There it is! Mortis is coming!"

Psalma couldn't outshout the all hysterical people around her. And even if she could, what could she say that they would believe? "It's not real? It's a lie that I made up!"

The woman screamed and the crowd began to compress and expand like an entity unto itself, inhaling and exhaling.

People were running blindly and the wall of bodies behind her shifted. Elbows were swinging, someone was actually trying to climb over her. She was pushed and fell to one knee, grabbing the clothes of the big man beside her to haul herself back up. When she fell again, all she could do was cover her head with her arms and roll through the slush. She was kicked and trod upon as the pandemonium seemed to go on forever.

As suddenly as the panic had begun, it was over. Psalma stared back into sky, trying to imagine what people had thought they had seen, the creature – a demon as big as a mountain, reaching down toward them. But in the glow from the screens, all she saw was the spiraling snow, the bodies and the blood.

Clearly, this monster was as real as it needed to be. And it was hungry.

Masks of Flesh

Preamble – Masks of Flesh

Boy, does this story have a long and chequered history.

It began as a 14,000 word novella somewhere around 1992. It was called "Masks of Flesh and Sanity" and it was a harrowing dark fantasy with a strange incestual subtext between the brother and sister protagonists. Somewhere along the way, the fantasy aspect was replaced with what I considered to be a very science fictional explanation for the Madness. Like many of my stories it was post-apolcalyptic.

If you've ever tried to sell a 14,000 word story, you can probably imagine what I went through trying to get it published. Lots of nice rejection letters saying, "it's good, just not quite good enough for us to dedicate a quarter of our publication and our budget in order to buy it." I worked very hard and finally got it down to about 12,000 words, which dropped it from the novella to the novelette category.

Lo and behold!

I was over the moon when I got a sort of conditional acceptance letter from *Pulphouse*. They wanted it and were trying to slot it. They ended up holding it for a very long time and before it actually saw the light of day, *Pulphouse* stopped publishing. After a few more submissions, I realized that my odds of having it published as a 12,000 word story were very poor indeed. So I cut it to 9,500, then managed to get it under 7,500. And in the end I managed to cut it to under 5,000. The title kept changing too – first to "Penetration Dance" and then to "A Valence for Violence" and then to "The Blue Butterfly (don't ask, the butterfly is long gone)." I had always considered it one of my very best stories and I had poured so much of myself into it that I was not only surprised and dismayed when it continued to get rejected – I was crushed.

There were other factors that contributed to my decision to quit writing in the early 2000s, but this was one of the main ones. It was the very best writing I was capable of producing and I couldn't even sell it to the smallest of small presses. I was loathe to look at it again – and completely unable to discern where I had gone wrong.

When I started writing again in 2010, I never though about this story. In fact, I didn't think about it until I started putting together this collection and realized that I really, really wanted this story to be in here.

So I read the latest version for the first time in ten years, and my reaction was, "No wonder nobody wanted it! In the process of cutting all those words, I've cut out it's heart and soul!" So I rewrote it again – coming up with an ending that felt deeper and more resonant.

Then I stumbled across the version that Dean had wanted for *Pulphouse*. Much better! But realizing how much I have grown as a writer since the early 90s, I did find it awfully – and unnecessarily – long. I merged the two versions and came up with a hybrid version that seemed to strike a nice balance.

Then I joined Wattpad. On a lark, I decided to serialize "Masks of Flesh" (I went back to a variation of the original title). After publishing the first two parts, readers were raving to me that it was one of the creepiest things they had ever read. Everyone was getting excited in anticipation of the ending. But the ending, in my opinion, was still something of a lunchbox letdown. The science fictional explanation created pages and pages of untimely and unlikely exposition. So I went back and massaged it some more, working out the kinks, getting rid of clunky dialogue, trying my best to maintain the sense of creeping dread that had captured my new fans on Wattpad.

The result may not be perfect, but I think it is now as good as it's going to get.

Ironically, that brings me back, full circle to *Pulphouse* and Dean Wesley Smith. I remember him and Kristine Kathryn Rusch speaking at a convention in Washington state in the mid-90s where they said, "There are no bad stories, just unfinished ones."

It took me twenty-two years to write the story you're about to read. I do hope you're happy with the final version but I find it more important – not to mention incredibly gratifying and cathartic – to be able to say that I am finally happy with it. It's finished.

Masks of Flesh

My father was a brilliant man, a professor of anthropology, but after seven years of his constant company, I understood why so many of his peers in the pre-madness world considered him a crackpot.

Not that his ideas were bad. Just unorthodox. Take the "scarecrows".

"What do you think of this?" Dad strode into the kitchen, carrying a huge tome in his good arm. Thumping it down in a valley between stratified mountains of books on the big oak table, he flipped it open, arraying candles on plateaus of literature. Theatrically running his long fingered hand through his eroded thistle of white hair, he beckoned us with the other hand.

My sister, Jan and I were standing at the kitchen counter with bowls of steamed carrots; me craving the taste of butter and remembering a time in my childhood when we would slather it on our food. Jan couldn't remember dairy products. In fact, a teenaged friend of hers at Windsor Stronghold had told her that milk and butter and cheese were the stuff of old wives tales; the notion of any animal allowing us to take its milk, as plausible as Santa Claus. Setting her bowl on the counter, Jan crossed the kitchen and leaned over the table.

Coming up behind her, I slapped her ass. "Move over fat-butt."

The pest spread her legs and planted her feet.

"Let him in," Dad said. And so she did.

A woodprint of bodies impaled on poles filled the top half of the page. Below it was a paragraph describing the legendary practices of Vlad the Impaler as landmarks in the psychological history of intimidation. I read aloud. "'Vlad's methods held off the Turkish army until it became apparent to everyone that his own history of torture and imprisonment had turned Vlad into a complete madman.' What does this have to do with us?"

"He held off the Turks. It might keep raiders away from the potato patch," Dad said to us, quite seriously.

"Heads on poles went out of style ages ago," I said. "We're supposed to have become a bit more civilized in the past six hundred years."

"In the 1970's," Dad whispered. "The Khymer Rouge built towers of human skulls. And that was back when we were still trying to pretend we were civilized."

I walked to the window, opened the shutters and looked out on our mountainside. Where our neighbours had once lived, terraces of glass shone in the moonlight like misshapen white spaces on a giant chessboard, greenhouses built out of salvaged glass over the foundations of the houses we had torched.

Human raiders had done more damage to our crops over the past the few months than animals had ever done.

I looked back at Jan and Dad. "How do you propose to do this? Want me to go over to the stronghold to find a few people who wouldn't mind being butchered for a worthy cause?" I asked.

"Something like that," Dad said with a smile.

The next day he took us to a place outside of Tillicum Stronghold, which had once been a shopping centre. When people had moved into the old shopping mall, they had cleared out the refuse. The unburnable mannequins, were good for nothing and so had been stacked in a mass grave and forgotten.

Two days after he seeded the idea, I was driving eight-foot wooden stakes through the lower backs of one-after-another of our 'signposts.' All around me on the mountainside, the still air reeked of molten plastic. I poured red paint over the points protruding from their chests and necks, flowing the blood-red paint down, to gush convincingly over the torsos. The shafts were tapered, so that the bodies locked into position half a metre off the ground. When I couldn't get the arms to flop back the way I wanted, I broke them with a crowbar. The hands and the fingers too. Then I wired the pieces together.

"Nice job, Picasso," Dad said, coming up behind me. "Can't tell they're not real unless you get real close. Reminds me of the Ice Capades."

"What are Ice Capades?" I asked.

"Like ice dancers, you know?" Then he laughed, "Who am I kidding, that's almost before my time. Anyway, the poses and the glaring surfaces somehow reminded me of figure skaters."

"Scary dance," I said.

"Danse Macabre."

"Not intended to be pretty."

"Don't worry," Dad laughed. "It's a message only a malice-puppet could ignore."

Malice-puppet was a name Dad made up last winter, after Grant Petersen came pounding at our door. We let him in figuring his wife or one of the kids might be in trouble. He swung at Dad with a hatchet, planting it deep in his arm before I shot Petersen in the head. Found out later that he'd butchered his family before coming to take care of us.

Dad survived, but developed the habit of carrying a handgun in his bellypouch. If he pulled it out and you ran and hid like a normal, he accepted it as proof that you weren't a malice-puppet and (usually) let you live.

"They look like they were once alive. You're a natural artist, Mark. I just wish we lived in a world where there were a few more practical applications for your talent."

Forgetting that my hands were covered in paint, I reached out to straighten the mannequin's wig. My fingertips slid down my victim's cheek leaving crimson claw marks.

My hand was shaking as I drew it back. I was too fixated on the face to hear what Dad was saying. It reminded so much of my mother's face. I hardly ever thought or dreamed about her anymore but in that instant, it all came rushing back: the bus window splattered with spring mud; me squeezing past Mom into the narrow aisle; Mom gliding up behind me as the door hissed open; me running ahead through wet leaves; Mom's shriek of alarm; me looking back, unable to see her face through a blur of flapping wings and splattering blood. Talons were tearing at her hands, a beak spearing at her eyes. I panicked and ran toward her. It gouged at me too. I remember handfuls of feathers, a tiny ribcage cracking underfoot. A Samoyed that belonged to one of the tenants came bounding across the driveway, hitting Mom from behind, not making a sound until it was tearing at her throat. I remember the weight and coarseness of the chunk of broken concrete I found in my hand, the relentless rhythm of my arm swinging down and down into a pile of bloody fur still whimpering. I remember the odd, moist texture of Mom's green sweater as I put my hands on her shoulders and shook her, looking for life.

I don't remember passing out but my next memory was in the hospital.

They kept me there overnight after the attack that killed my Mom; stitched me up, wrapped the hand with the two broken fingers and released me. The emergency ward was filled with the survivors of animal attacks. I remember one man swearing there were several raccoons and a housecat in the pack of dogs that had nearly killed him.

By the time people clued in enough to start putting their much loved, part-of-the-family pets to sleep, old Rover often managed to wipe out entire families. And the death rates kept climbing. When the domestic animals were all dead, the wild ones moved in. Then the insects. Mosquitos, wasps and locusts. Pestilence-a-plenty. Ninety-four percent of the human population was wiped out over the next Thirty-six months. Concrete barricades were built around apartment blocks, that reconceived themselves as strongholds. The strongholds took down all the trees and burned down all the empty houses in their neighbourhoods. They rounded up all the bullets and gasoline and pesticides.

As natural pollination became rare, starvation grew common. Strongholds became serfdoms. Dad said they were all ruled by nasty little fascists who thanked their individual Gods every night for the Madness that had given them power that otherwise would have been out of their grasps forever. Dad was even more eloquent on the subject of the strongholds than he was on most things.

We stayed in our house, reinforcing it until it looked like Fort Apache. Dad described the house once as Beaver Cleaver's dream fort – 50's suburbia in full battle armour. Under layers of plywood and sheet metal, you can still make out the shape of a big, gabled split level home, like a bottle in Christmas wrap.

Once I started thinking about the past, I got lost in the fugue for the rest of the afternoon. Astonishment and fear had long since turned to tedium and bitterness, but I could still while away hours recalling moments of joy or contentment from before the Madness.

I was in a black mood when Jan started bugging me for using gasoline to clean the paint off my hands.

"That's probably enough to run the generator for an hour. And it stinks up the whole house."

"You're starting to sound like Dad."

"And there's something wrong with that?" Dad came out of the back door and put his hand on Jan's shoulders. He smiled, something he seldom did since Mom died.

He'd obviously been testing our latest batch of moonshine. "We got any more of those biscuits, Daddy's girl?"

"Sorry, they're all gone," Jan said.

"Already? Which of you two's been pigging out?"

"Hey! It was three weeks ago you found that tin of whole wheat flour. It only made five dozen biscuits..."

"All right, all right. What do we have, then?"

"Rabbit jerky."

Dad rolled his eyes. "No potatoes?"

"I'll get some tomorrow," I promised before going into the living room and turning on the radio. Nothing happened. I checked to make sure it was still plugged into the wall outlet. "Who's been screwing with the stereo?" I shouted.

Dad came in, chewing vigorously on a piece of dried meat. The upper plate of his false teeth had broken in half a few weeks earlier and we still hadn't found new ones or a way to fix the old ones. Soon after it happened, I suggested it might not be such a bad thing, because his food lasted longer that way. He cuffed me for that one, but it was worth it.

"I shurn off na generator," he said.

"What?? I just turned it on."

He swallowed a painfully large mouthful and yelled, "We waste too much gas listening to the damn radio!"

"How we gonna hear the local news?"

"We can get by without it."

"If you'd said that a few months ago, we might never have heard of the Breth."

A gangly, grizzled man, my father looked more like a truck driver than an intellectual, especially with that totally goofy smile of his. Mom used to say that people often thought he was dour because he wouldn't risk undermining his dignity through a careless display of mirth.

Dad's new, post-Mom, post-Madness smile was different. It was a sad-clown mask, like one of those pressed cardboard 'paintings' Jan had on her bedroom wall in our old house. Wistful was the happiest anyone got in the wake of the madness. This smile was more smug than wistful.

"There is no more gas, Mark. Either production has stopped or there's issues shipping it out to the island. We need to find another way to do things. Let's start by getting that old car battery from under the workbench in the garage."

Here we go again, I thought. It was the third time in as many years he'd sent me to look for something that didn't exist. Neither Jan nor I remembered ever having seen it. Arguing with him would be putting off the inevitable, so I went without protest, taking my time, making a show of it. That way he wouldn't be pissed off when I came back empty-handed.

When I returned he spoke before I had the door half-opened. "Nothing, eh?"

"A box of shirts."

"Shirts?"

"Yeah. Those red plaid flannelette shirts Uncle Vern used to wear all the time."

"Did you bring them in?"

"What for?"

"Might be able to trade them for batteries or something."

I rolled my eyes. Batteries were almost as hard to come by as gas. But there was no sense challenging Dad when he set his mind on something.

The cardboard box was so damp and flimsy, the bottom came open and shirts flopped and tumbled all over the oil-stained concrete. I ended up stacking them and delivering them in two separate loads.

Jan modelled one of the huge shirts for us. I laughed at the time, but Uncle Vern haunted my dreams that night. He came back from the dead to tell me his secret; that he was a demon, elaborately disguised in an enormous fat suit. And he told me that I was a spy, programmed to fool everyone including myself, right up to the crucial moment. It made perfect sense in the dream, since I'd always felt different from those around me – an outsider, even from other family members, although I couldn't imagine ever betraying them.

I looked at Uncle Vern and screamed, "You're a liar!" But he was already gone.

I touched my face. The skin was numb. I dug my fingernail into the flesh of my cheek. It didn't hurt. I pushed harder, twisting it like a drill and sinking it in up to the first knuckle, then pulling and prying at the area around the hole. My face split in two. Peeling off first the top half and then the bottom, I gazed in terror at the bisected face. I held a stare in my right hand and a smile in my left.

There were no mirrors to show me what I looked like underneath the mask.

The lips of the mask moved, began to form words. "Traitor," they said.

The next morning, I sat up in bed with my eyes closed, trying to fill out the foggy patches of the dream.

"I'm taking those shirts to Viewtower instead of Ocean Point." The sudden conversation startled me. I turned to see Dad rooting through the cupboards behind me. He reached for the jam, the one jar of strawberry from the cupboardful of home preserves we'd scavenged during our Colwood trip the previous summer. We were all getting sick of plum.

"We should get going soon regardless," I said.

Dad glanced at me and said drily. "You're not coming."

"You're not going alone?"

"No, Jan's coming."

"She went last week!" I protested.

Swallowing a large spoonful of jam, Dad said in his don't-mess-with-me voice, "I need you to take the .22 and go digging potatoes." We'd planted over a dozen patches, each small enough that other scavengers wouldn't be likely to find them.

"Why can't she do it? It's not like there isn't a map! It's even colour coded, with planting and harvesting dates, so she can't screw it up!"

Jan stuck out her tongue as Dad countered, "You know where the plots are, Mr. Atlas. And we need someone with a strong back to roll them up here. So, fill the damned bin before the raiders decide your wall of death is all bluff and attack us in force. I need Julia Child here with me."

Dad put on his jacket and stuffed several pieces of rabbit jerky into a pocket, before hoisting the Browning automatic down from the wall rack. He checked the magazine, plucked some fresh shells out of the box in the hutch and dropped them into the same pocket as the meat then slung the bundle of shirts over his shoulder with the extra rope we'd tied on for that purpose. Turning without looking at us, he marched abruptly out the door.

"You got a boyfriend at Viewtower? How did you talk Dad into taking you again?"

"Maybe I do," she said as she hurriedly got on her own coat and followed. Before she pulled the door closed, she said, "Cheer up, idiot. It's your birthday on Friday. He doesn't want you to see what you're getting."

"Oh, c'mon. We don't have enough to trade for gas and food, why would he get me a present?"

She looked at me as though I'd left my brain in the garage the night before. Dad hadn't neglected a birthday yet. Somehow, they had become more important.

So I got to dig potatoes and haul them up the mountain by myself. Nice birthday present, I thought as went to the living room after working all day.

Jan had left an old science book open on the couch with instructions for making something called a crystal radio. The accompanying article explained how they worked without batteries or electricity.

I thought of making one myself until I realized that it was probably going to be my gift from Jan. It would serve her right if I beat her to it, I laughed to myself.

Right around when I started feeling guilty for wasting so much time, the back door slammed open and Jan screeched, "Mark! Are you still here? We need you!"

That was a mighty strange statement coming from my sister! I jumped up from the couch and ran to the kitchen.

She actually looked relieved to see me. "It's Dad. He's hurt bad."

"What? How? Where?" I asked without giving her a chance to answer.

"He collapsed at the bottom of the mountain. He was losing a lot of blood."

"What? Did he get shot? Attacked? What's going on?"

"I think he stepped on something." She answered all the questions at once, but vaguely. She hauled on my coat sleeve almost pulling me over while I put on my boots. "I didn't see it happen. Now hurry!"

I saw a crumpled shape in the middle of the road about hundred metres distant.

"Where's your gun?" I asked, putting my arm around his waist and pulling him to his feet. Dad's usually strong hand feebly grasped the fabric of my shirt.

"Dropped it," Dad muttered, barely coherent.

"Where?" I insisted. We couldn't afford to lose our best rifle. He didn't answer. Jan got there a second later. Even with both of us propping him up, it took several minutes to get him into the house and lay him down on the couch.

As I began unlacing the boot, Jan came in with a bowl of water, some bandages and disinfectant. When she saw how serious it was, she said, "Don't take it off yet, I'll get some towels."

But I wasn't listening. As I pulled off the boot, my father screamed and kicked with his injured foot, pushing me to the floor.

"I told you to...oh, Jeez," Jan cried. She wrapped a towel around the foot and applied pressure from underneath. Our father screamed and writhed then abruptly stopped struggling.

I couldn't find his pulse, so Jan took his wrist and immediately sighed. "You've gotta learn to do this better." She nodded. "He's alive."

I held a finger under his nose and felt his warm breath, then lifted one eyelid.

"What are you doing?" my sister asked.

"Aren't you supposed to be able to tell something from that?" I muttered as I pulled my hand back.

"So, what, exactly, can you tell?" she asked.

"His pupils are dilated."

"Yes? Telling us what, exactly?"

I stood up and yelled, "I get it! But what was I supposed to do? How can I help him?"

She stopped and said, "I think there's something in it. Big nail or... something."

She inserted her finger into the wound and pulled it back as though it were an electrical socket. "It's quivering. Like it's alive."

"Bullshit." I didn't want to think about what this might mean. I had never seen a malice worm, but like everyone, I knew what they were supposed to look like. Less worms than snails in slender conical shells that were needle sharp on one end and widened to the diameter of a man's thumb at the other. The same size as the hole in Dad's boot. They were rumoured to travel underground like clams without the seaside.

"Were you with him when it happened."

"Let's talk about this later. I need tweezers or something."

"Where do you keep them?" Then I thought of an alternative and said, "Oh, nevermind."

I came back a moment later with needle nose pliers, washed them with soap and water, then poured alcohol over them.

"Is there a cup you can soak them in?" Jan asked.

"Not a clean one," I said and by the time I turned back, she was already digging in the wound.

I watched in terror. It simply couldn't be a malice worm. It just seemed to Jan that something was quivering because Dad's whole leg was trembling from the shock. Malice worms couldn't move that fast, couldn't attack someone like that. Could they?

By the time Jan came out empty for the third time, the blood was spurting. Jan lowered his foot back to the couch and pressed the sodden rag to the wound.

"You have to keep trying," I said.

"I can't," she replied. "There's nothing in there to grab. He's bleeding to death. If I keep trying it will kill him. I don't have the equipment or the knowledge. You asked what you can do? Go to Viewtower Stronghold."

"Windsor's closer. I'll get Dr. White.!"

"They all went to fucking Viewtower to see the Breth. I saw Dr. White there."

"The Breth is at Viewtower? What for?"

"How the fuck should I know? I was with Dad. He'd said he'd chop it into little pieces before listening to its lies." She screamed, "Hurry!"

I tried to remember where I'd propped my .22 on the way into the house with Dad. I was just as worried as Jan. What right did she have to order me around? I was a capable adult. Certainly more of an adult than she was. I only obeyed because...she was right. We were out of our depth. I slammed the door on the way out.

If Dad wasn't such a tightass with his rules we might have known what was going on. Why had the Breth come to our stupid freaking island of all the places on Earth?

A raccoon watched from a tree as I dashed past the stretch of wilderness at Kinsman Gorge Park. I ran to the middle of the bridge before turning around with my gun poised. But amazingly, it didn't attack.

A few blocks later, a wasp zipped past, inches from my face. I froze, trying to track its trajectory. Where there was one wasp there were usually many. I could see no corpses along the curb or in the tall grass along the shore. Perhaps this wasp had simply strayed too far from its nest. I listened for buzzing and heard only the hiss and patter of tiny raindrops on leaves and grass.

Twenty minutes later, I reached the walls around the stronghold. Choking my way through a pesticide haze, I pounded on the front gate. The sentry was wearing a gas mask. She asked if I'd seen any wasps and looked relieved when I told her how far from the stronghold my sighting had occurred.

"I need Dr. White. Emergency. Do you know where he is?" I asked while walking backward into the courtyard.

"At the meeting in the main lobby most likely," she said.

Through the big glass doors of the main apartment building, I could see a large crowd gathered. Good luck finding him in here, I thought. Inside the door, I came up beside a man who was all curly black hair and bushy beard. I tapped him on the shoulder.

"I'm looking for Doctor White, from Windsor Stronghold."

The man shrugged.

"Where's the clinic?"

He pointed down a hallway. "But it's closed."

I had to shout to be heard as the din of the crowd grew several notches louder, "There must be somebody on standby for emergencies!"

The man shrugged again and I leaned in and shouted, "Why is the Breth here?"

"You haven't heard? It's cleared out almost all the malice worms. It's tracked the last of them here."

A voice said over a loudspeaker, "Here's Mayor Peter Shaver of Viewtower to introduce our very special guest."

I'd never even seen pictures of the Breth, but I'd heard it described as a giant slug moulded into a vaguely humanoid shapes. From across the room I could see that the description didn't do it justice. The Breth was slightly taller and bulkier than the humans surrounding it – with the mottled colour and apparent texture of an overripe banana. It wasn't wearing any sort of clothing.

The inanities coming out of the mouth of the Mayor melted to babble as I pushed my way through the crowd toward the Breth, with no plan other than getting a closer look. It seemed to have a human-like face, but instead of a skull, the back of its head looked like a half full sack of potatoes. Its fingers were almost as long as its stubby arms. Tyrannosaurus slugs, I thought. As I watched, the Breth grew a foot taller and as it did, its flesh seemed to become more translucent. I could now see that the face had two eyes but no mouth. Those eyes locked on mine.

Alien thoughts slithered into my consciousness.

The Mayor stopped talking. Everyone in the crowd turned simultaneously and looked at me.

"You have encountered the valent we are searching for." The voice was a bagpipe drone, overlaid with a squishy whisper. And even as I heard the words, I realized that the alien wasn't actually communicating in an Earthly language. These words were supplied by my own mind, organizing the information and feeding it back to me in a format I could understand.

As the concept of 'valents' tried to form itself in my consciousness, it came with a whole host of confusing and contradictory definitions. The primary meaning seemed to be, 'part of ourselves', but it also meant 'ambition', 'reward', 'beautiful aggression', 'your pestilence' and simply 'malice worms.'

"My Dad," I said, "needs your help."

"Your parent is beyond hope," the Breth said. "But there are others we must save, are there not?"

"That's Mark Hoag. Damon Hoag's son."

"You must guide us to the valent," said the Breth as it slid down off the podium. "Now."

"I know where they live!" someone shouted. "Follow me!"

Other voices rose up, "Yeah, let's go!"

The crowd roared its agreement.

"Kill ourselves a malice worm!"

More comments were buried in pandemonium.

"Stop!" The Breth's mental exclamation pummeled all other thoughts out of its path. "Only Breth can contain it. Terrestrial life-forms are too fragile. Anyone nearby is in danger. This human alone will guide me."

As we left the building, nobody followed. I looked back twice more before we reached the already opened gate and nobody even stepped out of the building.

"What did you do to them?"

"Simply told the truth."

"Why aren't they coming out?"

"They know not to interfere."

"Did you hurt them?"

"Not at all," said the Breth, and I knew he was telling the truth. Those people would be fine. I took one last look and still saw no movement. Despite the Breth's assurances, my stomach did a little flip. In fact, I realized, it was because of the Breth's assurances.

Twisting the top part of its body like taffy, the Breth managed to convey the effect of cocking its head. "Are you not coming to rescue your family?"

"My Dad thinks you put the malice worms here to eliminate us, so you can use this planet to plant crops or whatever you do with planets you conquer. Why should I believe anything you tell me?"

"In our society, thoughts cannot be hidden, deceit is impossible," the alien said. I felt the creature's bewilderment and fascination with the concept of dishonesty.

"We must hurry," said the Breth. "This valent is aware of our proximity – clinging to its autonomy."

The alien moved faster than I, flowing as much as walking with a strange bipedal gait. I ran as fast as my already exhausted state would allow. Stopping several times to wait for me, it suggested, "We could carry you."

"Don't even fucking touch me," I said as I slogged past.

"How distant is the victim?"

"You can read my mind," I replied aloud. Then I simply thought the rest of the question, "Why don't you tell me?"

"Spatial relationships are complex calculations for Breth. We require your navigational assistance."

Exhausted, I stopped, bending over with my hands on my knees as I gasped for breath.

The alien went on for a ways, then came directly back, stopping in front of me and regarding me with eyes that were spinning black orbs. The more often it communicated with me, the more seamlessly its thoughts merged with my own. There was less a sense of being spoken to than simply understanding something. I couldn't distinguish my own thoughts from the slithery voice telling me, "Speed is imperative. Your sibling's life is in extreme danger."

I can't tell you how much it bothered me that it knew about Jan without my telling it.

I said, "I came here to fetch the doctor, not you. I don't trust you."

"Trust," it said. "A peculiar human concept. You know as well as we do that we are here to help. The escape of the valents was a tragic accident. We are attempting to minimize the impact on your environment."

"If you expect my help, then I need to know more about you."

"A biology lesson is worth more to you than your sibling's life?"

"She can take care of herself. She has the gun. Now tell me something about your kind."

"You are impressively strong-willed to resist our imperative. If your sibling shares this trait, its survival is conceivable."

The next conversation took place in a few seconds because I barely had time to consider the questions before I knew the answers. Nothing was spoken aloud.

"You speak and think of yourself in the plural," I observed. "Why?"

"In our natural state, Breth hosts are formless and listless. We eat, excrete, reproduce...."

I had a clear mental image of these things, like giant pancakes, lying together in a swamp, overlapping and rubbing together, but otherwise not moving much at all.

"Our relationship with the valents is symbiotic," explained the Breth. "We interact chemically, hormonally, mentally. We harness their rage and purpose and their valence completes us. Fuels our ambition, fills us with motivation, forces us to apply our intelligence. Through us, they can aspire to do more than simply drill through the muck and fill the air with the stench of their discontent. Within us, they are part of God's own civilization."

"And without you, they run around and kill things!"

"Without us, they are profoundly unproductive – toxic and acidic – and they find a savage joy in that." The positive spin was restored immediately. "Through the valents, we gained the ability to communicate with one another – a path that ultimately brought us to the stars. When Batch 4320 Prime crashed on your planet, the host died and all of its valents escaped."

I stared into its eyes which seemed deeper and darker than before. The spinning effect had all but stopped.

"The malice worms are a part of you?" I said.

"That is correct," said the alien.

"How many valents did he have? This Breth that crashed."

"We will discuss nothing more unless we resume progress towards the valent's location."

Rather than spinning around, the face simply melted into the Breth's body and it started flowing away from me. As I ran up beside it, the Breth proceeded to answer my question. "Batch 4320 Prime contained two hundred and seventeen valents. One hundred and eighty-two survived. Once orphaned, they each went their own way."

"Spreading the Madness," I said.

"Aggression is already abundant in the lifeforms that have evolved on your planet. Whenever the valents were able to establish any sort of mental interface, their own aggression served to increase the levels in the host, while the host's aggression built up inside of the valent."

Like a feedback loop, I understood.

"As the energy escalated, psychic fields filled with pure rage grew around them, affecting every impressionable creature within range. A frenzy that would not stop until the host died, setting the valent free, so that its search for a more compatible host could continue. Humans are only affected through direct interface, but they die quickly."

The Breth stopped in mid-thought, rising up to a height of seven or eight feet. "We have arrived at your residence, have we not? I feel the valent nearby."

"One more question. How many valents are inside you?"

"One hundred and seven when our mission began," it said. "Plus one hundred and eighty-one from Batch 4320 Prime."

All pretence of looking human was abandoned as it flowed rapidly up the hill.

"And if you were killed?" I hurried to get in one final query.

"Our valents would be free once more."

As I stood staring at its receding shape, I wondered if I had done the right thing bringing it here.

"You don't believe the Breth's bullshit, do you Mark?" Dad's voice came from the air itself. I looked around but couldn't see him. "You know they don't really care about you."

"Dad?" I turned in a slow circle. " Where are you? What's going on?"

"The valent is using us to relay and amplify its thoughts to you," came the slithery voice of the Breth.

"Where is it?"

"We are unable to locate it…."

"The Breth are lying," said my father's voice.

"They can't lie, Dad," I said.

"Their lives are lies."

"They can't even grasp the concept of lying," I insisted.

"Then they bend the truth. They are masters of rhetoric. You remember what that is, don't you, Aristotle?"

He called me Aristotle. If Dad was already dead, as the Breth had told me, then how come it sounded just like him? I directed my question to the Breth, but it didn't respond.

I marched on gamely. The door of the house was open when I got to the hilltop. I tried to ignore my pounding heart and rasping breath – to not be tired – but I felt like I was going to fall over.

The Breth was standing in the kitchen twirling like a corkscrew. "This dwelling is empty," it told me.

"Where's Jan?" I asked.

The alien responded with the mental equivalent of a shrug. "Not here."

"How can you not find them?" I shouted. "You can read its mind…."

"All our senses tell us that it is here. Right where we are standing."

I smelled the gasoline, just before I felt the heat coming up through the floor.

"The basement! There's a fire in the basement!" I yelled as I turned and ran for the front door. It never even occurred to me that Dad had made a bomb until it went off, the impact launching me out the door and through the air to the centre of the driveway. I landed on my shoulder and moaned with pain.

I didn't realize that the Breth had survived as well until pain of a whole different magnitude hit me in a wave from behind. The searing heat had bubbled the alien's flesh and I felt every inch of it. As I turned and looked back at the house, I saw the Breth, still more-or-less alive – a monstrous amoeba squirming and flowing down the steps.

And I wondered for a moment if the creature was going to die; before I understood that the valents inside it would simply not permit it to give up. It wasn't even feigning speech anymore, jusy filling me with information. I knew that the uncompromising will of the valents inside the Breth would speed repair of the tissue to mere hours. I understood that this was far from a fatal injury for a Breth and wondered briefly how Batch 4320 Prime had managed to die.

As I framed the question, I knew that getting caught within the inferno would have damaged it beyond repair, without necessarily killing the valents.

Then I saw Dad. He must have gone out the basement door and circled around the house. He came around the far side of the garage, carrying a pitchfork.

He walked straight towards me, hefting the implement like a spear. Every muscle in my body hurt, but I managed to get to my feet and turn to face him. I didn't feel like I had enough coordination to dodge out of the way, but I was prepared to fight him anyway.

I was surprised as hell when he walked straight past me and plunged the pitchfork into the puddle that was the Breth. Alien flesh rippled and flowed up the wooden handle of the pitchfork which nailed the Breth to the ground. Then it stopped moving and just lay there, quivering.

After the initial jolt of pain, I heard and felt nothing more.

"Is it dead?" I asked aloud.

Dad shook his head and walked back past me, kicking open the garage door and stepping inside. His thoughts were no longer being relayed by the Breth, so I knew the thing must be hurt pretty badly.

"Where's Jan?" I shouted to no one in particular. Unsurprisingly, no one answered.

From the garage came a roar and Dad stepped out, wielding a chainsaw. When he started walking back toward the Breth, I picked up a rock, which was the only weapon I could find, and blocked his way. He lunged at me, swinging the heavy tool so awkwardly with his single arm that I was able to jump out of the way. But I fell and smashed my own ankle with the rock. Through the pain haze, I could see Dad looming above me. And from my ground level vantage point, I could see something he didn't – a fluid limb extending out of the fleshy puddle and coiling around Dad's ankle.

The Breth pulled Dad's legs out from under him. He lost his grip on the chainsaw, which carved up soil inches from my face as it bounced and twisted over the stony ground and finally stuttered to silence well out of Dad's reach. The Breth's tentacle pulled him into the centre of the puddle and the yellow skin of the Breth flowed over his legs like an oily sheet.

"Help me, Buffalo Bill!" The voice came back into my head. "You can save me. Use the chainsaw. Stop the Breth. They've come to enslave us all. Please!"

The Breth covered him like a glistening blanket.

I stared at the slimy, writhing cocoon. Through the pearly, translucent flesh, I could see the outline of my father's face, his open mouth a small crater on the smooth surface, two smaller hollows for the eyes.

"Can you get the valent out and keep my father alive?" I demanded, pulling my hunting knife from its scabbard on my belt.

The Breth did not respond.

Gently but insistently, I pushed the tip of the blade into the Breth's flesh, into the centre of Dad's mouth. Yellow goo oozed out, more like tree sap than blood.

"Can you keep my father alive?" I repeated. Again, no answer.

I cut through, careful not to push it in too far I turned the blade sideways, preparing to cut open the sticky envelope, and pull my father from within, but his head burst out through the tiny opening like an eager newborn, already screaming.

The Breth screamed as well, its pain pouring into me from wherever I touched it, searing into my mind and down through my body – as though my own flesh had been torn open. Its thoughts were fractured, semi-coherent, bordering on delirious.

My father was shaking yellow blood from his hair like a dog shouting, "Cut them again – cut them to pieces!"

I wanted badly to believe that my father was still alive but there was too much wrong. His eyes were as dull and depthless as stones. He had consistently referred to the Breth in the plural – something Dad wouldn't have known or bothered to do. In that instant I understood and accepted that my dad was indeed already dead.

So I did nothing as the Breth's flesh clenched around the inside of the wound and Dad's eyes bulged out and his mouth gaped. I turned my head away as the Breth pushed a pseudopod of flesh into his mouth and blood gurgled out around it. My dad's eyes rolled back in his head, and he began to shake as if he was having a seizure.

I said to the Breth, "I won't release you unless you destroy this valent. The one that killed my dad."

The Breth's voice was a whisper. "It is already inside us. The joining is too advanced."

"It's an evil little fucker and it deserves to die," I pressed the blade against the alien's flesh once again. "Spit it out – or whatever it is you do…."

I lowered the knife, since it knew I was bluffing. I wouldn't risk killing it by cutting it again.

"The valent's memories are a part of you now?"

"Yes."

"Then tell me where my sister is?"

"She…wanted to be Florence Nightingale." The voice in my head, the Breth's voice, sounded just like my dad's. "But I thought she should be Michelle Kwan."

"Michelle Kwan?" I shook him. "What does that mean?"

"A *figure skater.*" The Breth's suggestion crawled through my mind and down my spine.

I saw images of bloody mannequins, one of them with Jan's face. Leaving my father's corpse, I got up and ran past my burning house down the hillside, screaming her name.

I found her lying on the ground behind the house, still alive despite a ragged slash across her throat. I tore off a piece of my shirt, rolled it up and put pressure on it, but had no way to judge how deep the cut it was. The ground was soaked in her blood.

"Sorry," she muttered, blood bubbling at the corners of her lips, her voice little more than a whisper. "I couldn't kill him."

"It wasn't Dad. You know that don't you? It was the valent; the malice worm."

"Yeah," she acknowledged, gripping my hand with blood-slicked fingers. "Did you bring the doctor?"

A doctor might be able to save her. But instead, I had brought the Breth – one of the creatures responsible for everything that had happened, for everyone who had died.

And I had left it pinned to the ground.

If it died, two hundred and eighty-nine malice worms would be released, almost certainly destroying whatever was left of our Earth. But it didn't matter. It had already cost me everything I cared about.

Staring down into my sister's beautiful face, I amended that thought. Almost everything. Jan was still alive.

"Don't die," I told her. I placed her hand on the makeshift bandage. "Don't give up!"

I lifted her in my arms and carried her back up the hill. Remembering how the valents had prevented the Breth from dying, I said, "Get angry."

Mentally, I shouted to the Breth. *I'm bringing her to you. You have to help her!*

But when I got back to the front of the still burning house, all I found was Dad's body and a trail of yellow slime.

You can't just walk away!

I can't remember if I thought it or screamed it. All I know is that I got no answer.

The Breth was gone.

It took me two hours to get Jan to Windsor Stronghold.

Now I'm doing all I can to help her stay alive.

As my own bitterness and hatred grow like a tumour inside of me, I stay at her bedside, feeding her my rage in tiny doses. "They almost destroyed us all. As soon as they got what they wanted, they just went away. We meant nothing to them. You can't let them win."

Sometimes, I just chant, "You *can't* die. You *have* to stay and fight."

Of course, there is nothing left to fight but memories.

Some nights I still wake up dreaming of Dad, speaking in the Breth's voice. "They're inside us all, Bruce Banner. Straining to get out."

It's a recurring dream – a variation of the one I had just before the malice worm killed him. In this dream, Dad is the one who peels off the fleshy mask. Beneath his face is mine. And beneath mine is my very own valent – a maelstrom of confusion and rage trapped within a thin, transparent shell. I howl, knowing that one day I will hit the right frequency, and it will shatter.

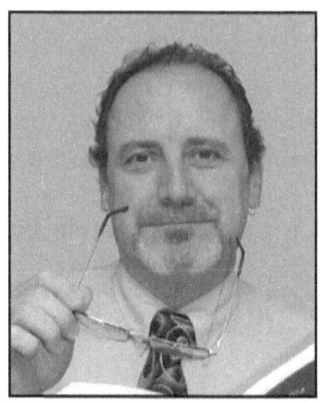

About the Author

In his thirty year writing career, Dale L. Sproule has published over fifty stories and poems and been nominated for seven Aurora awards.

With Sally McBride, he published and edited *TransVersions* - Literature of the Fantastic and did a stint as editor of the SFCanada Newsletter, *Communique*.

As an artist, his illustrations have appeared on the covers of numerous books and magazines. He designed the SFCanada logo. His sculpture won him the Chair's Choice Award World Fantasy Art Show 2012 and can be viewed at sculptorstouch.com.